Also by Lynda Allen

<u>Fiction</u>

Flashes of Insight

<u>Poetry</u>

Grace Reflected

Wild Divinity

Illumine

Rest in the Knowing

<u>Nonfiction</u>

The Rules of Creation

Praise for Flashes of a Dying Hour

"A rare Edgar Allan Poe poetry collection possibly concealed somewhere in Fredericksburg, VA. A feisty group of middle-aged women hot on its trail. An amateur sleuth navigating both menopause and premonitions. Add in a huge dollop of humor and FLASHES OF A DYING HOUR checks all the boxes for an entertaining, satisfying, edgy cozy read. The Liv Wilde series has fast become one of my favorites!"

Lori Roberts Herbst, Silver Falchion Award winning author of the Callie Cassidy Mysteries

"Flashes of a Dying Hour is where an intricately woven mystery unfolds against an unexpected element—menopause. This innovative narrative not only keeps you on the edge of your seat with its suspenseful twists and turns but also invites you to explore the deeper layers of human experience and resilience.

"Lynda Allen's unique contribution to the literary world redefines traditional narratives by weaving the theme of menopause into her captivating mystery novels. Her portrayal of this often-overlooked chapter of life adds depth and intrigue that resonates with readers, making her characters relatable and profoundly authentic."

Suzie Housley, Midwest Book Review

FLASHES OF A DYING HOUR

A Liv Wilde Mystery

Lynda Allen

Living Heartfully Press

For my women friends who inspired these characters.
Your friendship is one of my life's greatest gifts.

For my daughters,
who fill my life with love, laughter, and sass.
Infinity squared.

CHAPTER ONE

Finding a dead body is nothing like how it looks in movies or on TV. Happening upon one as I did in a dank, deserted underground storage room all alone was not only frightening, it was also nauseating. I didn't scream like they do in British detective shows. My hand didn't cover my mouth in horror. I didn't faint. When I entered the room and saw his body there on the cold, dirt floor with stark shadows cast by a small lantern on the ground beside him, my mind was consumed with the image of my husband's body, completely still and quiet in a hospital bed, his skin as pale as the sheet pulled up under his chin.

I don't know how long I stood there lost in my memories before I returned to the new misery in front of me. When I did, I realized I felt queasy and had to consciously swallow the bile I felt rising. I unlocked my phone, ready to call Detective Gomez, then edged closer to the body.

I wasn't brave enough to touch him with my fingers to check for a pulse. After all, it was the first dead body I'd ever encountered - outside of a hospital and visions at least. Instead, I reached out with the tip of my shoe, which along with my jeans was muddy from sliding down the slope behind the building to get in the back door. I gave his shoulder a little nudge to see if the body was stiff.

That's when he groaned, and I threw up.

Normally, it might be considered bad form to vomit on a dead body. However, I think that even Miss Manners would make an allowance if the aforementioned dead body came alive.

I'd seen his body on the ground in a vision a month ago. Obviously, it would have been helpful to have seen he wasn't actually dead, but it doesn't work like that. I don't always get all the pertinent information. In fact, if my visions had a personality, I would say they were more impertinent.

The other big difference between what I saw last month and the reality before me, was that in the vision I hadn't recognized the dead man. Now, I knew whose boots I'd thrown up on.

CHAPTER TWO

Despite the frustrations, I think I prefer the ambiguity of my visions, whether waking or in dreams, to the stark realities of watching them play out in my daily life. The best part is I can awaken from a vision. In this particular case, when I first saw the man in the tunnel in a dream a month ago, I may have awakened drenched in sweat and shivering, but at least I woke up. At the time, I was convinced he wouldn't be as lucky.

After awakening with his image in my mind, I'd reached for the journal my septuagenarian neighbor Lucia Leto had given me. In her flowing handwriting she'd inscribed it with "Liv Wilde's Flashes of Insight." She thought tracking my moments of clairvoyance and capturing any significant details from what was revealed as soon as they happened might help me better understand what I was seeing. So, I carried a small notebook in my purse for when I had waking visions and kept the journal by my bed for those that came while I slept.

Since the visions began in the midst of hot flashes two years ago, Lucia and I had discussed them frequently. She gave me books to read and sent me links to websites with information about psychic abilities. She'd become my go-to person for anything spiritual.

Lucia grew up immersed in mystery, raised by a mother who was well-known for the salons she hosted on topics considered occult and spiritual. I don't know what I would've done when the premonitions first started if it hadn't been for her wisdom, unconditional acceptance, and her own mystical insights.

I still occasionally had a hard time believing I saw things before they happened, but in general, I'd gotten used to the idea. Though I was rarely a participant in what I saw like I had been in this one. Usually, I just watched things happen to someone else like a psychic voyeur.

While I had plenty of hot flashes without accompanying insights, when the visions started happening on a more regular basis, I knew I needed to find a way to better understand them because they weren't going away.

I quickly learned that going down rabbit holes on the internet wasn't the best way to gather information. I needed a source I could trust. That's where Lucia came in.

With her help, I'd come to understand that when what I saw was intense like this one, I needed to pay attention. So, I wrote down what I remembered of the dream I'd just had. When I was done, I checked the clock and decided that while Lucia might be awake, 5:30 was too early to call her. I sent her a text instead, asking her to call me after she'd had her first cup of tea.

My phone rang as I reached to put it back on the nightstand.

"You've had tea already?" I asked.

"Good morning, Liv. My tea's almost ready. I can sip it while we talk." In the background I heard the sound of her spoon hitting the sides of her teacup as she stirred in the wildflower honey I knew she liked. "What's up, besides us?"

I smiled.

Our friendship had begun over cups of tea (once in a while with whiskey added) as Lucia helped me gradually understand my newly discovered clairvoyance. Our friendship had deepened through long conversations about family, men, spirituality, sex, children, joy, nature, and the loves of our lives. I was so grateful to have her friendship and wisdom in my life.

It was a gift having someone with whom to discuss the visions and dreams who wasn't skeptical about them. My other girlfriends were supportive and intrigued, but also occasionally still slightly wary of them, and understandably so. After all, it's not always a good thing to see the future. With Lucia, I never had to worry. She didn't bat an eye when I first told her what was happening. She treated it like a normal part of life, which is what it had become for me. Well, relatively normal.

"What did you see in your dream?" she asked.

"I was underground. I didn't recognize the location. Although it was pretty dark, I could still see. I'm not sure why."

"Hmm," she said, with a tone I've come to learn meant what I've said is important.

"I came out of what seemed to be a small tunnel into a cave or underground room, and a man was lying on the ground, dead."

"And?"

"And what? Isn't a dead man enough?"

"Enough for what?"

She often reflected my words back to me with a gentle, knowing tone.

"Enough for me to have to see. Too much for me to have to see." I was unnerved by the image of me approaching his unmoving body, which kept replaying on a loop in my brain. "This is the first time I've seen a dead person in a vision."

"I'm sorry. It must be quite upsetting," she said with genuine concern, and then paused. I suspected that in the pauses during our conversations she was listening to things I couldn't hear. "Are you certain he was dead?"

"I didn't look that closely. He wasn't moving and didn't appear to be breathing."

"What else do you remember about him or the space?"

This was a typical question she asked. It helped me focus on what I saw rather than the emotions I was feeling.

"How old was he? What was his skin color like?" she asked.

I closed my eyes, trying to focus on the lingering details without trying to interpret what they meant. "His hair was salt and pepper. His skin was white and very pale, almost translucent. This will sound strange, but he reminds me of Indiana Jones in some way."

"Interesting. Is there a whip anywhere around him?" She snickered.

More than once, Lucia told me dreams I'd had were about sexual fantasies.

"Great. Now you're going to tell me I'm into kinky sex with dead people?"

"Maybe he was only mostly dead," said Lucia, quoting *The Princess Bride*, one of my favorite movies. Since we'd met, I'd introduced her to the film, and now she could quote it almost as accurately as me.

I laughed. "Just my luck, my Farm Boy turns out to be the Dead Pirate Roberts."

"Don't tempt the fates," she said. While her tone was light, I heard a more serious undertone.

A shiver having nothing to do with the temperature made me pull the blanket I had draped over my shoulders more tightly around myself.

"What else do you remember? Were there any scents in the air? Anything on the floor or walls?"

"Other than a whip?" I asked.

"Yes, other than that," she said.

I tried to put myself back in the scene. "The walls were made of brick, so it wasn't a cave. It had either a dirt floor or a layer of dirt covered whatever flooring was there. It smelled dank and moldy, but I also smelled a hint of some kind of spice in the air." It had been strange to discover I could smell things from the visions. Now it was just another question to ask about what I'd experienced, another bit of information to glean from them.

"Good. What else do you see?"

I suspected, in a strange way, Lucia's questions helped make my visions clearer even as they happened. It was as if knowing the questions to ask in advance had helped me learn to be more observant in the midst of them.

"He was wearing jeans and a light blue shirt with a light-weight khaki jacket. The jacket had lots of pockets."

"Was he wearing a fedora or perhaps a black mask?" she asked.

"Very funny. He looked like neither Harrison Ford nor Cary Elwes, thank you very much." After a pause I said, "He did look vaguely familiar though. I feel like I've seen him somewhere before, but I don't know where. It's frustrating."

"Don't focus on the frustration, just focus on the images. Is there anything else you noticed?"

"A battery-operated lantern was on the floor beside him."

"How close did you get to him?"

"Not very. As soon as I saw him, I froze. I was scared." The feeling of fear was still very present in my body, as the memory of Nate's face was lingering in my mind. "Then I called out. I woke up trying to say something." I sighed in frustration. "I haven't been able to remember what it was."

"Keep a notebook with you today in case you remember what you were saying."

"Lucia?" My voice was almost a whisper. "If he was really dead, is there anything I can do to prevent it? What if I can't? What's the point of knowing something in advance if I can't do anything to change it?"

"No matter what is true in the vision, his life is not your responsibility."

"But—"

She spoke over my protest. "Each life has its own path and its own forks in the road. We each have choices to make and no matter where they lead, there are lessons to be learned along the way. One of your lessons to learn, I'm afraid, is that not everyone needs or wants saving." She paused for a sip of tea before continuing.

"I have a friend who is a healer. Once she desperately wanted to save a young man she knew who was very sick. She began to contact other healers to get them together for a ceremony to help this man, who had so much more life to live, so much more to do. One of the elders she contacted asked her if she had permission from the young man for the healing, which she had to admit she didn't. So, my friend went to him and told him her plan to save his life. He got angry. He called my friend arrogant. He told her that it was not her life to save and that she was undervaluing the life he had lived to that point in thinking he had more work to do here. My friend told me it had never once occurred to her the young man wouldn't want to be saved, that he might feel complete in the life he had lived."

"What happened to him?"

"He died peacefully several months later. My friend was by his side. She told me she'd come to realize her desire to save him was more about her own grief at the prospect of losing him than about what he wanted. I was glad she told me the story. It was a powerful lesson for us both."

"And now it's an important lesson for me?"

"That's for you to decide," she said in her maddening way.

CHAPTER THREE

Lucia isn't the only woman in my life whose friendship I rely on. My life wouldn't be complete or as full of laughter without my circle of friends: Sophie, Mary, Jane, Hannah and Claire. We've been through everything together—divorces, new loves, joys and struggles with our kids, the loss of my husband Nate, and last year Jane and I helped the police catch a thief. We gather each month for a dinner party we affectionately call our "Monthly" and get together in various configurations between dinners, too.

A few weeks after my conversation with Lucia, I met Sophie and Mary at Hyperion coffee shop where we occasionally meet for the day's first caffeine infusion before going to work. We sat at a table near the window and engaged in one of our favorite activities, people-watching.

"Are there an unusual number of people dressed in black?" Sophie asked. She's my counterpart in sassy attitude, which she brings unapologetically to her work at the downtown branch of the local library system.

I glanced up from blowing on my tea just as two youngish men wearing old fashioned, black suits walked by. One had long sideburns and the other wore a black top hat.

"I don't know of any big funerals happening," Mary said, a slight southern lilt to her voice.

And she would know. Mary's our source for news concerning local people or events. She's from an old Fredericksburg family, so she's hard-wired into the grapevine. Around here, news can travel faster by word of mouth than electronically.

"I don't think it's a funeral," I said, as a woman walked by wearing a full-length, black, period dress with a puffy skirt. She fanned her face which was shaded by an elaborate hat trimmed with black flowers. "Is there some kind of reenactment in town this weekend?"

It wouldn't be unusual for there to be a Civil War era reenactment in the area.

I turned to Mary, but she was focused on her phone, texting furiously. She was always the epitome of understated elegance, right down to her phone's subtly gold-edged case.

"It's better than a funeral!" she said.

A couple of people around us glanced our way at her comment.

"Gee, what could be better than a funeral?" asked Sophie.

Mary still didn't respond, reading whatever text she'd received.

"Earth to Mary," I said waving my hand in front of her eyes. "What's better than a funeral?"

She looked up, her brow creased. "That's a weird thing to say, Liv."

Sophie and I laughed.

"I didn't say it. You did."

"Never mind," she said, waving me off. "Listen to this. Momma M said the foundation has been getting calls nonstop from people wanting to know if Edgar Allan Poe or his brother Henry ever visited the city."

"I've never heard of any connection between Poe and Fredericksburg, have you, Soph?"

As a reference librarian, she would be the most likely to know, and because, well, Sophie knew an awful lot about most everything. Though, I would never tell her I thought that.

She was already on her phone, tapping away. I glanced between the two, smiled, and sipped my tea. Whatever was happening, I knew the mystery would soon be revealed.

Sophie looked up from her phone, her eyes alight in a way I'd never seen before.

"You'll never believe this."

She turned her phone around to reveal a series of headlines, which all included Edgar Allan Poe's name.

"A letter was found from Poe's brother Henry to a Wallace Jackson. The letter references a collection of Poe's poems that he included with the letter to Jackson." Her voice kept rising as she spoke. "Based on when Henry died, they believe the only collection he could have been referring to was *Tamerlane*." She ended the statement with breathless excitement.

"And *Tamerlane* would be?" I asked.

Sophie seemed disappointed that neither Mary nor I were expressing the appropriate amount of excitement at the news.

"*Tamerlane and Other Poems* was Poe's first published collection of poetry. He paid a friend to print copies of it for him in eighteen twenty-seven. Historians think there were around fifty copies printed. There are only twelve known to have survived." Her voice rose. "One sold a few years ago for more than six hundred fifty thousand dollars."

"That's a lot of money for a collection of poems," I said.

"Exactly. And a copy of *Tamerlane* was stolen from UVA's Alderman library in the seventies which was never recovered." she said.

"Wait, you're not even reading from an article. Did you know all this already?" I asked.

"I might have," Sophie said, with her trademark know-it-all-librarian smile.

"And this is all connected to the invasion of the goths, how?" Mary asked.

"Apparently, the letter they've discovered was addressed to Wallace Jackson here in Fredericksburg. Do you have any idea how exciting this is?"

Mary nodded. I felt a bit bewildered.

"Poe never lived here in Fredericksburg, did he?" I asked.

"No. He may have passed through on his way from Baltimore to his home in Richmond or vice versa, but there's no record of him having stopped here. He lived in Richmond with his adoptive parents for part of his life. That's why The Poe Museum is there. And you can peek into his dorm room on the lawn at UVA, though he wasn't at UVA for long because he spent what little money he had on gambling and couldn't pay his tuition. He was born in Boston and lived in a variety of places, including London. However, because he spent a portion of his life here, he's still claimed as a Virginian."

"I had no idea you were such a fan of Poe," I said.

"I think he's creepy," said Mary. "I read 'The Tell-Tale Heart' as a teenager and couldn't sleep for days because I thought I heard a heart beating under the floor." Mary shuddered.

"Come on," Sophie said. "Poe was a genius."

"A genius?" Mary asked, her eyebrows raised.

"Yes, and he didn't just write horror. He's credited with writing the first detective stories. Arthur Conan Doyle cited his work as an inspiration for Sherlock Holmes. So, he should be of particular interest to you," she said, looking pointedly at me.

"I hear Marilyn Manson is a fan too," I said. Sophie ignored me, so I didn't bother to tell her my mental image of Poe looked exactly like him.

My phone rang, saving me from hearing more of Poe's biography. "It's Bailey. I'll be back in a sec."

Whenever my daughters Bailey or Izzy called, my friends understood my need to take the call. I carried my phone outside and sat at the end of a row of tables in the warm September sunlight.

"Hi B. What's up?"

"Have you heard the news?" Her voice was filled with excitement.

Thinking she meant some celebrity gossip, I said, "No. What news?"

"The letter linking Poe's *Tamerlane* to Fredericksburg."

"How on earth did you hear—" Then I remembered she worked at the Smithsonian.

"Everyone here is talking about it. It's a huge deal."

"I get that it's rare, but why is there so much excitement? There are already people here wandering around dressed like Poe's contemporaries."

"Already? Wow, that was fast. It's not just that *Tamerlane* is rare, it's become kind of a holy grail for collectors of Poe's work. It was his first poetry collection, and a mystique has grown around it."

"Are the poems that good?" I asked.

"It almost doesn't matter if they're good or not, though no one considers it his best work. Apparently the critics of his time didn't exactly praise it."

"So, again, why all the fuss?"

"Because it's Poe. He has a cult following that bridges generations. There's fan fiction, Poe conferences, Poe raves, Poe impersonator poetry battles. You wouldn't believe the fanaticism."

"Poe raves. Seriously?" I tried not to laugh at the picture forming in my brain. "Shouldn't they be called Rave-ns?" I asked.

Bailey groaned, and I snickered.

"How do you know all this anyway?" I asked.

"I wrote a paper on him at VCU. The Poe Museum in Richmond has a lot of events for Poe enthusiasts. I kinda got into it for a while."

"Ah, that explains all the black clothes in the laundry your junior year, though maybe not the black underwear."

She laughed. "You don't want to know about those."

And she was right. I didn't want to know.

She returned the focus to Poe. "Brace yourself. People are obsessed with him. I'm sure more will show up. I may have to come home for a visit this weekend."

"Any excuse to see you is OK with me."

"I'll let you know if I plan to come down." I heard voices in the background. "I've got to get to work. Love you, Mom."

"Love you too, sweetie." She ended the call and I found myself smiling at the idea of her coming home.

When I sat back down at the table with Sophie and Mary, they were on their phones. Mary was reading and Sophie was talking animatedly, heedless of the other people around her. She's never been good at discretion.

"Get your ass over here now. Let Ellie take care of the store," Sophie said. She paused to listen. "She has a lot of nerve taking the day off." Laughter emanated from the phone. "OK, I'll come down there. See you soon." She ended the call and turning her attention to me asked, "How's Bailey?"

"She called about the whole Poe thing. She's as worked up as you are. She might come home this weekend to be part of all the excitement," I said.

"That's great. She and I can wander around downtown and enjoy the show," Sophie said.

Mary started packing up her Marc Jacobs bag. "I've gotta go. Momma M says they need all hands on deck at HFFI."

Mary was named after her mother. It got too confusing to call them both Mary, so for years she and everyone else have called her mom Momma M. They volunteer at the Historic Fredericksburg Foundation, Inc., known as HFFI. Her mom doesn't like driving much anymore, so Mary drops her off or they volunteer together. Mary's part-time job in the advancement office at the University of Mary Washington, her alma mater, allowed her the luxury of a flexible schedule.

After quick hugs, she was out the door, leaving the slight scent of Calvin Klein's Eternity to blend with the smell of coffee. Strangely, it wasn't a bad combination.

Sophie put her phone in her purse too and started to clean up the table. "I'm heading over to the store. Wanna come with?"

The store meant Past Present, our friend Jane's antique store on Caroline Street six blocks from Hyperion. "No. I think I'll take a short walk, then go home. I have some proofreading work to catch up on."

Sophie threw on a light fleece zip-up jacket over her "I Read Banned Books" T-shirt, gave me a quick hug, and left for Jane's. I wasn't surprised that's where she was going. Rare books are a specialty of Jane's, so I had no doubt she was thrilled by the prospect of a copy of *Tamerlane* being found in Fredericksburg.

I decided to finish my tea before leaving. As I took the last sip, I noticed a man turning the corner from William Street onto Princess Anne. I only caught a glimpse of him. The sight sent a shiver through me, and not in a good way. I felt as if I knew him, but I couldn't place him.

I quickly put my tea things on a tray above the trash receptacle and headed out the door. It was almost as if I wasn't in control of my actions. I crossed the street at the first break in traffic without bothering to even walk to the intersection to use the crosswalk. In a rush, I rounded the corner onto Princess Anne Street and bounced off the plump form of a middle-aged woman, who turned out not to be plump at all. She was surrounded by yards of fabric in the form of a dark, navy blue dress with puffy sleeves and lace across the top of the bodice and sleeves.

"I'm so sorry," I said trying to disentangle myself from her skirt.

She laughed and said, "It's this dress. I'm always bumping into things when I wear it."

She spoke in a high voice with a slightly nasal, southern aristocratic tone to it.

I tried moving around her to see if the man was still in sight, but she put a hand on my arm to stop me.

"Can you tell me the local places where Poe visited? Edgar Allan Poe," she added as if an average person like me wouldn't recognize his name.

"I'm afraid you wasted a trip. There's no record of him ever having visited Fredericksburg," I said, parroting some of what Sophie told us earlier.

She looked taken aback, then tapped me playfully on the arm with her folded fan and said, "You locals can't keep him all to yourselves. We'll find out eventually." She winked and opened her fan, waving it in front of her face. I wondered if it was simply an affectation of the character she was playing or if wearing so much fabric made her hot.

Noticing her age again, I thought I knew what else might create a need for a fan. I briefly imagined what fits G.G. would throw if she was forced to wear a similar dress and the corset underneath while having a hot flash.

G.G. stands for Grumpy Gal. It's the nickname I gave my moody perimenopausal personality when she first reared her feisty head in my late forties. Giving her a name helped me deal with the mood swings with a bit of humor. G.G. almost made the mood swings bearable. Almost. While the frequency of the moodiness had lessened over the years, she still shows up "periodically," and my friends never miss a chance to call her out when she's around.

I wished the woman luck and had to admit I admired her commitment. Though I still rolled my eyes as soon as I was past her.

Free of the haze of lace and skirt, I realized I'd lost sight of the man I'd seen and began to wonder why I was following him in the first place. As I turned toward home, my thoughts turned toward Poe. I'd never really given him much consideration. I found I had a vague image in my head of someone clothed all in black, hunched over a piece of parchment with a quill pen in hand, spilling the dark ink of his mind onto the page. Dressed all in black, like the young men who'd walked by the window earlier.

I was starting to wonder if I truly knew what it meant to be a fanatic. Previously, I'd imagined young women screaming and swooning at the sight of the Beatles, Harry Styles, or hell even Taylor Swift. I'd pictured lunatics in 40-degree weather with no shirts on so they can show off a single letter in the name of their favorite team's name written in grease paint, with what there is of their chest hair caked in the stuff. It now seemed likely I knew nothing of fanaticism.

CHAPTER FOUR

"I'm home," Bailey called as she dropped her purse on the table by the door on Friday night.

I met her halfway down the hall to the front door and hugged her until she begged for air.

"You nearly squeezed the life out of me," she said, laughing.

She looked more and more like me as she got older, our brown eyes and our smiles so similar. Though her lighter brown hair was curly like her dad's rather than slightly wavy, mostly frizzy like mine. Izzy was the one who'd gotten Nate's blue eyes and my mom's deep brown hair.

I put my arm around her and we walked to the living room together, where she flopped on the couch and dropped her phone on the coffee table.

I sat beside her, pulling my feet up under me and turning to face her. "How was the traffic?"

"Not too bad for a Friday night. It only took me an hour and forty-five."

"Ugh, I'm sorry."

"It's no problem. I just listened to a podcast."

"Which one?"

"A true crime podcast about Poe's death."

"I'm already sick of hearing about him. Wait, was his death a crime?"

"No one knows for sure, but the circumstances around his death were sus."

"Sus as in suspect?"

She nodded and grimaced at my oldness simultaneously. "Or suspicious."

"OK, how so?" I asked, surrendering to the inevitable.

"He was supposed to be traveling from Richmond to Philadelphia and showed up in Baltimore instead. He was wearing someone else's clothes and couldn't remember anything after having left Richmond."

"Sounds like a bender to me."

"There's more. He ended up in the hospital, where he was delirious for several days, talking to people who weren't there and calling out the name Reynolds repeatedly before he died."

"Who was Reynolds?"

"Nobody knows." Her eyes were lit with enthusiasm.

We both jumped at the sound of a voice in the hall, "Anyone home?"

"Nope," I called back.

Bailey jumped up from the couch and ran to hug Sophie as she walked into the room. "Sophie the Great. It's so good to see you."

When Bailey was little she'd misunderstood Sophie's last name, Grace. Since then she and her younger sister Izzy have called her Sophie the Great.

"I've told you not to call her that. She takes it too seriously. I think she has it on business cards now."

"It's only in the fine print," Sophie said. She sat on the large, squishy, moss green armchair perpendicular to the couch. "How're you doing, B?"

Sophie was the only one of my friends who also called Bailey by my nickname for her.

"Who cares how I'm doing? Fill me in on all the *Tamerlane* news. Are there any leads?"

Sophie leaned forward, radiating excitement. "I've been keeping my ear to the ground. There are now treasure hunters in town in addition to the Poe fanatics. The treasure hunters are reluctant to share any information because obviously they want to the be the one to find it. However, I've made a couple of interesting discoveries this week. First of all, it's fairly well-established Poe did send a copy of *Tamerlane* to his brother Henry in Baltimore. Henry even had two of the poems published in the Baltimore newspaper *The North American*."

"So, he was trying to help his brother by sharing his work," Bailey said.

"It seems that way," Sophie said. "I was also able to dig up some information about this Wallace Jackson, the man Henry wrote to."

B leaned forward, so she wouldn't miss a word.

"He was a local business owner. Not a big name in town. He owned a small cobbler's shop somewhere near the Old Stone Warehouse. There isn't a lot of information on him." She paused, looking up at me. "You OK?"

The heat had started to rise in my body, along with a familiar tingling feeling running down my spine as Sophie talked. She must have noticed the shiver it induced.

"I'm fine. Just a hot flash," I said while reaching for a tissue to wipe the sweat off my forehead and upper lip.

Sophie raised her eyebrows at me but didn't pursue it. She knew I hadn't broached the subject of my hot flash-induced visions with B or Izzy yet. The few times I'd tried to, I chickened out.

To avoid B's inquisitive gaze, I asked, "All you know is that he was a cobbler?"

"Yes and no. I was able to dig up a reference to a literary journal here in Fredericksburg from the same year as the letter to Wallace. I found an ad in the *Virginia Herald* newspaper calling for submissions of poetry or short stories. The interesting thing is the journal was called *The Lasting Word*."

I was amazed how much Sophie had learned since the news about the letter had broken only days before.

"That doesn't sound like such an unusual name for a literary publication," I said, and B nodded in agreement.

"Not on the surface, but something about it intrigued me. I don't think it would have caught my attention if it'd just been called The Last Word. *The Lasting Word* seemed odd, so I started doing some searches related to the title and came across a reference to terms used by cobblers. Lasting is part of the process of making shoes. A last is the wooden form that's used in place of a foot. The leather is wrapped around it and nailed in place in a process called lasting."

"I've got goosebumps," B said.

I had them too, but I didn't mention them. "So, you think Wallace Jackson was the person behind *The Lasting Word*?" I asked.

"I think there's a pretty good chance he was. And if it's true, then he clearly had an interest in poetry—" Sophie said.

B jumped in. "So, it would make sense that Poe's brother would've sent him a copy of *Tamerlane*."

"Exactly." Sophie's knees bounced with excitement.

"Were you able to find any copies of *The Lasting Word*?" I asked.

Sophie deflated a bit. "No. I couldn't find confirmation any copies were ever made. It's possible it never got off the ground or only put out one or two issues. Paper was not as easy to come by then, and paying for printing may have been difficult for a cobbler. So, even if he was able to have it printed, it's unlikely there were many copies of each issue."

I had a brief flash in my mind's eye of an old wooden box. I'd discovered I could banish the images that would appear unbidden by blinking my eyes repeatedly. The memory of them would stay with me, even as the image dissipated. When I stopped blinking, I found Sophie looking at me.

"What does all this prove?" I asked.

"Nothing really," Sophie conceded. "But it does show there might be a legitimate reason for Poe's brother to have sent a copy of *Tamerlane* to Jackson."

"Have you told anyone else about the journal?" Bailey asked.

An impish gleam showed in Sophie's eyes when she replied, "I didn't want to share it prematurely."

❧

A half-hour later Bailey had changed her clothes and she, Sophie, and I were heading out the door for dinner.

As we walked down the few steps from the courtyard shared by the townhouses surrounding mine to the sidewalk, Sophie said, "Since the story broke, I've been able to glean a little information by sitting quietly in a coffee shop or restaurant frequented by the Poe enthusiasts."

"So, where should we go for dinner? Where are they hangin'?" B asked.

She and Sophie were walking shoulder to shoulder, leaning in to talk to each other like co-conspirators. I walked a step behind them, smiling contentedly. It was a strange and joyful feeling to see my daughter as an adult taking her connection to my friends to a new level, creating a friendship of their own.

Sophie said, "I doubt they've been here long enough to have established regular places, but we should probably try a kinda noisy restaurant. They'll want to be able to have conversations without being overheard."

"For goodness sakes, they aren't spies. Are they really gonna be so stealthy?" I asked.

They each glanced over their shoulder at me with such disdain I had to laugh.

"Don't be such a buzzkill, Mom."

"OK. OK. It's a huge conspiracy. Where would co-conspirators gather for secretive, yet public meetings?" I asked, playing along.

We walked in silence for a moment before Sophie said, "I know where I'd go if I wanted to have a private conversation at a restaurant downtown. The Sky Bar at Castiglia's. There's always music, and you'd have the street noise too, so it would be more difficult for people to eavesdrop."

"Which, at the risk of being a buzzkill, will reduce our chances of hearing any juicy tidbits," I said to more disdainful looks from the two of them.

"If only we had some extendable ears," B lamented.

"Still wishing you were a wizard?" Sophie asked. She'd introduced the girls to the Harry Potter books once they were old enough to be interested in them. Bailey in particular had always wanted to go to Hogwarts. I'd taken them to story time at the library as often as I could and had gotten them their own library cards, at Sophie's insistence, when they each turned five.

With B's long drive down, we were on the late side for dinner, so we didn't have to wait long for a table overlooking William

Street on the rooftop of Castiglia's restaurant. We found we were seated in the vicinity of at least two tables occupied by fans of Poe.

"They must all have it so easy at Halloween," I said nodding to the two tables of darkly clad diners. "I wonder if they dress their children up as ravens or mini Poes."

Seeing Sophie and B roll their eyes at me simultaneously made me snort into my freshly poured water.

I tried starting a conversation on a different topic as we perused the menus. Sophie and B silenced me with glares as they pretended to read their menus while trying to listen in on the conversations happening around them. I decided to let them have their fun.

After our drinks arrived - a margarita for Soph, a Fred Red ale for B, and a whiskey smash for me - I felt a hot flash coming on. I excused myself to go to the ladies' room.

As I walked toward the door to go back inside the main part of the building toward the restrooms, I noticed two men having a quiet yet heated discussion at a table in the corner. I couldn't hear what they were saying, but based on their body language, it was clear they weren't happy with each other. I felt a sense of recognition and unease as I looked at the back of the man facing away from me.

A glance at the other, larger, bald man revealed a tattoo on the right side of the broad canvas of his football player-like neck. From the glimpse I got, it appeared to be two paw prints with claws at the tips of slender toe pads, which climbed up from under the collar of his shirt. I looked away. I didn't want to be caught staring at this imposing man.

By the time I came back out onto the roof from the restroom, the man with the tattoo was gone. The uncomfortable feeling I had when I saw the profile of other man remained.

When I returned to the table, Bailey was leaning over picking up her napkin and glancing at the table behind her. I had a feeling her napkin hadn't fallen accidentally.

"Real subtle, B," I said, sitting down.

"Shhh." She glared while shushing me.

Sophie was sipping her drink as if nothing unusual was happening.

B leaned toward me and said in my ear, "They've been talking about *Tamerlane*. Unfortunately, they seem to be scholars more than treasure hunters, so they've only been discussing the poems in the collection."

"Yes, they've been most unhelpful," said Sophie, who had yet to master the art of whispering.

"Did you hear anything interesting on your way to the bathroom?" B asked.

It wasn't the first instance when I wondered if she had the ability to sense things without the need for hot flashes.

"I didn't hear anything, but I did see something."

I had their full attention.

"It may not be related to Poe," I warned them. "See the table in the corner where the guy is sitting by himself?" I pointed surreptitiously toward the table I'd noticed. They both nodded, glancing in his direction. "He and another man were having what appeared to be an angry discussion while intentionally keeping their voices low. The man who left had a tattoo of paw prints on his neck."

"That's not much to go on," said Sophie. She took a gulp of her drink and stood up.

"What are you doing?" I said, reaching for her arm.

She avoided my grasp and headed toward the corner. Bailey and I watched in amazement as she walked right up to his table and put her hand out to shake his. He gestured to the chair next to him, and she sat down. They talked for what was probably only a couple minutes but felt much longer. Then Sophie got up and walked back over to us.

"Oh my, he's hot," Sophie said sitting back down, fanning herself.

I watched as he glanced over his shoulder at us. When I saw his face, a wave of nausea hit me as I realized where I had seen him before.

"Are you sure you're OK, Mom?" Bailey's eyebrows were drawn together as we stood outside the restaurant.

"I'm fine. I promise."

"You still look pale," she said, not taking me at my word.

Sophie joined us, giving me a reprieve. "The bill's all taken care of. Are you feeling better?"

So much for a reprieve.

"I'm absolutely fine. Will you please stop worrying?" I gave Sophie a meaningful look, hoping she would get the hint to change the subject.

She put her arm through B's and started to move her along the sidewalk. She leaned closer to her and whispered loud enough for me to hear. "Fake swooning just to get me to pick up the bill for our drinks. What is the world coming to?" She shook her head and sighed in a world-weary way.

B smiled and glanced at me sideways to confirm I was walking along with them.

"Bailey," a female voice called from across the street. We all turned to find a young woman waving.

B waved back. "Ronnie."

Without a word to us she dashed across the street where there were hugs and voices raised in happy greetings.

Sophie slipped her arm through mine and whispered, "What did you see?"

I turned toward her, keeping my voice low. "It's not what I saw tonight. It's what I saw a while ago."

"Meaning?"

"I've seen him before."

The foreboding I was feeling must have come through in my voice, because Sophie followed up with, "I take it what you saw was not good?"

"It was the opposite of good."

I felt a slight shudder pass through her as she stood beside me. "Should we go back and talk to him? Warn him or something?"

"No," I said with more force than I intended.

Sophie raised her eyebrows but said nothing.

"It's just, well, what would I say? I can't walk up to a complete stranger and say, 'Hi. I'm Liv, and by the way you're gonna die soon. Have a nice day.'"

Sophie's jaw dropped. "You saw him die?"

I tried to backpedal. "No, I didn't see him die. I wasn't even certain he was dead."

Her eyes held mine.

"He looked dead, though."

"Holy shit, Liv. I never thought—I didn't realize—what do we do now?"

"I wish I knew."

B ran back across the street all smiles, so happy at the reunion with her friend, she didn't notice the dark expressions on our faces. I was glad for the opportunity to put a smile on my face before she slowed down enough to really look at us.

"Was that Veronica?" I asked, with a forced smile.

"Yeah. I haven't seen her in a couple years. We're gonna get together for coffee tomorrow morning."

"That'll be fun, give you a chance to catch up."

"Yup. And since she still lives in the area, she's up on all that's been happening, including all the buzz around *Tamerlane*."

This reawakened Sophie, who'd been silent since B's return. "You'll have to tell us everything she tells you."

"Natch," she said. "It's the least I can do since Mom tricked you into paying for the drinks. But if I'm going to share what I learn from Ronnie, you've got to tell us what you said to the guy at the corner table."

I was relieved to see B was back in a good mood. As the two of them began to walk, Sophie looked back over her shoulder at me, and I could see the concern had clearly transferred to her.

I fell in step beside them and attempted to distract Sophie. "Agreed. Spill it, Soph."

No doubt she saw through me. She let herself be distracted anyway. "I introduced myself as a local reporter working on a story related to *Tamerlane* and treasure hunters."

"What?" I asked, shocked.

"Good idea," said B. "Did he believe you?"

"Sure, why not? There's so much buzz about *Tamerlane* and there have already been stories about it in the paper. I asked if he'd be willing to be interviewed."

"He couldn't have said yes, your conversation was too short," I said.

"Yeah, he was nice about it, but said no. I did ask him a couple questions off the record and he's definitely one of the treasure hunters."

"Did he call himself that?" I asked.

Sophie paused. "No, that was actually the one weird thing he said. I asked if he was a treasure hunter and he said he was here conducting a legitimate search for *Tamerlane*."

"Interesting," B said. "Is he saying there are people here conducting illegitimate searches?"

"That's what it sounded like to me," Sophie said.

"I wonder if he was trying to direct attention to someone else or away from himself," I said.

B put her arm through mine and said, "Let's discuss it over dinner. I'm starving."

"Me too and since I ruined our plans and poor Sophie had to pay for the drinks, how about I spring for delivery and we have dinner at our place?"

"I guess it will do," Sophie said, with a tone of long-suffering.

CHAPTER FIVE

I moved around the kitchen quietly the next morning, knowing B would want to sleep in. I nearly dropped the coffee cup I had just pulled out of the cabinet when I turned to find her watching me from the other side of the counter.

"Geez, B. You nearly gave me a heart attack. I didn't expect to see you for another couple hours."

"Sorry. Next time I'll stomp down the stairs like Izzy so you'll hear me coming."

We smiled thinking of her sister's less than dainty footfalls.

"Trust me," she said yawning. "I would still be sleeping if it was up to me."

"Who's it up to?"

She slumped onto one of the barstools at the counter. "I'm meeting Ronnie for coffee, and she has to be at work by ten."

I patted her hand. "The world can be so cruel."

"The struggle is real," she said.

"Coffee before you go for coffee?" I asked, holding up the cup.

"No thanks. I have to run."

She came around the counter and hugged me. I smiled as I held her, glad I hadn't asked what she was gonna wear, since she clearly meant to go out in what she'd slept in—a pair of soft, charcoal gray yoga pants and an oversized, lightweight, lavender sweatshirt. I kissed the top of her head, which I could only reach because it rested on my shoulder. She'd grown taller than me years ago, a fact she often reminded me of.

⁂

An hour and a half later my phone rang, interrupting my Saturday morning routine of doing absolutely nothing other than staring absently out my window at the birds on the feeder while drinking coffee.

"Hey, B. What's up? How was—"

"Mom, you have to call Sophie and get her to come over. Now!"

"Why? What's the matter?"

"Nothing. I just have lots of *Tamerlane* news to share."

She was either extremely excited by what she'd learned or she'd decided on espresso at the coffee shop.

"I can't wait to tell you what Ronnie said. I'm on my way home now. Call Sophie."

"OK, but I can't call her while I'm on the phone with you."

She laughed and hung up.

When I got a hold of Sophie, she was about to start cleaning her pet ball python Kaa's tank, her least favorite chore. She was thrilled to have an excuse to postpone it.

She arrived ten minutes after B who'd waited in her room so she wouldn't be tempted to tell me everything before Sophie arrived. When Sophie's not-so-quiet voice announced her arrival, B ran downstairs, breathless with excitement.

After a quick hug for Sophie, B said, "Sit. I have so much to tell you."

"Spill the tea," Sophie said. "And who's this Ronnie anyway?"

B smiled and hopped onto the armchair pulling her legs up under her. Sophie and I faced her from the couch.

"I've known Ronnie since kindergarten. We had a falling out in seventh grade. Who doesn't, though? Middle school is a shit show. We became friends again in high school. She ended up going to Germanna for college so she could stay at home to save money, and because her mom was sick."

"I remember. The funeral was so sad," I said.

"She and her mom were close. It was awful for Ronnie," B said, her sadness for her friend palpable.

Losing a parent was an experience they shared, and it had solidified their friendship.

"A year and a half ago, she started doing a podcast called *Tea with Jam*. It's a mixture of Fredericksburg gossip and news about the local music scene."

"I've listened to that," Sophie said. "Isn't the host's name supposed to be a secret?"

"It is. Only a few people know, so you're forbidden to tell anyone." She gave her a mock stern look and Sophie crossed her heart. "It's part of the allure. She's super smart, and she's savvy when it comes to marketing. Plus, staying anonymous has helped protect her from some of the people who weren't so happy with the things she's spilled."

"She doesn't share personal stuff, does she?" I asked. "That sounds mean and possibly dangerous. I wouldn't have thought Ronnie would be intentionally hurtful."

"No, it's not like that. She would never out someone or anything like that. A lot of the gossip is about local politicians or business people and their sketchy closed-door dealings. She does call out some unpleasant truths and has dropped hints about cheating partners. She doesn't name names, but—"

"But if you live here, you can usually figure out who's who," Sophie finished.

"Exactly."

I had an uncomfortable feeling as I listened, which increased when B shot me a momentary, quizzical glance.

"It still sounds dangerous to me. Can't people tell who she is by her voice?" I asked.

"She alters it electronically," B said. "She's thinking of ending the show because she's had a few threatening notes sent to the email address she set up for tips. Plus, she's been able to develop a good relationship with a couple sponsors. So, she may drop it and start a new show in her own name with the help of the sponsors. You know, start building a social media brand for herself."

"Wow, she has sponsors?" I asked.

"We're getting off track," B said.

"Yeah, what did she say about *Tamerlane*?" Sophie asked.

"She had some interesting dirt on the treasure hunters." B's eyes lit up again. "She has a friend who works at the Marriott downtown where several of them are staying. There was a dispute between two of them in a hallway the other night. It almost ended up in a fight. One guy had the other pushed up against the wall and was yelling in his face. They broke it up when another guest opened their door to see what was going on. The guest called the front desk and reported it to the manager. That's how Ronnie's friend found out. And based on the description of the guy who was doing the yelling, I think it was one of the guys we saw at Castiglia's."

Sophie and I spoke over each other.

"Which one?" I asked.

"The one I talked to?"

B smiled. "Not the one you talked to, Soph, but I think it might've been the one he was sitting with. The one you said he was having an argument with, Mom. Ronnie's friend said the guest described him as being bald and big like a football player. And he had a tattoo on his neck."

"Did her friend know what they were arguing about?" Sophie asked.

"No, they stopped yelling when the guest opened the door. He'd only heard raised voices, not what they were saying."

"Were the police called?" I asked, thinking I might be able to get something out of Detective Gomez if they had been. She was the detective who'd been assigned to investigate the break-in at Jane's store the previous year. We had a rocky relationship. She'd been alternately annoyed and amused by me when I was working on the case and helped discover the thief's identity. It was the first time I'd tried putting my visions to practical use.

"No. When the manager got upstairs to check on the situation, the men were already gone. Neither made a complaint and they weren't positively identified as hotel guests, so all they could do was increase the security presence in the public spaces to discourage any more incidents."

I leaned back, strangely relieved the man Sophie had spoken to wasn't the aggressor.

"Did she say what the man shoved against the wall looked like?" I asked.

"The only detail she got was he had a long ponytail," B said. "However, her friend did see a bald man who fit the aggressor's description in the lobby the next day. She overheard him introduce himself as Caleb."

"Does Ronnie have an idea how many people are here searching for *Tamerlane*, as opposed to those who are just Poe fanatics?" Sophie asked.

"From what she's been able to tell, there are four or five individuals or companies searching for it, plus several legit historians. The treasure hunters appear to be competitive, but again, legit." She took a dramatic pause.

"And?" I urged her on.

"She's been hearing rumors about one person with a more notorious reputation."

"Notorious?" Sophie leaned toward B.

"Yes. They don't even use a regular name. They're known only as The Falcon."

"Ooo, The Falcon. That's pretty cool," Sophie said.

"Sounds pretty lame to me. I mean, code names? This isn't a spy movie. It's Fredericksburg."

They looked at me as if I were unbelievably stupid.

"Yeah, and it's got to be the most exciting thing that's happened in Fredericksburg since—" B paused, struggling to think of anything equally exciting that happened here. She looked to Sophie for help.

"Since the Battle of Fredericksburg," Sophie offered.

"Yeah, since then." B's brow crinkled. "Though does that really count as exciting?" she asked.

"Well, if you want to be specific, I guess it was more disastrous than exciting," Sophie said.

"Or catastrophic."

"Or calamitous."

I watched them feed off each other, tossing words back and forth. Each one grinning.

"Cataclysmic," said B.

"Deleterious."

"At the very least, injurious."

"OK, Laurel and Hardy. Enough already," I said.

"At a minimum, hurtful," Sophie tossed in. She couldn't help herself. She loved both playing with words and having the last one.

I gave them each a stern look. "What does Ronnie know about this Falcon?"

The gleam was back in B's eyes. "The Falcon is a dealer in black market antiquities and art. Once Ronnie got wind of the name, she did some searching on the dark web—"

"Isn't that dangerous?" I asked. "How do you access the dark web anyway?" Curiosity momentarily won out over concern.

"I'll explain it later," Sophie said, shocking the hell out of me. She laughed at the surprise on my face. "What? I'm a librarian," she said, as if it explained everything.

"We will definitely get back to that another time. For now, tell us what she found," I said, turning back to B.

"Well, the dark web is a lot like the regular web in some ways, there are marketplaces and services—"

"Bailey Wilde Brown. How do you know about using the dark web?" I demanded.

"She's Gen Z," Sophie said. Again, as if that explained everything.

I was beginning to wonder if maybe I *was* unbelievably stupid.

"Anyway, Ronnie did some searching and found a reference to Falcon Finds in a forum. Eventually, she was able to get a link to their site on the dark web, and they list treasure recovery among their areas of expertise. They have a no questions asked, no questions answered policy. It also said they specialize in art from the World War Two era. Ronnie thinks that's a coded reference to art stolen by the Nazis and never returned to the owners."

My stomach turned over at the thought of someone like that being here in our town.

"If this person is so secretive and powerful, how come Ronnie's heard they're in town?"

"That's a good question," Sophie agreed.

"And wouldn't they have minions to send rather than coming in person?" I added.

"Minions?" Sophie grinned. "Now all I can see is yellow Popsicles with tiny legs running around town in denim overalls."

B laughed. "Popsicles! Now you've ruined the Minions for me."

Sophie laughed too. "It's what they look like. Lemon-flavored Popsicles."

"The way your mind works, Soph. It's one of life's great mysteries," I shook my head. "Seriously though, if some big deal criminal is involved, wouldn't they have people who work for them to do their dirty work? Why would they come to Fredericksburg themselves when there's no concrete evidence a copy of *Tamerlane* is even here? And why would they let it be known they're here?"

"It does seem odd," Bailey said. "Maybe just getting people to whisper their name around town creates the fear they need to keep the competition away?"

"Or maybe," I began, with a tingle traveling up my spine, "it's Poe." I trailed off, trying to pay attention to the feeling that was arising without completely surrendering to the vision just below the surface.

"What's Poe?" Bailey asked, confused.

I had to consciously refocus my attention on Bailey. "The Falcon could have an obsession with Poe, just like everyone else who's come to town."

"It's possible," Sophie said. I felt a twinge of worry at her mischievous expression as she spoke the next words. "Or it could be The Falcon isn't as smart as they think they are. Wouldn't it be cool if we helped catch an international thief?" She practically sang the words.

Before B had a chance to agree, I jumped in. "You mean a potentially dangerous, unscrupulous criminal?" I glared at Sophie, while also darting my eyes to Bailey, who she was enticing into a risky venture.

Sophie must have gotten my message. "Well, if you want to put it that way, it might not be the best idea I've ever had."

"You know what would be a good idea?" B asked. Sophie and I returned our focus to her, and she directed her words to me. "You getting together with Detective Gomez for a friendly chat."

I held up my hands. "Hang on. Most of the chats I've had with Gomez have leaned toward coolly cordial and occasionally slightly hostile. I doubt she'd get together for a cup of coffee and tell me everything she knows about our unsavory visitors."

"Oh, I don't know. I'd say at least one of them is pretty savory," Sophie said.

I smacked Sophie's arm and B laughed.

A familiar feeling caused me to close my eyes. For a moment I saw Gomez holding a tiny doll out toward me. When I opened my eyes, B was staring at me.

CHAPTER SIX

B left on Sunday without any further Poe-related discoveries. She made me promise to keep her updated on any news pertaining to *Tamerlane*. On Monday, I went for a walk downtown after lunch. I'd spent the morning revising an article on the reproductive habits of emus, which was equal parts boring and fascinating. Such is the life of an editor and proofreader. The small, DC-based company I work for has a wide variety of clients who write on a huge range of topics. I didn't always get my pick of assignments, but since I had the freedom to work from home rather than face the commute and had a flexible schedule, I didn't complain. Too much.

Needing to stretch my legs and get the images of mating emus out of my head, I strolled toward Jane's store. If I hadn't been looking at a text on my phone as I approached the entrance, I might have kept right on walking. As it was, I was putting my phone in my pocket and opening the door before I noticed who was with Jane. I would've considered closing the door and continuing on if she hadn't spotted me and waved me over. I didn't need him to turn my way, to know he was the man I'd seen on the street, and at Castiglia's, also known as the dead guy from my vision.

It was an eerie sensation to see a man so alive in front of me, while seeing his pale, still face on the ground in my mind's eye. A juxtaposition I hoped to never have to deal with again.

To have a moment to regain my composure, I waved back at Jane, then dropped my eyes and made a sharp left to walk down an aisle featuring antique chairs and sofas. I strolled slowly along the aisle but eventually had to turn up the next row. As soon as I did, Jane caught my eye and gestured for me to join them. I made my way to where they stood at a counter filled with jewelry once worn by people who were now probably long dead. Everything seemed to be taking on a foreboding Poe sheen.

"Come here. There's someone I'd like you to meet," Jane said smiling.

I couldn't interpret the gleam I saw in her brown eyes.

I approached, stopping a couple feet from the soon-to-be-dead guy's right. I silently scolded myself and insisted I find a new name for him. Jane supplied it.

"Liv, this is Tynan Foley. Ty, this is Liv Wilde."

His eyebrows arched at my name, and he was fighting off a smile. I prayed he would forgo the lame jokes I'd heard a million times.

We shook hands. His were callused and warm.

"Ty's a treasure hunter here searching for *Tamerlane*," she added in a conspiratorial tone.

"It's nice to meet you, Ms. Wilde."

"Please, call me Liv."

"Short for—?" he asked, leaving a blank for me to fill in.

"Olivia," I said.

He'd stopped fighting the smile. It annoyed me that my first thought was what a nice smile it was. It further irked me that I liked the trace of an Irish accent he had when he spoke. I wondered why he bothered me so much. It wasn't his fault he was going to die soon. Then again, maybe it was. I didn't know anything about the circumstances around his impending death. I reminded myself he wasn't responsible for my vision, even if he might be responsible for what happened in it.

I realized they were looking at me. Had I missed a question?

"Where were you?" Jane asked, a trace of suspicion in her voice. "You disappeared for a minute."

I forced a laugh. "Zoned out. I get sleepy after lunch."

"I was just asking if we've already met," Ty said.

Truth or lie? I wondered. I decided on a little of each. "No, but you met a friend of mine the other night at Castiglia's. Sophie Grace," I said.

It took a moment for the memory to surface, then he said, "Ah, the inquisitive Ms. Grace."

"She is the curious type. Though I guess most reporters are," I said.

Jane raised her eyebrows but didn't give me or Sophie away.

"You know what happened to the curious cat," he said.

Was that a threat? I stifled another shudder as I tried to block out the idea of curiosity being what would get him killed. "What about you, Mr. Foley?"

He interrupted before I could continue. "Ty, please."

"What about you, Ty? I would think people in your line of work are curious by nature."

He nodded. "Curious and cautious."

His attention was drawn to something outside. As it turned out, it was someone. All three of us shifted our gaze to the door. A gorgeous woman with flaming red hair opened it and leaned in. Not a freaking gray hair anywhere to be seen, I noted. She wore jeans that fit her just right and a snug, Kelly green T-shirt with the words, "Don't Make This Ginger Snap" in yellow letters.

She stood in the doorway without entering the store, gesturing for Ty to join her. In her left hand, she held a to-go cup, which she took a sip from.

"Looks like I need to be on my way. Thank you for your assistance, Jane." He turned to me. "It was nice to meet you, Liv."

We watched him walk toward the door, which the woman held open for him, heedless of the breeze blowing inside, carrying a faint scent reminiscent of chai tea with it.

As soon as the door closed, Jane said, "What the hell was that all about?"

I filled her in on Sophie's conversation with Ty at dinner.

"And she wasn't able to get any details out of him?" Jane asked.

"Nothing other than confirming he was in town searching for *Tamerlane*. He stressed that he's a professional. If she was going to include him in a story for the paper, he didn't want to be categorized as an amateur." I glanced over my shoulder out the window to reassure myself they were out of sight. "What was he doing here anyway? Did you get any information from him?"

"It was the other way around. He was trying to get information out of me." She did a quick scan of the store and gestured to her office with a nod of her head.

She closed the office door behind me. I took my customary seat in front of her desk, and she sat behind it.

"What was he after?" I asked, leaning forward.

"Well, of course he was interested to know if I knew of any rumors linking *Tamerlane* or Poe to Fredericksburg, which I could honestly say I hadn't. He also asked if I knew of any old literary journals from the time period."

"Sounds like he was aware of your area of expertise, doesn't it?"

"Yes. He said he heard I was the person to come to for rare books or documents in the area." A note of pride came through in her voice.

She'd opened her store over twenty years ago and much of her identity was wrapped up in it. It may be a small store in a small town, but she'd earned a reputation as a savvy businesswoman and carved out a niche for herself as an expert on rare books.

"I didn't have any information to give him, even if I'd wanted to."

"You didn't want to?"

"Are you kidding? If I knew where a copy of *Tamerlane* was I'd be the first to claim it. Then I'd retire to some tropical island."

"One with a variety of cabana boys?" I asked.

"Is there another kind?" she asked without missing a beat.

I was only a few years older than Jane. With the help of her stylist, she kept her dark, short, spiky hair free of gray. She also had an affinity for younger men, which she said kept her feeling youthful. Though her affair with Spencer, more than twenty years her junior, had been rekindled last year, the flame had faded. He'd since moved to Northern Virginia for a job, but at least this time the relationship had ended on a good note as opposed to when they'd first dated. That was a story she'd managed to keep hidden from us until it came out when we were questioned by Detective Gomez last year.

"I can't imagine you giving up the store and retiring."

Her expression became more serious, exposing tiny lines on her face. "Until last year, I couldn't imagine it either. Since I hit the back side of my fifties, I've started thinking more seriously about it. I still enjoy my work. I'm just not quite as passionate about it anymore."

"And what on earth would Ellie do?"

Jane smiled. "She'd become the new proprietor."

"Oh, lord. I'm not sure she has the temperament?" Ellie was a wonderful person and a great assistant manager, however she had a tendency toward the dramatic.

"You know, in a way, my partnership with Ellie is the longest relationship I've ever had."

"You certainly don't like being tied down."

With a sly smile she replied, "Well, maybe by one of those cabana boys."

I snorted. "Gives a whole different meaning to hitting the back side of your fifties." We both laughed, though mine quickly faded. "Are you really considering moving away after you retire?"

"I don't know. I'd love to move someplace exotic, but I don't have the money for anything too extravagant."

"I can't imagine our Monthlies without you." I was surprised by the catch in my throat. I'd never considered what would happen to my circle of friends once we started to retire. The thought was kind of depressing.

"I can't imagine it either." Her expression softened. "I guess we'll just have to create a village of tiny houses for all of us to live in."

I smiled. "What about the husbands?" Three of our friends were married.

"They will be welcome for conjugal visits," she said with a straight face.

"That's quite generous." I laughed.

She leaned forward. "Speaking of conjugal visits, what did you think of Ty?"

"Wow, that was a direction I didn't expect you to go."

"Oh, come on, why did you think I wanted to introduce you?"

"Seriously?"

"Of course. He's handsome. He's interesting. He's—"

"Here with his hot girlfriend."

"A minor complication."

"A minor complication?"

"Perhaps she'd be open to a ménage à trois." The grin was back.

I rolled my eyes. "Yes, that's exactly what I need as my first foray back into dating."

"Indeed. It might be just what you need."

"Yes, to compare myself to a gorgeous younger woman with a perfect figure and no gray hair. A real confidence booster."

"You don't give yourself enough credit, Liv. If you're going to get back out there, you're going to need to embrace your own hotness."

"I'll need to find it first."

"We will have to see what we can do about that."

"Sometimes you're terrifying, Jane."

She laughed her throaty, I-don't-give-a-damn-what-any-one-thinks laugh. It was one of her qualities I loved the most.

CHAPTER SEVEN

The second Friday in September was Jane's turn to host our Monthly dinner party. The rest of us loved it and hated it when we met at her house. She's an excellent cook, so, the meal would be delicious. However, her house was also the farthest from downtown, which meant if we wanted to take an Uber after an evening of good food and decent wine, it would cost more.

We were definitely not disappointed with the food. Since the weather had begun to cool, Jane had made a fabulous butternut squash, apple, and potato soup. Each bowl was topped with a sprinkling of lightly-fried prosciutto. It brought the perfect amount of saltiness to the mildly sweet soup.

It's also a pretty accurate description of the friends I gather with for our Monthly: They bring a little (understatement) saltiness to the mostly sweet soup of my life.

"Who thinks Liv needs to start putting herself out there?" Jane clearly had an agenda for the gathering based on our conversation at the store. She dove right in after we'd finished dinner and gathered in the living room with refilled wine glasses.

All their hands shot up. It was telling for me even Claire raised her hand. She'd been the one to support my desire to wait.

"I'm not ready," I protested.

"You say that every month," Hannah said.

"And it's still true. So, you can stop asking me every fucking month!" I said with more frustration than I'd intended.

"Whoa. G.G.'s in the house," Hannah laughed. Her voice was deeper than the rest of ours, so her laugh was too. It always made me smile.

Calling out G.G. was a surefire way to help me laugh at the moodiness, and so, temper it.

I put my hands up in surrender. "I'm sorry. The truth is I'm not sure how I'll know when I'm ready to date again."

Claire leaned toward me, her perfect blond bob swinging forward. "You know we all love and support you taking the time you need, but it's possible you'll never feel completely prepared. You may have to settle for being as ready as you can be."

The subject of my resistance to the idea of dating since my husband Nate's death was a regular topic at our monthly dinners. Especially if Hannah had too much wine.

"You're not gettin' any younger you know," Hannah said. She was known for her sometimes-brutal honesty.

"Yes, thank you for the unnecessary reminder. I'm well aware of it. Gravity reminds me every day." I put my hands under my breasts and lifted them. "Why can't they make a bra that doesn't wreck your shoulders and still provides some lift?"

"In the future they should have some anti-gravity device built into bras," Sophie said. "Ones that can make both nipples point in the same direction too. You just press a button and—" she lifted her breasts as I had, while attempting a sci-fi-spaceship-door-opening-whooshing-sound "—up they go and straight forward."

Hannah almost did a spit take. Upon recovering she said, "Can you visualize that? All these women walkin' around with their perky boobs floatin' in front of them." She hoisted her breasts with her bra straps and pranced around the room bouncing them like they were floating.

Claire did do a spit take, which made us laugh harder. Luckily, she was standing in the kitchen, having gone to refill her wine glass. We've learned over the years that when cleaned right away, red wine won't stain ceramic tiles.

"God, Han, I don't know if I'll ever be able to get that image out of my mind," Claire said reentering the living room.

Hannah patted her breasts and said, "There are worse things to have stuck in your mind."

"Honestly, that's part of my resistance to dating," I said.

"Hannah's breasts?" asked Sophie.

"Well, hers do pale in comparison," laughed Hannah. She sat on the arm of the couch beside me and put a consoling arm around me. "But they're not bad."

I leaned into her, laughing. "With friends like you, it's a wonder I'm not out there already."

"Wait a minute, what were you going to say, Liv? What's part of your resistance to dating? Besides Han's ample breasts?" Sophie was always paying attention. It was hard to sneak anything by her.

I took a breath, unsure if I wanted to say what I'd been thinking. Another sip of wine fortified me. "It's been forever since I started dating anyone. I was always nervous about the physical part in new relationships. You know I've struggled with body image, so the idea of being naked with someone now," I looked toward Sophie, "without an anti-gravity device is terrifying." Jane and Mary nodded in unison.

They were the other two who weren't in long-term relationships. Jane because she preferred short-term relationships and Mary because she was divorced and still saying she was one and done. We all wondered if the right man would change her attitude about it.

"Soph, you, Claire, and Hannah have gotten to age with your partners, you've seen each other changing over the years. When I start a relationship, all they'll see is me now."

"Hmm, I see your point. You should consider a convent. Then you can wear one of those shapeless, baggy habits," said Sophie. She threw a balled-up napkin at me across the coffee table that separated us. "Come on, Liv. You're gorgeous."

"And curves are in," added Claire. "Though I do understand what you mean. I think it would be terrifying too."

Sophie lightly slapped Claire's arm. "That's not helpful."

"What? You think it's better to be dishonest? I do think it would be scary at our age." Sophie opened her mouth, but Claire preempted her. "And before you point out that I'm the youngest, that doesn't mean gravity hasn't taken its toll on me too."

Of course, we all looked at Claire's breasts, which, while a smidge perkier than mine, were drooping a little.

"Time waits for no woman," Jane said.

"Well, this woman is going to do some more waiting," I said.

"Wait until what?" Sophie asked. "Seriously, what's the worst that can happen? Unless you're Jane Cougar Mellencamp over there, any guy you're likely to date would be at a similar point in his life."

"Meaning?" I asked.

"Meanin' his balls will be as saggy as your boobs," Hannah concluded, as eloquent as ever.

"Yeah, but you never hear some famous actor being criticized because his balls aren't as perky as they used to be," Claire chimed in.

"And even if they are saggy, I won't have to go searching for them," I said.

"What the hell are you talkin' about?" asked Hannah.

"Imagine I'm with a guy for the first time and we're naked and I lie back on the bed and he leans over me and says, 'Wait, where did your breasts go?' and then he has to go searching in my armpits for them!"

Sophie had to run to the bathroom and Hannah fell off the arm of the couch they were laughing so hard.

"Talk about images we won't be able to get out of our minds," said Jane.

After we had all caught our breath and Sophie had returned, Hannah said, "It's simple. You just adjust your dating profile to say, 'Lookin' for a man who likes to go spelunking'."

I snorted, making me choke on the sip of wine I'd just taken.

"I think we're missing something important," Sophie said with a mischievous glint in her eye. "Liv said when she starts a relationship, not if. That's a big step forward." She raised her glass to me.

I smiled and raised my glass in return, still terrified, but maybe a tiny bit closer to ready.

"I think she should step forward right into the arms of Ty Foley," Jane added.

"Ooo, who's Ty Foley?" Claire asked.

"He's one of the treasure hunters in town after *Tamerlane*," Jane said. "And he's got a nice ass."

"An important feature," Hannah chimed in.

"He also has a voice to die for," Jane added.

I cringed at the reference to Ty and death.

Sophie noticed and asked, "Is this the guy from Castiglia's?"

I nodded and she raised her eyebrows, knowing what I'd seen in his future.

"Why's his voice so special?" Mary asked.

Jane spoke up. "He has a hint of an Irish accent. It's sexy."

"And most likely fake," I added. "I mean why would he have only a hint of an Irish accent? Either you have one or you don't. It seems suspicious," I said.

"It seems like an excuse," Jane said.

I shrugged. "I have one indisputable excuse. She's around five-eight, red-haired, and gorgeous. And she looked pretty tough. I bet she could kick my ass."

"Well, that's probably true," Jane sighed.

"Who is she?" Mary asked.

I looked at Jane.

"Search me. He didn't mention her when we talked," she said. "He certainly jumped when she called, though."

"Yeah, he did leave as soon as she showed up. I wonder if she's his boss," I said.

"She looked like the kind of woman a man would like to have boss him around," Jane said with a wicked grin.

"Well, it is an obstacle, but not an insurmountable one," Mary said.

Hannah opened her mouth and I held up a hand to stop her. "Don't say it." I knew where her mind went at the word insurmountable.

She put her hand to her chest and batted her eyes. "What? I was just gonna suggest you ask him if he enjoys spelunking."

I picked a pillow and threw it at Hannah.

"I think I'll be staying above ground for a while." I struggled to suppress a shiver at my own words.

"I guess we'll have to wait and see," Jane said.

CHAPTER EIGHT

I t turned out I didn't have to wait long. Ty called me the next day. I suspected it was at Jane's suggestion. I was so caught off-guard by his call, I'd agreed to meet him for dinner the next evening before I'd had a chance to think better of it.

It had taken me an hour and a half and three changes of clothing to settle on a pair of curve-hugging, flared jeans and a red, short-sleeved sweater with two buttons below the scoop neckline allowing the wearer to reveal as much cleavage as they dared. I had them both buttoned closed. Even with the wardrobe changes, I arrived prior to Ty.

Sweat beaded on my upper lip as I waited for him at a table for two at Foode. It wasn't only a hot flash turning up the heat, though. I struggled with my mixed emotions about having dinner with him. Why was I there? Was it just for information or did I hope for more than that? Did I hope I could somehow save his life? Lucia would ask me what my intention was, and I wouldn't know how to answer her.

I had to admit I found him attractive. I also had reservations, given the tone of his comment about curiosity killing the cat at Jane's store and the fact that he was likely going to die soon. I'd never been attracted to "bad boys," which my gut warned me he was. They're too high maintenance when you get right down to it. Why be with people who don't care about anyone else's feelings? Besides, at this point in my life, I had no desire to play games in a relationship. *Shit, did I just think the word relationship in connection to Ty?*

I picked up the cold glass of water in front of me, took a sip, and then held it to my forehead, hoping to cool and calm myself. Closing my eyes to try to focus on the coolness of the glass, I also surrendered to the nagging feeling making itself known, an indicator of a vision arising.

Scenes formed in my mind, playing out like a movie. The redhead stands beside Ty, her right hand holding his left. They might be on a sidewalk somewhere in town. She leans toward him and whispers in his ear. My attention is drawn to her forearm, which is covered by the sleeve of a thin, sheer fabric. Through the sleeve I can tell there's a tattoo but it's shrouded by the fabric. It appears to be an animal, a dog maybe, with a bushy tail. I wished, not for the first time, my visions had a zoom feature so I could get a better look at the things that felt the most important.

"Are you alright?"

My eyes flew open to find Ty standing beside the table, look-ing at me curiously. The condensation from the glass I was still holding to my forehead had dripped onto the table and formed a small puddle. I tried to sop it up with a napkin while putting down the glass and casually wiping my brow with the back of my hand.

"I'm fine. Just a little warm." I gestured to the seat across from me.

He sat and said, "You were a million miles away. I said your name twice. It was like you didn't hear me."

He wore dark khaki pants and a hunter green button down, with a pair of dark leather boots. My traitorous heart skipped a beat when I looked at him.

"Long day," I said.

He was still looking at me like I was in a cage at the zoo when our server came to my rescue. He was a young man in his twenties, who I'd noticed didn't carry anything for making notes about people's orders, which always concerned me.

"Good evening. I'm Chad. I'll be taking care of you tonight. Thank you for joining us for dinner. Can I get you some drinks to start with?"

Ty picked up the drink menu, which I'd already read through.

"I'd like a whiskey and lemonade, if possible," I said.

"No problem," Chad said with confidence, even though it wasn't on the menu.

Ty glanced at me over his menu with what I hoped was approval and ordered a stout. I felt awkward in the silence left in Chad's wake. I was painfully conscious of the fact I hadn't been on a date with a relative stranger in decades. I had no idea why people put themselves through this. But this was more of a fact-finding mission than a date, so it was fine.

He broke the silence, which I'm sure was much shorter than it seemed. "How the hell do you pronounce the name of this restaurant anyway? Is it just food with a silent e for effect or is it foodie?"

I smiled, knowing it was a common question. "It's pronounced foodie. The chef, Joy Crump, is a well-known and well-respected chef. The food here is wonderful and locally sourced."

He rolled his eyes. "Ah, the farm-to-table trend. In other countries, we just call that a restaurant."

"Of course. I hear all the restaurants in London get the lamb for their shepherd's pie from the farms in Piccadilly Circus."

He smirked. I hated it and liked it equally. "Touché."

When I smiled back, I was struck by a wave of guilt. Whether or not this was officially a date, I couldn't help but wonder what Nate would think. I felt anxiety mounting and was afraid I was going to have a panic attack when Chad approached with our drinks. I'd never been so grateful to see a waiter.

He'd no sooner set my drink down than I picked it up and took a big swig. I enjoyed the heat of the whiskey in my throat and the citrus lingering on my tongue. It was a calming combination.

I asked Chad for a few more minutes to look over the menu and raised my glass to Ty. "To discovering hidden treasures."

A rakish grin lit his face when he raised his glass to meet mine.

I tried to ignore the implication in his smile and the tiny thrill it made me feel. I made a clumsy attempt to change the subject. "So, how'd you get my number?" I wasn't always good at subtlety.

He didn't bat an eye. "I would think that was obvious. I'm an expert at finding things."

"An expert?" my eyebrows raised in what I hoped was a doubtful expression. "Since it's unlisted, I'd guess Jane gave it to you."

He smiled a Cheshire cat smile and admitted to nothing.

I decided to try to focus the conversation on why I was there. "How does one become a treasure hunter? Is there a certification process? Treasure hunter academy?"

"Are you mocking me?" he asked with a dramatic expression of hurt on his face.

A smile came easily to my lips. "Seriously, did you watch a lot of pirate movies as a kid or read *Treasure Island* over and over? What got you into it in the first place?" My curiosity was genuine, which he must have sensed because he paused to consider my question, taking a sip of his beer.

"If you truly want to know, it started on my tenth birthday. My dad was a history buff. I think he always wished for more adventure than his life offered. So, when I turned ten he got me my own metal detector and taught me how to use it. I spent a whole summer searching every field and nook and cranny in our village for buried treasure."

The slight Irish lilt in his voice, with his soft vowels and occasional rolling Rs, drew me into the story.

"Did you find any?"

"Believe it or not, I did." A gleam had begun to light his eyes. "Beside an old, rundown cottage, I found a metal box. I imagined it was filled with gold Roman coins. It didn't occur to me at that age to look at the box itself to see how old it was before I got too worked up. I sneaked it back to my bedroom to open it in secret. When I shook it something metal rattled around inside, which confirmed my suspicion about the gold coins. When I tried to open it, I found it was locked."

"What did you do?"

Chad's voice preempted Ty's response. "Are you ready to order?"

Ty grinned at the look of exasperation on my face at the untimely interruption. We glanced at the menu. I ordered chicken and waffles and he ordered an Angus burger.

"Chicken and waffles?" he asked as Chad walked away.

"What? It's one of their specialties." I felt defensive. Hadn't we progressed beyond the days when women were supposed to only order a salad on a date? "If you weren't so judgmental, I might've been willing to let you try some."

"It just sounds like a very southern kind of dish. I was under the impression you weren't from around here."

Had I told him I was from New Jersey? I didn't remember having shared where I grew up. "What gave you that impression?"

He shrugged. "First rule of treasure hunting, always research the prize in advance." He held my eyes and I blushed, not knowing if he was flirting or just being honest about having asked around about me for other reasons.

"Anyway, back to the box you found. How did you get it open?"

"I didn't."

"You didn't? What happened?"

"I tried everything I could think of: a screwdriver, a pocket knife, one of my sister's hairpins."

"You have a sister?" I asked, not able to keep the astonishment out of my voice.

"And two brothers. Is it such a surprise I should have siblings? Or did you think I'd sprung full-grown from the loins of the devil?"

I laughed and said, "Fair enough, I guess even the devil's spawn can have siblings. How did you find out what was inside the box?"

"I had to enlist my dad's help, which was good and bad."

"Why bad?"

"Because he wanted to know where I'd found the box."

"Meaning you had to return it?"

"Yes, but not until after we opened it." He grinned from ear-to-ear. "He may have been an honest man, but he was also a curious one. He had a jar of old keys he'd collected over the years and after a few attempts, he was able to get it open using one of the keys and a bit of force."

"What was inside?"

"When the latch finally popped open, we looked at each other over the box and I swear his eyes were as wide as mine must have been. He let me open it, and inside we found a bunch of coins from the forties, a few bullets, an old German Luger pistol, and a medal from the war."

"Wow. That was quite a find. What did you do with it?"

"After my dad confirmed the gun wasn't loaded, we took it to the home of the people who owned the property I'd found it on. I'd tried to convince my dad we didn't need to return it, that it had been hidden there by someone they didn't even know. He wouldn't be persuaded, insisting we take it to them. He told me if they didn't claim it, we would take it to the local historical society and see if they wanted it."

"Did the property owners recognize it?"

"To my disappointment, they did. The name on the medal was one of their uncles on their mother's side, which was why we hadn't recognized it. He'd had a difficult experience during the war and had come home a different person. He'd become very secretive. They let him live in the cottage on the property, but he kept to himself. They never knew he had the Luger or how he'd gotten it."

"How did they react?"

"The grandmother, whose brother it had been, got all choked up over the medal. She thought it had been lost. She was so happy they'd be able to leave it at his grave where it belonged." He sounded choked up too and paused for a sip of beer.

"They donated the Luger to the local historical society and let me keep the coins as a reward for having found the medal. Even though they weren't worth much, I've been hooked ever since."

"Sounds like it's in your blood."

He nodded. "The box hadn't crossed my mind in a long time."

"This was a village in Ireland?"

His eyebrows raised. "How'd you know that?"

I grinned and said, "First rule."

His laugh was deep and genuine.

"Did you and your dad keep searching for treasure together?"

"Unfortunately, no. We moved the following summer to Boston." His Irish accent couldn't hide the evidence of his life there in the way he pronounced Boston. "His new job required long hours. I had to go on quests on my own. It can be a lonely business."

"Not too lonely, it seems."

His eyes held mine. "What're you implying?"

He caught me off guard. I wasn't exactly sure myself what I meant. "Well—" I stammered. "You and the woman I saw at Jane's store seemed pretty close." I felt like an idiot.

He smirked and enjoyed my discomfort for a moment, then responded. "Perry and I are business partners before," he paused for effect, "anything else."

For a moment, the glimpse of the tattoo on her arm flashed through my mind. Was it a coyote?

"How long have you been working together?" I asked.

"Five years, but our paths crossed frequently for years prior to that. We started out as competitors."

"What changed?"

"Let's just say we decided it was more profitable to work together than to work against each other." He picked up his beer, not willing to say more.

I pressed on anyway. "If you were competitors once, I would think it would be hard to trust each other as partners." I wondered if I pushed on because I wanted more information or because I felt a twinge of jealousy.

He was able to avoid responding to my statement because Chad arrived with our food. My plate featured a single, large Belgian waffle with two pieces of crisp fried chicken on top and two small metal cups on the side, one filled with warm maple syrup and the other with cardamom, honey butter. Ty's burger was topped with melted blue cheese, lettuce, and tomato on a toasted brioche bun and was accompanied by thin, crisp fries and fresh slaw. He raised his eyebrows at my plate.

"If it's possible for the devil's spawn to be on good behavior, you might earn a taste."

"Oh, I think I'd be willing to be well-behaved for a little taste."

I blushed as red as my sweater when I saw he was looking at me, not at my food.

Grasping for a change of subject, I said, "You lived in Boston, so you must be a Red Sox fan."

He laughed at my discomfort and said, "Luckily, I never picked up the American obsession with baseball."

My horror must have shown on my face.

"Not the right thing to say, I take it."

"I grew up in a baseball-loving family. My dad's a huge Orioles fan and so am I, though I make it to more Nationals games than O's games now."

"You go in person? How can you stand it? They're so boring."

"You should stop talking now."

"Baseball's a deal-breaker?" he asked with surprise.

I raised my eyebrows, happy for an opportunity to put him on the spot. "Deal-breaker? I didn't realize we were in negotiations."

"Didn't you?"

Throughout the rest of the meal we talked of inconsequential things. I did offer him a sample from my plate, but I'm happy to say I put it on his plate rather than offering to feed it to him. Based on the groan of pleasure he made upon tasting it, I think I convinced him of the allures of chicken and waffles, if not of my own allures.

I admit I was aroused by the sound of his enjoyment, which must have shown on my face because I blushed again when I saw the twinkle in his eye as he continued chewing while smiling at me.

I wanted to wipe that smug expression off his face or at least distract him from what felt like making fun of me. "Is *Tamer-*

lane the biggest prize you've hunted for in terms of potential payout?"

He finished chewing and took a sip of his beer, while glancing around at the tables near us. He leaned toward me. "You make it sound so mercenary."

"Isn't it? I mean you're a treasure hunter, not an archaeologist, right? You're in it for the money, aren't you?"

"If I was only in it for the money, I would try to find it and sell it to a different kind of buyer."

I wondered how well he knew those types of buyers.

"Despite what you apparently think, most people in my field work with local authorities when searching for lost items. Yes, there is a monetary reward - it is a job after all - but there is also the benefit of being able to illuminate the history of the find. Much like what happened after you helped find the Monroe letters."

I was surprised he knew of my involvement in the discovery of a secret cache of letters written by James and Elizabeth Monroe last year, though I guess I shouldn't have been. There'd been a great deal of publicity about the letters and how they'd come to light.

"You did your homework."

"Yes, I did." He leaned toward me. "What wasn't clear in what I read was how you knew where to look for the letters. There were some who hinted you have psychic abilities which helped you find them."

His gaze was intent on mine, and I realized why he'd asked me out to dinner. I felt disappointment flare up in my chest.

"Surely you don't believe in psychics," I said.

He shook his head. "Come now. Why wouldn't the devil's spawn believe in the supernatural?"

"Touché," I said, smiling in spite of myself.

His smile faded a little. "One thing I've learned in this business, is there are some unexplainable things in this world."

I was intrigued. "Tell me more."

"Don't try to change the subject." He placed his forearms on the table, a serious expression on his face. "Are you psychic?"

"Can I tempt either of you with our desserts this evening?" Chad asked with impeccable timing.

Ty held my eyes for a moment longer before acknowledging Chad. "I couldn't eat another thing, thanks."

I agreed, and Chad began clearing our dishes away after offering to box up what was left on my plate.

Ty returned his attention to me. I did my best to hold his gaze.

This wasn't the first time a stranger asked me about my abilities. Ever since I'd helped find the letters, there'd been sporadic messages from people via social media or texts to my phone, asking me to help them find things, pets, or people they'd lost. It was heartbreaking to read their messages and sense their desperation. It was the reason I'd gotten an unlisted phone number. My friends were still encouraging me to open G.G.'s Investigations, which I was considering, but it was something I thought of as happening in the future. I wasn't ready to hang out a shingle yet. I had a long way to go to better understand and make use of my so-called gift before I could consciously use it to help others.

I decided to be honest, yet keep it simple. "I don't know what the correct term is for the abilities I have, but I do experience prescient visions and dreams."

His gaze was so intent, I felt like he was trying to read my mind with his own psychic abilities. It made me wonder if he sensed I'd had a premonition about him.

"Maybe we can help each other," he said in a way that left me feeling vaguely uncomfortable.

"Maybe we can," I said. "What can you tell me about a dealer who's known as The Falcon?"

His eyebrows shot up and he leaned forward, keeping his voice low. "I wouldn't go throwing that name around."

I lowered my voice too. "Why not?"

"Like I said, most of us in this business work with local authorities. However, there are those who're less scrupulous when it comes to reporting what they find. They also tend to use less scrupulous means to find it."

"Meaning?"

"If the find is particularly valuable, they won't hesitate to—" he paused, searching for the right words. "Hamper the competition," he concluded.

"Like the bald man you were in a heated conversation with at Castiglia's?"

He was confused for a moment, then his brows raised. "You're full of surprises, aren't you?"

"Who was he?" I asked.

He leaned back in his chair, considering me. "I see you directed the conversation away from yourself." As he opened his mouth to continue, he was distracted by the rumble of his phone vibrating on the table. He picked it up and held it so I couldn't see the message or who it was from and sent a short reply.

"We'll have to continue this conversation another evening. I'm afraid I have to be on my way." He signaled to Chad, who brought the bill to the table along with my to-go box. I reached for my purse, but Ty said, "It's on me," and placed two hundred-dollar bills on the tray with the bill and told Chad to keep the change, leaving him a generous tip.

"I'm sorry to have to run off. I'll be in touch."

"What's the hurry?" I asked. "A break in the hunt for *Tamerlane*?"

Did I imagine it or did it get quieter in the restaurant at my words?

Ty stood and grinned down at me. "Rule number two, never answer questions about how the hunt is going." He leaned toward me, kissed my cheek, and left without another word.

I was torn between being annoyed at his abrupt departure and noticing how warm and soft his lips had felt on my cheek.

CHAPTER NINE

As soon as I walked out the door, I called Sophie. She picked up after one ring.

"How'd it go?" she asked without preliminaries.

"Weird. Good. Weird. Annoying."

"In that order?"

I laughed. "Not necessarily."

"Are you on your way home?"

"I just walked out of the restaurant and am heading that way."

"I'll meet you there soon," she said.

I looked at my phone, surprised and not surprised to see she had hung up without a goodbye.

I'd been home only fifteen minutes when she came in, calling hello from the hallway. I was sitting on the couch when she walked in and sat beside me, pulling one knee up so she could turn sideways to face me. I did the same.

"Tell me everything he said."

I shared our conversation, the innuendos, the blushing, the story about his tenth birthday, the text bringing an abrupt ending to our conversation. I didn't leave any embarrassing detail out, knowing I could trust Sophie with all of it.

"I was hoping for some information about how close they are to finding *Tamerlane*. I guess I should've known he wouldn't divulge anything useful." She sighed. "Do you think he was telling the truth about how his interest in treasure hunting began?"

"It hadn't occurred to me he might be lying," I said, pausing to reflect on his childhood story. "It felt genuine to me. He had a gleam in his eye when he talked about it, like the little boy with his metal detector was still having fun searching for treasure."

"You have a crush on him, don't you?"

Damn my face for blushing again. "I wouldn't go that far. I think he's good-looking. However, he's also over-confident, which you know I don't find attractive."

She nodded in agreement.

"It felt strange to have dinner with a man who wasn't Nate."

"I'm sorry it felt weird. I guess it's to be expected, but that part will shift eventually." She put her hand on my arm.

"I kept feeling guilty. Like Nate was somehow able to see me and disapproved."

We sat in silence for a few moments.

"Do you believe in ghosts?" I asked, feeling a bit childish.

"Do I believe that our loved ones watch us from the afterlife, whatever that is?" she asked. "No, I don't. Whatever's next, I don't think they would waste their time watching us grieve or do the stupid human things we do." She paused, thoughtful. "I do believe the people we've loved stay with us in some ways, and I even believe they can communicate with us once in a while, just to let us know we're still connected. I don't think that's the same thing as ghosts, though."

"But do you think there are ghosts? I mean, there are ghost tours around town."

With our long history (relatively speaking) and handful of local battlefields, Fredericksburg has many rumors about ghosts.

"Well, I don't know if there are disembodied spirits wandering around downtown, but some spooky things have happened at the library."

She hesitated, which was odd for Sophie, and I shivered. It's one thing to tell ghost stories to entertain tourists. It's another thing to hear experiences with the paranormal from someone you trust.

She seemed to need a nudge. "What kind of spooky things?" I asked.

"They were mainly small things. An item of no value went missing from someone's desk and was found in an unusual place. There was a period when employees kept finding trinkets from their desks lined up, like soldiers in formation, on top of one of the high shelves." Now Sophie shivered. "That was unsettling because once we spotted them, a special ladder had to be brought in to reach the top of the shelf to retrieve them. Not an easy thing to pull off anonymously as a prank."

Goosebumps rose on my arms. I felt like we were gathered around a campfire sharing scary stories.

"Then one night I was working late on a presentation for a school group coming in the next day. Everyone else had already left. It's not all that unusual, and it had never worried me to be there on my own before. Besides, I'm generally not alone for long because the cleaning crew comes in around nine.

"I'd gotten up to use the bathroom and while there, I heard somebody whistling and humming in the hallway. I figured it was the cleaning crew, and so didn't give it much thought."

The goosebumps multiplied on my arms.

She continued, "It did strike me as odd that I didn't run into anyone on the way back to the office. When I sat down at my desk, I looked out at the empty parking lot and watched as the van with the cleaning crew drove into the parking lot."

"Oh, my God! I would've been so freaked out," I said.

"No kidding. It was lucky I had just been to the bathroom. Otherwise, I would have peed my pants," she said with a grin. "My first instinct was to bolt out of there. Then I thought about all our precious books and worried what might happen if someone with bad intentions was locked in the library after hours." I had to laugh at how protective she was of the books. She added, "Not to mention the danger the cleaning crew would be in if they came upon an intruder. So, I called the police and explained the situation. They sent someone over to walk through the library with me, while the cleaners waited outside."

"What did you find?" I asked, enthralled by her story.

"Nothing. We didn't find anyone. Not a soul."

"Not a living one at least," I said with a grin. "I can't believe you didn't tell me about this when it happened. Why didn't you?"

"I was going to, but it creeped me out. It took a while to get rid of the sense of dread I felt when I saw the van arriving. Once it had faded, the last thing I wanted to do was bring the feeling back up."

I nodded, understanding the difficulty of letting go of unsettling feelings. I still had flashbacks to the moments on the Falmouth bridge last year when I almost went over the side. Nightmares in which I was falling continued to jolt me awake.

I took a deep breath, recalling myself to the present. "It's fascinating though, isn't it? There's so much we can't explain or understand. There might be things happening all around us we just can't see."

"Some of us can see them," she said.

"Seeing and understanding are two different things."

She was thoughtful, then said, "I'm kinda envious of your new talent."

I was shocked.

"Not envious in an 'if I can't have it no one can' kinda way." She held up her hand with an imaginary knife and made a Psychoesque stabbing motion. "I just mean, well, you know, life can be so ordinary and repetitive. To have this glimpse into a whole different aspect of the world, that's pretty cool."

"It never occurred to me anyone would be envious of it. I was worried people would think I was crazy."

"You don't worry about it anymore?"

"Well, I still do a little."

She raised her eyebrows at me.

"OK, more than a little. It's also been eye-opening. I've been amazed at the number of people who have not only accepted it but also wanted me to use my clairvoyance to help them. I just wish I could make the visions appear when I want them to, not out of the blue. It's hard to use them to help someone when I can't make them happen on demand. It can be very frustrating."

"And it would make opening G.G.'s Investigations more challenging." She smiled, and I rolled my eyes.

I knew my friends hoped I would become a psychic private detective. In moments of honesty, I could admit I loved the idea of changing my life so drastically. I'd let myself become too introverted since Nate died. I just needed to figure out how to harness my insights and use them to help people.

Sophie interrupted my train of thought. "You seem to be getting better at interpreting them."

"Yes, I've been making progress, but I'm still occasionally baffled by what I see, especially when there's no context. Like with this whole Poe thing. I had a vision I now think was related to all this months ago. Only, I had no idea what it was about at the time."

"Months ago? What did you see?"

Warmth started to stir in the center of my back. "It happened when I was sleeping, and it was so short I didn't pay much attention to it, but I always write down what I can remember of dreams. Let me go grab my journal." I'd like to say I leapt off the couch, but it's more accurate to say I pushed myself up off the couch and went upstairs.

I returned with my journal in hand. Sophie had wrapped herself in the blanket from the back of the couch. I flopped down beside her and flipped through my journal, searching for the entry.

"Here it is." I started to scan the words, but Sophie was having none of that.

"No fair reading it to yourself first. Read it out loud."

I smiled at her eagerness. "OK, settle down. There's not that much to it." I read from the journal. "I was walking from my place towards HFFI. The sky was dark—"

"Was it a midnight dreary?" she asked, smirking.

"You want me to read it or not?" I asked with false impatience. I began again. "It was a midnight dreary." She slapped my arm. "OK, the sky was dark with storm clouds. I heard a strange rasping noise. At first I thought it was a person coughing or clearing their throat. Then I saw a large black bird in a tree beside the library."

"A raven, I presume."

I smiled. "When I first saw it, I assumed it was a crow, so that's what I wrote here." I continued to read. "The crow kept calling out and calling out, so I paused to watch it to see if it was in distress. As soon as I looked up, it swooped down a few feet from my face, blocking my field of vision. I had thrown up my arm to protect my face from it as it descended, and when I put my arm back down, I was no longer next to the library. I'm not sure where I was, but the crow was now on the roof of a building pecking at the slate shingles. It just kept digging and digging with its beak. It didn't act like it found anything. Just as I started to give up and turn away, I swear it squawked my name, and I turned back." I looked up at Sophie.

"And?"

"One of the tiles he'd been pecking at came loose, slid down the roof, and shattered at my feet."

"Then what? Did you climb up on the roof?"

"No, the crow or raven flew down and started pecking at something on the ground. Then the dream ended."

"That's it? What the hell? That's not enough information. How frustrating."

"Yup," I said, glad for the sympathy.

"How can you be certain it's related to Poe or *Tamerlane*?"

"I can't be, but it's like you said, it's a raven."

"I was joking."

"Well, I'm not. Since all this started happening, it did occur to me that it might not have been a crow. So, I did some searching and compared photos of crows and ravens. Based on the size and thickness of its beak, I believe it was a raven I saw. I don't think it can be a coincidence."

"Hmm, it had a *large* beak. Maybe Ty is the raven."

I smacked her arm, laughing.

"What? It's a possibility." She grinned, then became more serious. "Even if it was a raven, what would it mean? How can it help now?"

"I don't know. Lucia's been helping me try to understand all this. From what I've learned so far, I think it meant one of two things. It was either a general premonition that all this Poe madness was going to happen."

"Or?" she prompted when I paused.

"Or it's related to where the raven was. The location could be a clue. As much as I've tried, I can't remember anything else significant from the dream, and there haven't been any others with the raven since then." I threw my hands up and let them slap back down on my thighs. "It can be maddening."

"Well, like you said, it might've been a general warning about the Poe-mania coming our way." She sounded slightly disappointed.

"That's probably all it was."

"But?"

"It just feels like the raven was trying to give me a message."

"Maybe it was Poe himself, trying to communicate with you."

"And now we're back to ghosts," I laughed.

"I think you should concentrate on what you saw. What did the building look like?"

I closed my eyes, trying to bring back the image of the raven on the roof. "I can't see the whole house, just part of the roof and the sky."

"You said the roof was slate. Was it dark gray or a lighter gray? Smooth or rough?" she asked.

I concentrated on the picture of the roof's tiles in my mind. "They're kind of rough. They're dark gray, but I think they're wet, so that would make them seem darker."

"And what is the raven doing?"

"He's pecking at one of the tiles and pushing it with his beak. Then I turn away and as soon as I do, he calls out and there's a scraping sound. When I turn back, I watch the tile fall from the roof and smash on the sidewalk at my feet."

"OK, so you see a sidewalk?"

"Yes, I do." I'm surprised I didn't remember that detail before.

"Good. Did you see anything else when the tile fell?"

I watched it fall over and over. "When it falls, it's sort of blurry with the motion. I think there's something green behind it as it drops."

Just then a crow called from a nearby tree, the sound drifting in through an open window. My eyes flew open, and we stared at each other, wide-eyed.

"I think whatever is green behind it is important," Sophie whispered.

CHAPTER TEN

I awoke early, groggy from a night of restless dreams featuring ravens with the face of Poe. I set out for a brisk walk around town to clear my head before getting to work. I walked along Sophia Street down to Riverfront Park, where I sat on a bench in the sunshine and watched several children running and climbing in the play area.

I was just beginning to relax when a car door closed behind me, which was followed by Detective Gomez's voice. "May I join you?"

I looked up as she gestured to the bench. I assumed she was on duty based on the navy-blue Fredericksburg Police Department polo shirt she wore with her gray slacks. Her thick, dark, wavy hair was a little longer than when we worked together last year. I still wasn't sure how old she was, though I figured she had to be in her fifties like me.

I smiled and said, "Of course."

We sat in silence, enjoying the sounds of laughter and joy.

After a couple minutes, I said, "My money's on the blond kid as the main suspect. He's got shifty eyes." I peeked at her out of the corner of my eye and saw her smiling.

"The blond kid's almost never the main suspect."

I turned to her and saw her smile was gone. I wondered again what had driven her from a high-profile position as a detective in DC to a job in a city the size of ours.

"But it's suspects I do want to talk to you about," she said.

"Suspects? In relation to what? Wait, were you out looking for me?"

"Should I have been?" She looked at me with one eyebrow raised and I was happy to see her smile had returned.

I held up my hands in surrender. "No. I promise I've been on my best behavior."

"I will reserve judgment on that until I have more facts. Especially given all the intrigue around *Tamerlane*. I have a feeling I should be keeping an eye on you."

"A feeling? Do detectives rely on intuition?" I asked.

Her gaze drifted from the children and locked in on my face. "Intuition, ESP, maybe it's all the same thing."

She'd caught me off guard. "I guess they could be. I'm no expert." It wasn't a lie. I was far from being an expert on the topic.

"That's not what I hear," she said, still looking at me.

I let my attention shift back to the children. "Well, you should know by now you can't believe everything you hear in a small town."

"Oh, it works the same in big cities. You have to be able to sift through the mierda to find the truth." She leaned forward, resting her forearms on her thighs.

"Sounds messy," I said.

She shook her head and smiled. "It can be. It can also be dangerous. That's what I wanted to talk to you about."

"Me? Why me?"

"From what I've seen, you have a way of ending up in the middle of things. And from what I've heard, you're already finding your way into the midst of these so-called treasure hunters."

"From what you've heard? Who's been talking about me? Or have you actually been following me?"

"I've got eyes and ears everywhere."

I couldn't tell if she was joking or not.

She sat back up. "Ms. Wilde, you seem like a nice person, and I don't want to see you get hurt. Most of the people in town after *Tamerlane* appear to be harmless enough, but there are some rumors going around—"

"Regarding—?" I prompted when she didn't continue, the familiar tingling starting at the top of my spine.

"Some of the people who might be here searching for the manuscript. Unscrupulous types. The kind of people you need to steer clear of. The kind of people who wouldn't care if they hurt a few locals to get what they want."

I debated what to say. Keeping my voice low, I asked, "Do you mean The Falcon?"

Her expression shifted to anger. If steam could have shot out of her ears like in the cartoons, no doubt it would have. "I knew you were nosing around already. You need to stay out of this. If The Falcon is involved and you try to interfere, you could get hurt. This is a cold-blooded, calculating person."

"Surely they wouldn't kill someone over a Poe manuscript, even if it is worth over a half million."

"Nothing's ever been proven in connection with The Falcon. However, when I reached out to a few colleagues who work in this field, they told me people who tangle with them tend to end up hurt. It's a competitive business. Highly prized items like this one don't surface every day, so when one does you can bet there'll be a fight over who gets to claim it and who gets to sell it. From what I've been told, an artifact like *Tamerlane* could sell for a lot more than half a million to the right collector. People like The Falcon are well-funded enough to be able to wait for the right buyer once they have the item in-hand. In fact, not selling it right away allows them to build interest and adds a bit of mystique to the item."

I waited, wondering if I should push her. I decided it was worth a try. "Do your contacts know who The Falcon is?"

She shook her head. "No. They've never been identified."

"What are the odds they're really here?"

"Normally, I'd say the odds were slim to none. The target is fairly inconsequential in terms of selling price, especially compared to other items The Falcon has been associated with. I would think it would only be a draw for mid-level thieves and

Poe fanatics. If The Falcon is involved at all, I would think they'd have associates to do the grunt work for them, but something's got me wondering."

"One of those secret sources of yours?"

"Yeah, a couple of them. It's possible The Falcon's not here in person. Even if that's true, it doesn't mean one of their associates wouldn't go to the same lengths to get what they want. You need to stay out of it for your own good. Remember how upset your daughters were last year when they almost lost you?"

"Emotional blackmail, detective? It may not be a criminal offense, but it's a low blow."

"Whatever keeps you out of harm's way." She stood. "I have to be going. You have my number if you need it, right?"

I nodded.

"I hope you won't need it." She held my eyes for a moment longer, then turned and walked away.

"Here's hoping," I said to her retreating back.

CHAPTER ELEVEN

My conversation with Gomez left me feeling annoyed, making it a challenge for me to settle into work once I got home. I did some of the deep breathing I'd practiced with Lucia to let go of my aggravation.

I then spent a productive morning and most of the afternoon proofing multiple chapters of a biography on Astrid Lindgren, the author of the Pippi Longstocking books, who it turns out led a fascinating life. By late afternoon, my brain was tired, and I needed a break.

I remembered Gomez's warning to stay out of the search for *Tamerlane* and decided a quick trip to HFFI to see Mary couldn't be considered sticking my nose into the situation. I would be hanging out with a friend. A friend who I decided not to tell about Gomez's warning. No sense in worrying her over nothing.

I'd visited Mary several times while she was volunteering at HFFI. I'd even helped out at a couple events, but I'd never seen it so abuzz with activity. The three women in the lobby glanced up when I walked in. Two were women I recognized as volunteers and the third, who leaned against the front desk, was a Poe enthusiast decked out in period attire. There were four other people looking at the various displays on walls and large green shelves in the lobby. They were wearing less obvious Poe-related clothing, though as one of them turned, I saw he had on a T-shirt featuring a raven.

The women I knew nodded hello and went back to the conversation they were having. There weren't usually so many people there on a weekday unless an event was underway. I worried my purpose in coming by, to see if I could find any information on the building and roof I'd seen in my dream or the tunnel in my vision of Ty, would be thwarted by how busy they were.

Mary's voice carried down the hall. I followed its sound to the administrative office in the back half of the building. Since I didn't hear anyone responding, I guessed she was on the phone. Trying not to disturb her, I entered the office quietly. She was sitting behind a wooden desk, her legs tucked under its solid wood front and the phone held to her ear. She exuded an air of impatience.

"I'm sorry, but as I've said, we have no evidence Poe ever visited Fredericksburg." She listened for a moment. "Yes, on one of his trips north from Richmond the stagecoach he was traveling in may have stopped here to pick up or discharge passengers. However, there's no empirical evidence that he spent any time here or had any correspondence with anyone who lived here."

The last statement about the correspondence seemed to be tacked on as a preemptory measure.

"The Poe Museum in Richmond and the Poe Society of Baltimore have excellent websites for information on his life. I'm sorry I couldn't be of more assistance." She listened briefly and responded, "You're welcome." She hung up the phone with an exasperated sigh. "Good lord, the phone won't stop ringing. We've been telling everyone the same thing for two weeks. You'd think the word would spread, but they all want to have it confirmed for themselves. And whenever there's a new rumor of someone finding the manuscript, we get more calls." She stood and came around the desk to give me a hug.

She was impeccably though casually dressed in black, pleated slacks and a lightweight tan sweater embroidered with a subtle leaf pattern.

The phone was ringing again before we even finished our hug. Mary leaned into the hallway and called, "Can someone else grab the phones for a few minutes, please?" She gestured to the chair in front of the desk and resumed her seat behind it.

"What a madhouse." She ran her fingers through her thick, auburn hair. The auburn was mostly natural, but she got some help from her favorite stylist to disguise the inevitable grays.

"It's incredible how fast word spread about the letter and how tenacious people are being. They keep digging for information no matter how often they're told there's no Poe connection to Fredericksburg," I said.

"It's even more incredible how many Poe fanatics there are out there."

"Bailey warned me about the fanaticism."

"Given the subject matter of some of his stories, it's more than a little concerning so many people are fixated on him."

"I hadn't thought of it that way."

"Well, I have. Some of the people who've dropped by here have given me the creeps, bless their tell-tale hearts."

I laughed. Mary had a sharp wit which I appreciated.

"In spite of the chaos, you know we love it. The ladies here haven't seen this much excitement since the rumors started to swirl about the tunnels under downtown a decade ago. What a disappointment that turned out to be. Now every one of these Poe—" she paused, searching for a word. "I've been trying to think of a term for them. Maybe Poe-its?"

I pondered it. "Poesers?"

She laughed. "Good, but too obvious."

"And the yoga studio by the same name probably wouldn't appreciate it," I said.

"Let's see—" She thought for a moment, then started riffing on Poe puns. "Poeems. Poedunks. Poesies. Poester boys. Poelo ponies."

I threw in poe-liticos and Poekemons. It went downhill from there until I said, "I think we're suffering from over-expoesure."

Her smile faded as the phone rang once more, "I think I'll call them Poechers since they're killing my peace of mind." She picked up the phone and managed to say in a cheerful voice, "Historic Fredericksburg Foundation how can I help you?"

I closed my eyes as I listened to her side of the conversation. I felt warmth rising in my body along with the sense I was forgetting something important. Or was it remembering?

"No, I—" A voice on the phone spoke over her. "Yes, I know there are websites that say there are tunnels under the city. They are out of date. It was disproved after an archaeological research company was brought in to investigate the claim. While they did find one underground storage space..."

I zoned out on her voice and tried to tune in to the voice within me, while ignoring the hot flash kicking into high gear. What was it I was forgetting? The mention of the tunnels had brought up the image of Ty dead on the ground. Something related to the vision nagged at me. I saw the dimly lit underground space in my mind and this time noticed an iron gate covering an opening at the back of the room. The image shifted to a quick succession of unconnected pictures. A room I didn't recognize with dark wood rafters, slanted ceilings, and hardwood floors. It made me think of France, though I wasn't sure why. Then a hand holding a heavy flashlight raised overhead like a sword raised in battle, a piece of some kind of object made of brown leather, a man with a shadowed face standing very close to me, an old door made of wooden slats painted red with a strange wrought iron keyhole, two hands clasped with their fingers interlocked.

"Liv." Mary's hand touched my shoulder.

I opened my eyes.

"Are you OK? I called your name repeatedly." Her concern was evident. "You didn't respond. It was like you weren't here."

I sat up straighter in my chair and wiped the sweat from my forehead. "I'm fine. I must have dozed off for a second."

"Cut the crap. I'm not blind. Were you having a vision?"

I refrained from making a pointless joke about blindness and visions not going together. "I, well,—" I stammered.

While all my friends knew my insights were increasing in clarity, I still felt self-conscious when they happened with other people around. Unexpected tears rose in my eyes.

"Oh, sweetie." She reached for a tissue and handed it to me. "What is it?"

I dabbed at the corners of my eyes with the tissue and took a deep breath. "I'm still a bit wary of sharing what I see with people, even with you guys."

"How many times must I tell you it's y'all, not you guys? I fear we'll never make a Virginian out of you," she said in her best southern belle accent, pronouncing Virginian *Vahginian.*

While I rolled my eyes at her playfully, my tone was tentative when I spoke. "I worry that you'd prefer to send me and my visions back to Jersey."

"Seriously?" She sounded shocked. "Come on, we have all sorts of Appalachian magic and witches and seers in Virginia. Hell, my dad's Aunt Bitsy talked to dead relatives all the damn time. You couldn't shut her up at family gatherings, she was so busy telling some ancestor or another what was happening in the family."

Now it was my turn to be shocked. "Why have you never mentioned Aunt Bitsy before?"

"Well, Daddy doesn't like us to talk about her." Her eyes widened, realizing her mistake as soon as the words were out of her mouth.

"See! That's what I mean. People will think I'm like loony Aunt Bitsy and will talk about me in whispers."

"Oh, you know how Daddy is. Besides, he's from a different generation. And I'm not just people. I'm your friend, and I can assure you, none of us would ever call you crazy. At least, not to your face."

I smiled. "Thanks. That's super reassuring."

She smiled back. "Now tell me what you saw." She leaned against the front edge of the desk.

"I didn't see just one thing. It was a lot of things kind of jumbled together. Normally, it's like a scene in a movie. This time it was more of a montage of random, unrelated pictures. It didn't make any sense."

"I thought it was getting easier for you to interpret or understand them."

"It has been. Lucia's been a big help with learning to understand what I see. This one was just so much so fast it was difficult to take in the images before the next one popped up."

"You should try to write it down. Like a dream journal."

"Oh, yeah." I reached down for my purse and pulled out my notebook. "Lucia convinced me to start carrying around a notebook, and I keep one by my bed too." I flipped to a blank page and paused. "You know, she recently reminded me to carry one around with me during the day."

"Sounds like she and Aunt Bitsy would have gotten along swimmingly."

I smiled and turned my attention to my notebook, alternating writing and talking. "Do you know of any old buildings in town with a room with dark wood rafters and hardwood floors?"

"Any number of homes and businesses have wood beam rafters. Do you have more detail about the floors? Color? Size of the pieces of wood?"

I recalled the image. "They were wide planks and sort of a reddish color."

"Red floors? Sounds like you're getting caught up in the Poe furor. Maybe the 'Tell-Tale Heart' is influencing your visions."

"Were the floors in the story red?"

"Might as well have been. Red floors, red walls, beating hearts—" Mary shivered.

"Sounds like you're the one having tell-tale visions."

She grinned. "OK, red plank floors. In a house or a business?"

"I said redd*ish*. They were more cherry than blood red. I'm not sure if it was a home or business. I couldn't see the whole room. It might be either."

"Nothing comes to mind, but I can search our database."

Mary walked behind the desk and sat down, reaching for the mouse on the desk.

"Do you remember any other details?"

"It had white walls."

"Not exactly narrowing it down, are we?"

I shrugged, feeling helpless. "This may sound strange, but something about the room reminded me of France."

"France? You mean it's in France?"

I shook my head. "I don't think so. It didn't feel—" I searched for the right words. "That far away."

She was looking at me with curiosity. "You could feel how far away it was?"

"I'm not explaining it very well," I said with exasperation. "It didn't feel like it was in France. It just had a French vibe."

"I'll see if there's anything with French decor." She turned back to the computer.

As she typed, I closed my eyes, trying to bring the images back up. "I saw a person holding a flashlight overhead in their left hand like it was a club. Like they were going to hit someone with it."

Mary's typing paused. "Can you tell if it was a man's or woman's hand?"

"No. They were wearing long sleeves and gloves, only a sliver of the wrist was visible."

Mary returned to clicking and typing.

"In another part of the vision, I saw an iron lock with an old-fashioned keyhole."

"There are plenty of iron gates around town. Any details?"

"It wasn't on a gate. It was a lock on a red wooden door and there was a shape around the keyhole." I rubbed my forehead, willing my brain to remember.

"What would Lucia tell you to do?"

I smiled, eyes still closed. "She would tell me to take a deep breath and concentrate on something else." I opened my eyes. "Any luck with the red room?"

"It's starting to sound like redrum, which is disturbing."

"Now we're mixing up our creepy authors," I said trying to put Mary's mind at ease. I ignored the eerie feeling brought on by the reference to Stephen King's reversal of the word murder in *The Shining*.

"You're going to have to give me a few minutes. Try looking through some back issues of the journal and see if any photos or articles spark anything for you."

I stood up and went to the bookshelf on the wall to my left. I pulled a volume of the HFFI journal off the shelf at random and began flipping through the pages. I came across an article on the history of newspapers in Fredericksburg, which made me think of Sophie and the ad for the literary journal she'd discovered in an old newspaper.

Since the library was across the street, I left Mary to her searching after making her promise she would text me if she found anything.

The phone on her desk was ringing as I walked out the door.

CHAPTER TWELVE

"I'm on my way over now," I said to Sophie on the phone as I stepped out of the HFFI building.

"I'll come down and meet you out front."

"You don't want me to come up?"

"No. I don't want anyone to overhear us."

I waited on the sidewalk for the traffic to clear before crossing the street.

"Why? Did you learn something new?" My heart rate increased.

"I'll tell you in a minute."

I started to respond but realized she'd hung up on me. She came through the front door moments after I reached the library's steps.

"Let's go to your place," she said as she put her arm through mine.

She wouldn't say another word until we were inside my townhouse next door.

"For goodness sake, why all the secrecy? What did you find out?"

Sophie went straight for the kitchen and helped herself to a glass of water before joining me on the couch.

"I reached out to a former colleague I've remained friendly with who now works in the UVA library system." She was almost breathless with excitement. "I asked her to see if there were any references to *The Lasting Word* in their databases."

"And?"

"She didn't find a thing."

I opened my mouth to protest, but she held up a hand to stop me.

"However," she said with emphasis, "she put me in touch with someone she knows at the Library of Virginia who is an expert on historic publications in central and eastern Virginia."

"That's pretty specific."

"She did her dissertation on the history of literary publications in Virginia. You know how obscure and focused dissertations can be. Anyway, she was able to find a couple references to *The Lasting Word*. It was short-lived. She confirmed there were at least three issues published in Fredericksburg from 1827 to 1830 by—drumroll please—" she drummed on her thighs. "Wallace Jackson!"

"So, you were right. He was the person behind the journal."

She smiled and reached up to pat herself on the back. "Yup."

"Wonderful. Was she able to find copies of the issues?"

"She's still working on that part. There's no guarantee any copies remain."

"One step forward—"

"Two steps back," Sophie finished. "At least that means we're dancin," she said with a grin.

I leaned back into the couch cushions, realizing I'd been leaning toward her with the excitement of her discoveries.

She leaned back too. "Now we just have to wait."

As the excitement ebbed, a thought occurred to me. "You were worried people would overhear our conversation. How can you trust this woman you don't know to keep quiet about the journal?"

Sophie's eyes sparkled with mischief. "She won't say anything."

"OK, I'll bite. How do you know she won't?"

"Because she is under the impression I'm doing research for the FBI."

I sat up. "First you're a reporter for the newspaper. Now you work for the FBI?"

Sophie shrugged.

"How did she get that impression?"

"Well, the FBI does handle the recovery of stolen art and artifacts, you know. I may have hinted they are involved because there's a chance it's the copy of *Tamerlane* stolen from UVA and—" She at least sounded a little apologetic at this point. "I may have indicated they'd been in contact with me through the library."

"You told her you were working with the FBI?" My voice rose. "Why on earth would she fall for that? Doesn't the FBI handle their own research?"

"That's not the point. The important thing is you'd be amazed the doors that will open if you mention The Bureau."

"I'm not even going to ask," I said, even though, part of me longed to know more. The wiser part of me knew I was better off not knowing, for the sake of plausible deniability. "Sometimes you're a hazard to yourself and others, Soph."

She just smiled, her eyes still sparkling.

"I don't see how it could be related to the copy stolen from UVA," I said.

"I'm sure it's not. I just threw that in there because everyone who works in research in a library in Virginia knows about the copy of *Tamerlane* stolen from UVA."

I laughed. "I'm gonna need to bail you out of prison one day."

"That'll be difficult since if I'm in there, odds are you'll be in there with me."

"Truth," I said, shuddering at the idea.

"Hey, did you learn anything from Mary?"

"Nothing new. They're swamped with calls. But she's trying to do some research for me."

"On what?"

"I had a vision while I was there. It was mostly a jumble of different pictures one after the other without much detail except for a room with dark rafters and hardwood floors. It felt like a space in one of the old buildings in town, yet it had a French vibe somehow. So, she's doing a search to see what comes up."

"It's not much to go on."

"Her thought too, but you know the ladies over there. Some of them don't need a database. They have all the information in their heads."

"Let's call her and see what she's found."

"Trust me, calling is a bad idea. She's been on the phone all morning."

The text alert on my phone chimed. "It's from Mary."

I unlocked my phone and leaned toward Sophie so she could see it too. There were two images and some text. The first photo was of an old, red, wood door. The second was a close up of the iron handle and lock on the door. The text was short and to the point: *The Old Stone Warehouse. Is this the door you saw?*

It was—and it wasn't.

CHAPTER THIRTEEN

After a few texts back and forth with Mary, Sophie and I left, with her going reluctantly back to work after her extended break, and me heading back to HFFI.

As I crossed the street, I noticed two men standing on the corner. Their voices were low and intense. As I approached, they stopped talking and glanced my way. I recognized one as the bald man I'd seen talking to Ty at Castiglia's. The other was shorter with broad shoulders and a long, brown ponytail hanging down his back. I nodded and continued to the door.

I entered the lobby and as the door closed behind me, I heard them resume their conversation. Glancing around, I noticed a man who looked freakishly like Poe and a woman in a long, black, modern dress standing at the desk asking questions of the volunteer on duty. The volunteer directed her gaze my way. She smiled, recognizing me, and gestured over her shoulder toward the office, indicating where I'd find Mary. Looking from the two Poe fans to her, I rolled my eyes and gave her a conspiratorial grin which she returned before refocusing on them.

As soon as I walked into the office, Mary said, "What do you mean it is and it isn't?"

I held up my hand. "Shhh."

I tiptoed to the window, trying to peek around the edge of the frame out toward the street.

The two men were still there. Their discussion had become more contentious. Their voices, while still muffled by the thick, old-fashioned glass, were loud enough for me to make out a few words.

The bald man I'd seen at the restaurant was facing my direction so I could see him more clearly.

His expression was serious. He raised a hand, pointing in the other man's face. "I'd think twice before spreading rumors about The Falcon if I were you. It might be—"

"Who are they?" Mary said from over my shoulder, making me jump.

I turned and put my finger to my lips to shush her.

The movement in the window must have caught his attention because when I peeked back outside the large man was looking my way. I jumped back out of his line of sight, though I was sure he saw me. A moment later he walked past, then turned abruptly back toward the window. Our eyes met before he turned back and continued up the hill.

The coldness in his eyes made me shudder.

"That was creepy," Mary said.

"Extremely."

"What were they saying?"

I filled her in on the little we'd learned about The Falcon and the others searching for *Tamerlane*. "We think the big guy's name is Caleb. The smaller one fits the description of the man he was fighting with at the hotel."

"It's like a Tim Burton version of *National Treasure* around here lately," she said, returning to the chair behind the desk.

I laughed. "That's a perfect description."

"Who'd have guessed one pamphlet of poems would cause so much commotion?"

"It's bizarre."

"Back to the matter at hand." She gestured to her phone. "What did you mean by it is and it isn't?"

I refocused on the photos she'd sent me. "Can you show the pictures to me on the computer?"

I walked behind the desk and stood beside her. She turned the monitor in my direction to show me a photo labeled Old Stone Warehouse.

"Well, the color is right. The handle and lock are different, though. It wasn't a handle you could lift, and I think the door was larger."

Her shoulders slumped a bit as she reached for the mouse and began scrolling through more photos.

"Wait." I reached out and put my hand on top of hers to keep her from moving to the next photo.

On the screen was an old black-and-white photo from the Library of Congress. Mary read the information below the photo and said, "This is from 1930 when it was a fertilizer company."

"It's so different."

"What are you looking at?" asked a feminine voice with a soft southern accent. Momma M leaned against the doorframe. She was dressed in a pair of beige, linen slacks, a pale blue, silk blouse, and flat, brown loafers made of leather too fine for my budget. She made her way to the desk to peer over my shoulder. At eighty-one, she may have been slowing down, but she was fairly steady on her feet.

"The Old Stone Warehouse," Mary replied. "But it doesn't look right, Momma. I don't remember there being a door on the second floor like that."

Pulling a pair of glasses off the top of her head and placing them on her nose, Momma M leaned in to get a better look. "Well, that's before they raised Sophia Street after the flood of thirty-seven and covered the lower floor. The door on the second floor in the photo is the door you enter through from the street today." Her annunciation, though slowed by her southern cadence, was as impeccable as her clothing.

Mary and I spoke over each other.

"They covered half the building?" I asked.

"Oh, I forgot they did that," Mary said.

"Yes. They wanted to try to avoid all the damage another major flood could do along Sophia Street, so they raised the street level near the entrance to the bridge. Now the lower door in the photo and that whole level are underground on the front side."

My whole body tensed in reaction to the word underground. I knew it was important.

Momma M gave me a squeeze. "Hi Livvy." She was the only one other than my mom who got away with calling me Livvy. "How's life on the wild side?" she asked with a wink.

"I think she's envious of your name," Mary said. "If only you'd had a name you could've used as an excuse for being a hell-raiser back in the day, right Momma?"

Momma M reached behind me and gave Mary a playful tap on the shoulder. "What do you know about my life back in the day?" Her gaze became unfocused as some memory from those days brought a smile to her lips. She leaned closer to me and whispered, "What she doesn't know about my life would fill volumes. I didn't need a name like Liv Wilde to inspire me to raise a little hell."

I was pleasantly surprised by the mischievous twinkle I saw in her eyes.

Turning back to the photo, I said. "I've seen the river flood, but it's hard to imagine it that high."

"You don't have to imagine it." Momma M walked to one of the bookshelves, where she pulled a coffee table-size book off a shelf. Opening it, she flipped through a few pages until she found what she was searching for. She handed the book to me.

"That's the flood of nineteen thirty-seven," she said.

Mary stood and looked over my shoulder. Spread across two pages was a black and white photo taken from William Street facing the old Chatham Bridge with the water all the way up over the span of the bridge. To the right was the Old Stone Warehouse looking almost like it does today, except the lower level was submerged in the floodwaters rather than hidden beneath the street.

"The water came all the way up to Caroline Street. Some people still called it Main Street then. It submerged Scott's Island and washed away the old structures out there," Momma M said.

"Scott's Island? Where's that?" I asked.

Mary jumped in. "It's the small island under Chatham Bridge. In the late eighteen-hundreds and early nineteen-hundreds, they used to have music, rides, Fourth of July celebrations, and parties out there."

"The bridge collapsed a few hours after this photo was taken," Momma M said.

"Wow. It's so easy to forget how powerful the river can be," I said.

"Oh, she has ways of reminding us," Momma M said. "Why do you want information on that particular site? It's not for one of these Typoes, is it?"

"Typos?" Mary asked.

"I got tired of calling them Poe-types. Typoes is easier to say and since they look like mistakes walking around dressed the way they are—"

We shared a collective sigh at their lingering presence.

I debated whether or not I should explain to Momma M why we were interested in the building. I glanced at Mary, who nodded.

"It's not for one of the Typoes. I was just wondering if there's anything under the warehouse," I said.

"Under it? Like what?" Momma M asked. "Oh, this isn't about the mythical tunnels, is it?"

I forced out a laugh and hoped it didn't sound as false as it was. "No. I'm thinking more of a storage space. How many floors does it have?"

"There are three levels and an attic. Only the one main level and the attic are visible from the street anymore. The other two floors are visible from the back. I doubt there's anything underneath those."

"Didn't they do some excavating in the basement not too long ago?" Mary asked.

"Yes. They uncovered part of the original brick floor from when it was built as a tobacco storehouse, but no secret tunnels." She winked and walked back to the door. "It was nice to see you, Livvy."

"You too, Momma M. Thank you. Try not to get into too much trouble. I don't want Mary having to bail you out of the slammer."

She laughed, waved and wandered back toward the lobby.

"Typoes," Mary laughed. "She's a trip, that one. She may be getting around slower than she used to, but there's nothing slow about her mind, and her memory is as sharp as ever. She never forgets a thing."

"I don't doubt it," I said, smiling. "I think we need to invite her to one of our Monthlies and after a couple glasses of wine get some of the stories about the good old days out of her."

I sat in the chair across the desk from Mary, who sat back down too, a grin still on her lips at the idea of Momma M at a Monthly.

I closed my eyes, trying to put pieces together. "I was convinced the building was important, but if there have been excavations there and they didn't find anything—" I was frustrated. I wanted to better understand all the things I'd seen. I was also frustrated because I knew the name of the warehouse had come up in another conversation since all this began. I just couldn't recall when. "It feels like a dead end." I felt a sense of uneasiness at my own word choice.

⁂

I'd come home from HFFI and worked for a few hours on my read-through of the Lindgren biography. It felt good to focus on something normal, not Poe-related and not related to the mating habits of emus. I felt productive and the distraction was good for me.

Afterwards, I found I was exhausted. It was 7:00, too early to go to bed. After the plate of smoked Gouda and crackers I'd had for a late-afternoon snack, I realized I wasn't quite ready for dinner either.

A power nap seemed like a good compromise. Thanks to what I call menopause-induced inzombia, naps had become an important part of my life. Inzombia's defining characteristics are sleeplessness, mindless wandering around the house, a maddening restlessness, and hunger.

I meant to close my eyes for a cat nap. Which is what I thought I'd done, until I jerked awake on the couch to find I'd slept for six hours. It was dark outside my window, which reflected the foreboding I awoke feeling. Between the darkness and the disorientation from having slept far more than I'd planned, I felt more than a little unsettled and a bit hungry.

I turned on the lamp on the side table and took a few deep breaths to calm my sense of unease.

As soon as I closed my eyes, the image of the hand raised holding a metal flashlight appeared in my thoughts. This time it was moving. It swung downward, striking someone's skull with a terrible thud of metal on bone. And this time, I was certain I knew who the someone was.

Should I have called Detective Gomez, or anyone sane, prior to leaving? Probably. Yet, why alarm anyone if I didn't know if the attack I was seeing was happening now or if it was still in the future? All I could think was if it was happening now, maybe I still had a chance to save Ty's life.

I wasn't completely irresponsible. I sent a quick text to Lucia explaining where I was going and why. While I knew she wouldn't be awake, I figured at least one person should know where I'd gone.

Despite her warning that not everyone wanted to be saved, Lucia would understand my need to go. If I didn't and Ty died, I wouldn't be able to live with the what ifs.

I pulled on a pair of sneakers and walked out the door in my jeans and a long-sleeved T-shirt with nothing more than my cell phone and front door key. I shook my head to try to clear the sense of disorientation I was feeling.

I wasn't sure if I would find anything, but I knew where I would start looking.

CHAPTER FOURTEEN

Only one car drove past on my short walk to the Chatham Bridge. One o'clock on a Monday morning was quiet in Fredericksburg, for which I was grateful. After I crossed over William Street to the corner where the Old Stone Warehouse stood, I inspected the cement wall leading from the edge of the bridge to the nearest wall of the warehouse. It closed off access to the back of the building. I peered over the wall and saw a hill sloping into the backyard. It was somewhat steep at the top but looked manageable.

Even though I was blocked from view from the opposite end of the bridge, I could see the headlights of a car approaching from the other side of the river. With a quick glance down Sophia Street, and a complete lack of intelligence, I hoisted myself up and over the wall, landing none too gracefully in the dirt on the other side. I stayed crouched behind the wall for a minute, in part to see if there was any reaction from the driver of the car who was now waiting at the light on this side of the bridge, and in part to listen for any sounds below me. After the car moved on, I slid down the hill on my backside, taking a lot of dirt and pebbles with me. If anyone was hiding in the vicinity, they had to have heard my descent. So much for the element of surprise.

With the light from the nearby streetlights filtering through the trees beside the bridge, I took in the imposing stone wall of the back of the edifice, rising three stories above me. I walked quietly to the center of the building to a red, wood door with no handle or knob on the outside. It hung ajar and a bit crooked on its hinges. I worried opening it would make a terrible noise, attracting unwanted attention, but I had to take the risk if I wanted to get inside.

I inched the door open. Whenever it creaked, which was frequently, I froze and listened for sounds from inside. I had a brief flashback to my conversation with Mary about the "Tell-Tale Heart" and hearts buried under floorboards and almost lost my nerve. What the hell was I doing, anyway? I had no means of protection if a flashlight-wielding maniac lurked inside. My heart raced, and every fight or flight primal instinct in me screamed flight. The panic almost won—until Ty's handsome, smiling face appeared in my mind.

I steadied myself as much as I could and eased the door open just enough to squeeze through. I was glad I'd entered timidly, because I found I was standing on a narrow piece of stone between the door and a one-foot drop to the floor. In the dim light, I saw the basement I'd entered ran the width of the building. Most of the floor was dirt, except for a section in front of me which I guessed was about three feet across and eight feet long. The dirt had been removed there to reveal a brick floor. I didn't detect any movement or sound, so I stepped down into the room.

In front of me stood a row of columns set in concrete. I stepped up onto the concrete, grateful to feel the firm surface beneath my feet. I knew it was a risk to turn on my phone's flashlight, but I didn't feel safe moving any further into the basement without more light.

Shining the light around the room, ready to bolt at the slightest sound, I saw only stone walls in every direction. Other than a wooden staircase rising to the next floor at the end of the room to my left, there appeared to be nowhere to go from here. Leaning against the side wall beyond the staircase, there were a few tools I guessed had been used in the excavation of the floor.

I began on the right, making my way back towards the stairs which rose from the floor into the ceiling above, with no wall under the front side of them for support. Approaching the stairs, I found stones stacked up beneath the first few steps. Continuing past the pile of rocks, I saw a faint glow, which they'd been blocking.

The light emanated from the hole in the wall created by the removal of the stones. It looked large enough for me to crawl through, but small enough to cause a twinge of claustrophobia. I peered in and saw it widened into a larger space after six feet or so, where the light was somewhat brighter.

I wasn't sure what to do. Should I call out? If I did, it was possible I'd endanger myself. Should I call Gomez? I was trespassing. If I called her and she found no crime had been committed other than by me, I might be arrested. I could just go home and pretend none of this ever happened and chalk it up to taking the visions too literally. Thinking of my visions reminded me that Ty's life might be in danger.

Nothing bad happened to me in the dream, I reminded myself. And this was not the best moment to give in to doubts about what I see.

On the other hand, I was hoping in this instance the part where I found Ty dead would be wrong.

I took what I hoped was a steadying breath.

I decided to try calling out first. I figured if my voice prompted the attacker to come after me, I'd have an advantage because they'd be slowed down by having to crawl through the short tunnel.

With my head at the opening in the wall, I called out, "Ty? Are you in there?" I held my breath and waited. I heard no response, no rustling of clothing, nothing. Feeling resigned to my fate, I turned off my flashlight, put my phone in my back pocket, got on my hands and knees, and muttered, "If he's not dead, I'm going to fucking kill him."

I worried the stones above me would cave in while I attempted to crawl through the short entry tunnel without making a sound.

In the midst of the tunnel, I felt transported to a canyon with towering cliffs on either side of me. As I looked up, the canyon walls began to fall in on me. I tried to raise my arms to keep them from crushing me, but something prevented me from lifting them. I gasped for air, overwhelmed with a feeling of panic and a claustrophobia I hadn't felt in years.

It was the pain of my knees pressing against the hard-packed earth that brought me back to the present. I shivered and crawled forward, trying to catch my breath. As eager as I was to escape, I still paused at the end, to look around.

The space opened onto an underground passage with brick walls and dirt floors. I stood up, the ceiling a foot or two over my head. In spite of the vision of the canyon I'd just had and my reaction to it, I was ready to turn and crawl back through the tunnel at the first sound of movement.

The glow I'd seen was coming from around a bend in the tunnel ahead of me. My eyes had adjusted to the dim light, but I pulled my phone out of my pocket and turned the flashlight back on anyway, taking comfort in having more light.

Every sense was on high alert, including my sense of smell, which was bombarded by a combination of musty bricks, dirt, and a faint odor that made me think of Christmas. Since it was likely what I'd seen in my dream of Ty was what I'd see when I turned the corner in the passage ahead, I shouldn't have been as scared as I was. But the biggest adventures I usually have are our Monthlies. The most danger I've ever been in, other than the incident on the bridge last year, was being the mother of two teenaged girls. I was way out of my comfort zone.

After a couple deep breaths, I walked down the passage, turned the corner, and stepped into my dream. The space was as I'd seen it and described it to Lucia, right down to Ty's body on the ground, the clothes he was wearing, and the lantern beside him. What I hadn't counted on was the body triggering the memory of Nate, dead in the hospital. It stopped me in my tracks and it took me a few moments to recover enough to look around.

Scanning the room, I didn't see anyone else, so I moved forward. At the back of the space was the iron gate I'd seen in the dream. Now I could see a passageway beyond it. The light from the lantern wasn't bright enough to allow me to see much beyond the gate, so I returned my attention to Ty.

I'd reached the point where my vision had ended. I didn't know what would happen next. I got my phone ready to call Gomez and inched closer to Ty. If I'd seen myself nudging him and throwing up on him in advance, I could've changed something, like the direction I faced when I got sick. No such luck. What little was in my stomach ended up on his boots. Perhaps the next time I have a premonition of a dead person, I'll think to bring a barf bag with me when I go to find them, but after all, I'm still learning how to navigate this future-becoming-the-present stuff.

Since Ty didn't move after his initial groan when I'd nudged him, I decided to call Detective Gomez. I wasn't surprised to find the call wouldn't go through from underground. Another groan from Ty nearly made me drop my phone. His eyes fluttered open for a moment, then closed.

I ran down the passage and quickly crawled back into the basement to try again. The call connected and Gomez picked up on the second ring.

Her voice was groggy and disgruntled. "Carajo! What time is it, Ms. Wilde?"

"Seriously? It's two freaking a.m. and you're still gonna call me Ms. Wilde?"

It must have been the frantic tone of my voice that caused her to dismiss the aggressiveness of my first words to her. "What's the problem?"

"I thought I found Foley dead. Luckily, he's alive. I may have thrown up on him a bit. I'm not sure how alive he is, though. He needs help."

"Whoa, slow down. Where are you?" Her voice was now clear and commanding.

"In the basement of the Old Stone Warehouse at the corner of Sophia and William. There's an opening in the wall under the stairs that leads to a tunnel and a passageway under the street. Do you know where the warehouse is?"

"Yes."

"To get to the basement, you have to hop the wall on the left side of the property and come down the slope to the back entrance." I realized explaining the route of my breaking and entering wasn't helping me. "The door was open when I got here," I threw in, as if it would excuse my presence there.

She was silent for a beat. "You're certain the assailant is no longer there?"

I peered into the shadows. "There's no one else here as far as I can tell."

"I'll have an ambulance there shortly. Don't do anything else until I arrive."

I started to tell her to be careful, but she'd already disconnected. I took a deep breath of the night air and forced myself to go back through the tunnel. I paused prior to turning the corner when it struck me that maybe the vision I'd had was of this moment, not the previous one. What if when I got back to him this time he really was dead? My feet felt like lead as I made my way around the corner.

Ty's eyes were still closed. As I squatted beside him, I was relieved to see he was still breathing.

I touched his shoulder and whispered, "Don't worry. An ambulance is on the way, and Detective Gomez will be here soon."

His eyes flew open and he said, "Why the hell did you call the police?"

Startled, I fell backward and landed hard on my backside on the floor. Luckily, I had some padding there.

He tried to sit but immediately laid back down. He closed his eyes and put his left hand to the back of his head.

"Holy crap, you scared me to death." One hand was on my chest. My heart was pounding.

Remaining prone, he glared up at me. "Gomez will have a crime scene team swarming all over this place any minute. I need to look around before she gets here. Help me up."

It was an order, not a request, which I was inclined to refuse.

Seeing his trademark smirk I was torn between helping him and smacking him. I opted for the first choice since he had already received the latter from someone else.

"Please," he said with an obvious lack of sincerity.

I crawled back towards him, remembering how hard the ground was with each movement. My knees were not pleased.

He raised his head tentatively, and I slipped my arm under his shoulders. He grimaced as I helped him into a sitting position. Once upright, he was able to put his hands on the floor behind him and prop himself up. I kept my hand on his shoulder to prevent him from falling over.

He glanced down at my hand and said, "Don't worry. I'm not going to swoon."

I snatched my hand away and stood up.

Smiling, he waved his right hand up at me as if he wanted me to pull him up.

"I don't think you should try to stand yet."

He let his hand remain suspended in mid-air, reaching out for mine. I gave in. Leaning over, I gripped his hands with my own. I braced myself, spreading my feet out so I'd be able to keep us both steady. "Ready?"

"For what?" he asked, his gaze moving from my eyes to my breasts, which I now noticed were at his eye level as I bent over to help him up.

Without thinking, I let go of his right hand and with my now free hand smacked him upside the head. I didn't hit him hard, but he did swoon, swaying where he sat.

"Shit. I'm so sorry. I forgot—" I checked my hand to see if I'd gotten blood on it. I breathed a sigh of relief when I saw I hadn't. He'd been lying on the ground since I arrived, so I hadn't been able to see where the blow that had knocked him out had landed. Apparently, it was on the left side of the back of his head.

Wincing, he said, "Lucky for me you have bad aim."

"I'm sorry, but if you weren't such an ass I wouldn't have had to do it."

He grimaced. "Let's try again. Without any violence."

With some struggle and my assistance, he was able to get to his feet. He swayed slightly yet remained standing. He took a step and reached out for the wall to steady himself. "I think you're going to have to do the looking for me." He closed his eyes. I took a step toward him, but he put his hand out to stop me. "I'm fine." He opened his eyes and glanced down at his feet. "Christ, what is that smell? And what is all over my boots?"

I'd been hoping he wouldn't notice. "I may have thrown up a little when I found you." I spoke over whatever rude comment he started to make. "I thought you were dead, and then you suddenly moved. It scared the—well, you can see what it scared out of me." I gestured to his feet. In an attempt to redirect him I said, "Wasn't there something you wanted to look for before Gomez gets here?"

He held my gaze, probably debating whether or not to comment on the state of his boots.

He opted to address more urgent matters. "Check the gate at the back of the tunnel to see if it's unlocked."

I walked to the iron gate. As I stood in front of it, I knew it was the one I'd seen in the jumbled vision I'd had when I was with Mary. I pulled on one of the gate's bars. It swung open with a terrible screech.

"Go through and tell me what you see."

"Go in there alone? No way. What if whoever hit you is still in there?"

"Trust me, if they'd still been here when you arrived, you would've been lying on the ground beside me."

When I hesitated, he added, "Go! We have to hurry."

I glared at him over my shoulder.

"Please."

Against my better judgment, I took a step through the gate, using my phone's flashlight to illuminate the dirt floor. As I walked I called out, "Whistle or something, so I'll know we can still hear each other."

After a pause, he began whistling "Take Me Out to the Ballgame", which pissed me off and made me snicker.

I continued walking another fifteen feet or so until the tunnel opened up into a small room. "Can you hear me?"

His whistling stopped. "Yes but talk louder."

I raised my voice, creating a soft echo. "There's a room similar to the one you're in. It looks like it was for storage. There are shelves covering one wall with a couple old crates on them and a trapdoor in the ceiling. I don't think it's been opened in a long time."

"Can you see into the crates? Are they open?"

I approached the shelves. The adrenaline rush of finding Ty was wearing off, and with the knees of my jeans damp and cold, I started to tremble. I tried to steady my hands as I lifted the lid off the first crate. "Yes, this one's open. It's full of empty old jam jars," I yelled.

"What about the other one?" he called back.

I opened the second crate. "There are some scraps of paper. They look like the corners of pages that fell off and there's a piece of brown leather. Nothing else."

"Bring it here," he ordered and added an insincere, "Please."

I considered telling him to come get it his damn self, then recalled him unconscious on the floor and sighed. I pulled the crate off the shelf and made my way back, awkwardly holding my phone and the crate, which was heavier than I'd imagined.

When I walked back through the gate, he was leaning against the wall where I'd left him. His eyes were closed and his face was pinched in pain, so I let go of the snide remark on the tip of my tongue.

"We need to get you to a hospital."

"I'm OK. Just let me see the crate, please."

I brought it over to him without comment, set it on the floor at his feet, and pulled the lid off. He used his phone's flashlight to illuminate the box's paltry contents, an expression of fury on his face.

He pulled a small slip of paper from the box. It didn't reveal much about the document it was torn from. At the top it read *II, August 1828.* The tear was right in front of the *II.* I assumed other words had proceeded it.

"Bastard. He must have just taken whatever was in here with him."

"Who is he?" I asked.

"Yes, Mr. Foley, who is he?" Detective Gomez said as she emerged from the dimness of the passageway. "And what do you think was in the box?"

His sole response was a scowl.

The ambulance crew arrived before she could ask more questions. In short order they had Ty on a portable, sled-like stretcher. Ignoring his protests, they carried him to the entrance of the tunnel.

Gomez stopped me from following them. Even though I had a silver emergency blanket wrapped around me that an EMT had given me, I was still shivering. "Go home, get changed, and meet me at the hospital. Then, after you explain what possessed you to do something as stupid as come down here on your own, you can tell me what you know about all this, since Mr. Foley doesn't seem like he'll be very forthcoming."

I was getting tired of people ordering me around, but I knew with Gomez I didn't have a choice. We walked to the tunnel entrance without another word.

CHAPTER FIFTEEN

I texted Gomez before I left, so when I arrived at Mary Washington Hospital's emergency room, she was waiting for me outside the main entrance. We walked to a bench and sat down. The night didn't feel as cold when my clothes weren't damp. I had a brief moment of gratitude towards Gomez for sending me home rather than just hauling me to the police station. A very brief moment.

"What the hell were you thinking?"

I was caught off guard by the intensity of her question. "I guess, well, I hadn't thought—"

"That's the problem. You hadn't thought at all or you would have known it was a bad idea to walk in there alone. You knew nothing about the situation and didn't let anyone know where you were going. What an idiotic thing to do. And I'd warned you about how serious these people are and expressly asked you to stay out of it." She threw her hands in the air. She spoke with her hands almost as much as I did.

"If you would shut up for a second and give me a chance to explain before jumping to conclusions, you wouldn't have to give yourself an aneurysm."

With what looked like great self-restraint, she crossed her arms and waited.

"Thank you." I tried to calm down before I spoke again. "First of all, Lucia did know where I was." I knew this wasn't entirely truthful since Lucia wouldn't have known my whereabouts until after she awoke.

"Well, that would have been a great help when we were searching for your body," Gomez grumbled.

I ignored her. "Second, I had my phone at the ready to call you in case I ran into any trouble."

"And how did that work out for you?" Each word was heavy with sarcasm.

"As you very well know, getting a signal underground was difficult. But I was able to call you from the basement after I found Ty, and we are still very much alive."

"Only due to dumb luck. If you'd been there a little earlier, both of you would've been left for dead. Why would you go in there by yourself?"

I didn't know how to answer the question. Could I tell her I went into the tunnel knowing I wouldn't get hurt because I'd already seen it happen? Even if I hadn't entirely believed it myself? We'd struck up not quite a friendship, but at least a connection since she worked on the break-in at Jane's store last year. And while she'd hinted she knew about my psychic abilities, I didn't know how she would react to the truth about them. Besides, I wasn't ready to tell her.

"Can I just say I had a feeling I wasn't in any danger?" I stared at my hands and still felt her scrutinizing my face.

"A feeling, huh? It will have to do for now. Lucky for you, I have more pressing questions than ones regarding your personal choices. Although, we will come back to those in a minute." She pulled her notebook out of the breast pocket on her jacket. "Tell me what happened."

"I'll tell you everything, after you at least tell me if Ty's OK."

She hesitated long enough to make me think she'd refuse but finally relented. "All we know so far is he does have a concussion. He had to get several stitches in the back of his head. They're waiting for the results of a CT scan to check for hemorrhages in his brain. He's not pleased to be stuck in the hospital."

"Thank you."

She nodded and waited, her pen hovering over her notebook.

It didn't take long to explain finding what appeared to be a dead body and then realizing he was alive. I skipped over the part where I threw up and explained everything up until the moment she'd arrived.

"You didn't see anyone else nearby when you got there?"

"No, and I was keeping an eye out so no one would follow me behind the building."

She raised an eyebrow, but didn't comment. "Do you know who Mr. Foley thinks attacked him?"

"He didn't volunteer the information, and I didn't get a chance to ask, other than what you heard."

"Do you have a guess?" She paused. "Or a feeling?"

I wasn't sure if the last part was a dig or a legitimate question, so I didn't address it. "Honestly, I don't. It could be any number of people with all the treasure hunters in town."

"So, you think it's related to the search for *Tamerlane*?"

"Since that's what brought him to Fredericksburg, it would make sense. I wouldn't think anything else would have drawn him to the warehouse." I paused. "He's not from around here, so I can't imagine he has any enemies in the area."

"Do you know of any enemies he has who aren't from here?"

It annoyed me when she noticed the things I didn't say. "No one other than the guy he was talking about when you arrived. And he didn't mention his name."

She held my gaze before asking, "Do you have any other information on Mr. Foley other than his name?"

I debated what to do. Should I tell her I'd seen him with Caleb at the Sky Bar? I didn't want to lose Gomez's trust, but I found I didn't want to lose Ty's either. Gomez won. I shared I'd seen them having a dispute at the restaurant and described Caleb.

"A tattoo of paw prints?"

"Yes, right here." I pointed to the right side of my neck. "It looked like it continued under his shirt."

"Thank you for telling me." She paused, like she wanted to say more, but changed her mind. "That's enough for now.

There is an officer outside Ty's room. You can see him for a few minutes if you'd like."

"Thanks," I said as I stood.

She stood too and faced me. "At the moment you are off the hook. However, the City owns the property and may want to have you and Ty charged with trespassing." When I opened my mouth to protest, she spoke over me. "They will be considering their options in the next few days. If they pursue charges, it might bring more attention to the fact the space is there, which they don't want. They could still decide to press charges as a deterrent to others, though."

"Would I be arrested?" My voice went up an octave.

"I've already had a call from the mayor. She was quite concerned and with good reason. You were on private property and broke into a potentially unstable underground storage space."

"I didn't break in. The door was open when I got there."

"This isn't a joke. You could be arrested." Her tone was harsh.

"What would that mean? I wouldn't have to go to jail, would I?"

Her voice was quieter when she responded. "Trespassing is a class one misdemeanor, which can carry jail time—"

"But I was—"

"Let me finish."

I closed my mouth and took a deep breath through my nose, just like our yoga teacher had taught us.

Gomez had an amused expression on her face, and the frustration was gone from her voice. "For a first offense, it's unlikely you'd get sentenced to any time, but you would have to pay a fine."

She took a sizable pause, then quietly said, "In Virginia, a trespassing charge is dependent upon the offender having been given notice they were not allowed on the property either orally, in writing, or through the use of signs."

"I don't remember there being—"

She held up her hand indicating I should stop. "I'm just sharing with a citizen what the code says."

I was astonished and grateful and knew enough to keep my mouth shut. I didn't try to suppress a grin though.

She raised a signature eyebrow and changed the subject. "Didn't you want to visit Mr. Foley?"

"Yes. I think I'll go do that." I turned to leave, then looked back at her. "Thanks, Gomez. For everything."

She smiled and said, "It's four freaking a.m. Call me Gina already."

⸻⧜⸻

I gave my name to the police officer sitting in a chair outside Ty's room, and he waved me passed.

When I entered, I swear I saw movement. It was almost as if he'd been getting back into bed.

"Oh, it's only you," he said.

"You say the sweetest things."

He grinned. "I thought you were the pesky nurse."

"Pesky? What are you, a villain in an episode of Scooby-Doo?"

He laughed. "Well, it's better than saying what I was thinking."

Before he could elaborate, I asked. "How're you feeling? Have they gotten the results of the CT scan yet?"

"Been talking to Detective Gomez, have you?"

"You didn't think she was gonna let me slide, did you? She was waiting for me outside."

He sat up straighter. "What did you tell her?"

"Wait, did you get your test results yet?"

"Screw that. What did you tell Gomez?"

I held up my hands, gesturing for him to sit back. "Calm down. Until you know you're OK, you need to keep your blood pressure down." He relaxed a little, leaning back on the pillows. "I didn't have much to tell her. I just explained what happened." I paused. "She asked if you had any enemies I knew of, or if I knew the name of the person you were talking about when she arrived in the tunnel."

"And?"

"I told her you'd mentioned a rival but I didn't know his name."

He relaxed into the pillows even more.

"I also mentioned the guy I saw you with at the Sky Bar."

"The Sky B—" Recognition dawned on his face.

"Remember, it was my friend Sophie who spoke to you that night."

"The reporter?"

"Yeah, well, she's not actually a reporter."

He grinned. "You're craftier than I thought you were."

"I'm full of surprises, remember?"

He looked at me with suggestively raised eyebrows, and I blushed.

"You don't seem upset I told her about him. Who is he?" I didn't let on I knew his name, hoping he'd give me some details.

"You have your secrets and I have mine," he said.

I'd expected nothing less.

I tried to fill the now awkward silence. "Well, I hope you won't be stuck in here too long. Gomez limited my visit to a few minutes, so I'm gonna get going." I turned and walked toward the door, hoping my ass looked good.

"Hey."

I paused, turning back toward him.

"Thanks."

"For what?" I asked.

"For finding me."

I didn't know if he was being sincere or not and didn't want to read more into his words than he meant. Unsure how to respond, I took the coward's way out and just nodded. As I turned to leave, his mouth spread in a mischievous smile.

"I'll send you a bill for the dry cleaning and for new boots," he said.

I let him think he'd had the last word.

CHAPTER SIXTEEN

I slept most of the day on Tuesday after getting home from the hospital just before dawn. By late afternoon, Mary called. She reported there were already rumors about my adventures the previous night.

After I'd described the events to her satisfaction, we'd made a plan to meet Sophie the following day at the Virginiana Collection in the basement of the downtown library. We wanted to try to find answers to some outstanding questions about the warehouse and what building used to be above the underground storage area where I'd found the boxes. We wanted to find more information on Wallace Jackson and *The Lasting Word*, too.

I ran into Mary chatting with a friend in the lobby of the library. She extracted herself from the conversation and we headed toward the stairs together. Mary put her arm through mine and pulled me close.

"There are all kinds of crazy stories flying around town about your underground escapades."

"Word certainly does travel fast around here."

As we walked downstairs, she hummed "I Heard it Through the Grapevine."

"It's faster than the telegraph." I laughed as we continued our descent.

Sophie was already in the basement talking with a colleague at the reception desk. She walked towards us as soon as she spotted us, then proceeded right past us and back into the stairwell. Holding the door open, she gestured for us to follow her. Once we had, she closed the door and peered back through its narrow, rectangular glass window. She whispered, "Some of the treasure hunters are already in there."

"Do you know which ones?" I asked.

"One with a long ponytail came in an hour ago. Another matches the description of the guy you saw sitting with Ty at Castiglia's."

"Caleb," I said.

The door at the top of the flight of stairs opened.

I was surprised to find Ty looking down at us with a quizzical expression. "Ladies," he said and descended the half-flight of steps from the atrium. We moved out of the way to make room for him to pass. He had a bandage on the back of his head but appeared to be steady on his feet.

"I'm surprised you're out of the hospital already," I said.

He paused at the door. "I'm a quick healer."

"And Detective Gomez didn't arrest you for trespassing?" I asked.

His expression darkened. "I had to spend more time than I would have liked in the detective's company before I was allowed to leave the hospital, but I'm happy to say no charges have been filed. Which should be good news for you too."

"I'm glad to hear it."

Without another word, he gave us a facetious half-bow and continued on.

We didn't say anything until the door closed behind him.

"He is nice to look at," Mary said.

Sophie and I nodded in agreement.

"You sure you just had dinner with him?" Mary asked. "Nothing else? No...dessert?"

"Absolutely not," I said. "Besides, if I had, you'd have heard the news already."

"Truth," Mary said. "The grapevine always knows."

"What do we do now?" I asked. "Do we go in there anyway?"

"Yeah. Why not?" asked Sophie.

"What if they figure out what we're looking for? We don't want to give them any leads they don't already have."

"Good point," Mary said.

"Though the same applies to us. We can get leads based on what they're looking for," Sophie countered.

"Also a good point," Mary said.

In the end, we decided on a three-pronged approach. Sophie would search online at the desk with her co-worker Cora. They would read through insurance records to see who owned the properties in the neighborhood of the Old Stone Warehouse in the past. I would look through some of the bound copies of old newspapers for references to *The Lasting Word*. Mary would be the decoy, reading through a series of old diaries in the collection.

It turned out it was difficult to keep anything we were doing secret in the limited space once we entered. In the open area to our right, which was the size of my living room, there were four square, wood tables, two of which were already occupied.

Along the left side of the room were the stacks, which were on ten movable shelves. Each shelf had a hand crank at the end, which when turned, would move the floor to ceiling bookshelf either to the left or right, opening up a row between it and the next stack. Sophie had warned us to check between the rows before we turned the handle so we wouldn't trap anyone standing in an adjacent aisle.

The man with the ponytail, who I now realized was the one I'd seen arguing with Caleb outside HFFI, was seated at the table in the farthest corner with his back to the door. He scowled over his shoulder at our intrusion. He was leaning to his left with an elbow on the table, trying to shield what he was reading from prying eyes.

Caleb sat at a table in the corner to the right of the door. He didn't acknowledge our arrival, keeping his eyes on the book resting on the table in front of him.

Mary walked along the shelves until she found the heading she was looking for. After checking the rows to the right and left, she turned the handle, creating a new aisle among the stacks. It didn't take her long to find the diaries. She pulled down two books and sat at a table to read through them.

Ty turned the handle of one of the other shelves and walked down the row he'd created. I glanced up at the label at the end of the row he'd just entered. It listed Papers, Diaries, and Biographies. I glanced at him as I walked past the aisle. His back was to me so I couldn't see what he'd pulled off the shelf.

I continued to the aisle that held the bound copies of the *Virginia Herald*, the local newspaper that was available in 1827 when *Tamerlane* was first printed. I hoped to find an indication of when *The Lasting Word* was first published.

I turned the handle and was surprised by how easy it was to move the heavy shelves. I'd rotated the crank a few times when an angry voice called out.

It was Ty. I quickly turned the handle back the other way, the weight and momentum of the heavy shelf making it crash into the next stack. Ty emerged from the row ready for a fight. His expression eased when he saw I was the culprit.

"I'm so sorry. I forgot you were in there," I said. "I should've remembered to check the rows."

The sound of laughter behind us drew our attention. We all turned to find the guy with the ponytail snickering in the corner. When I glanced back, Ty's face had tensed again. He glared at the man, then turned back to me.

"You should be more careful," he said and walked out of the room carrying a book.

I glanced back at the man in the corner and didn't like the menacing expression on his face as he watched Ty leave. He turned his head and found me looking at him. My blood ran cold when our eyes met. He grinned and turned back to the book in front of him.

Caleb had remained silent throughout the incident, observing everyone else.

I returned to the stacks and cranked the handle tentatively. No cries were prompted by my actions, and I was able to enter the aisle. I chose the appropriate volume of editions of the *Herald* and took it to the table where Mary sat facing the door. I took the seat across from her, allowing me to keep an eye on long-haired creepy guy.

I'd been going through the copies of the newspaper for half an hour when my eyes began to droop. Mary had been taking occasional pictures of what I knew were random pages in the diaries. I perked up when she leaned toward me to whisper about something she found. I noticed long-haired creepy guy inclined his head our way. He was falling for our decoy.

"I'm going to see if Sophie can help me find more information on one of the people mentioned in here," Mary said. Her tone made me wonder if she had found a clue in the diaries after all, or if she was just a good actress. She left the room without looking back, but I knew there were eyes following her.

I was feeling sleepy, so I got up and went to the map cabinet a few feet to the left of long-haired, creepy guy. I pulled open the top drawer and began looking through the maps, pretending I was searching for one in particular, while trying to get a glimpse over his arm at the book in front of him. The words at the top of the page were small. I was able to make out the word Minutes before I realized he'd turned to stare at me.

The same look of menace he'd directed at Ty was now directed at me. I decided I preferred it focused on Ty.

I returned my attention to the maps for another minute or two, then went back to my table.

I considered what I'd glimpsed in the book he was poring over. I didn't see enough of it to know what the minutes were from, but speculated they were from a local government body. I wasn't willing to risk another peek over his shoulder. Instead, I decided to peruse the stacks to see if I could spot an empty space in a collection of minutes.

I found a row towards the end that listed county histories including the City of Fredericksburg. I turned the crank and created an aisle to walk down. I glanced at creepy guy before I entered. He was still engrossed in his book.

I walked between the shelves, reading the spines as I went. The door to the room opened and closed but I wasn't able to see who had come or gone.

I found a row of books labeled Fredericksburg Council Minutes, with a gap where a volume containing the minutes from 1825 through 1850 would have been. When I reached for the previous volume, it moved. I looked up and was overwhelmed with a sense of vertigo and the sensation the stacks were falling in on me. I recognized it as the feeling I'd had in my vision of the canyon walls caving in on me while I was crawling through the tunnel under the warehouse.

It took me a moment to realize they weren't falling as much as sliding. The space I was standing in was shrinking. I tried to exit the row, but the space had already narrowed too much for me to be able to turn. I couldn't raise my arms enough to use any real force to push back on the shelves.

"Stop," I yelled as loudly as I was able to, given the weight pressing on my chest. I was afraid in a moment I wouldn't be able to take another deep breath.

The space continued to diminish and the substantial weight of the shelves pressing on my chest and back became painful. With my claustrophobia kicking in, I felt a blind, irrational panic rising.

Between the pressure and the panic, I felt like I couldn't get any air in my lungs. Some deep survival instinct took over and I managed to scream.

The door opened and crashed into the wall. I heard angry voices. Their words were indistinct, overwhelmed by a rushing sound in my ears.

The stacks began to move in the opposite direction and Sophie rushed in. She put her arm around me and guided me to a table.

Ty and creepy guy stood a foot apart, staring each other down.

As soon as I was seated with Mary by my side, Sophie was gone.

"What the fuck is the matter with you?" She pushed Ty out of the way and was in creepy guy's face. "Are you crazy? You could have hurt her." I'd never seen Sophie so angry. She was a force to be reckoned with.

He didn't back down. Something about him was so unsettling. He opened his mouth to speak when a large security guard entered the room with Cora at his back.

"That's him," she said pointing at creepy guy.

He looked at all the angry faces around the room and stepped back from Sophie.

"I'm sorry. I forgot you were in there," he said, echoing the words I'd said to Ty earlier.

The security guard stepped toward him. "You need to leave, sir."

Creepy guy looked like he wanted to argue with him but chose to raise his hands in mock surrender.

"Accidents happen," he said and left the room.

We watched him go. When I turned back, I noticed the book he was reading was no longer on the table. Mary noticed it too.

"Where's the book?" she asked, looking around the room.

Caleb appeared at the door. He leaned on the frame, taking everything in.

"I don't think he took it," I said. "He was wearing a tight-fitting shirt. We would've noticed it if he'd tried to hide it underneath."

"He must have hidden it on another shelf," Mary said. "Did you see what it was?"

"It's what I was looking for when he closed the shelves on me." I shuddered at the memory. "A volume of minutes from city council meetings."

"Where was he when you stopped him?" Sophie asked Ty.

He gestured toward one of the rows. "He was using this handle." He reached out and turned it so the aisle beside it opened wider.

Sophie ventured in and scanned the shelves. She returned empty-handed.

"Try the other side," Mary said.

Sophie turned the handle in the opposite direction and went down the next aisle. "Nothing," she said.

I noticed Ty wasn't helping in the search.

"Try the next row," I said. "Maybe Ty was mistaken about which handle he was using."

He glanced my way.

Sophie turned the handle on the next stack. She reemerged with a book in her hand.

She glared at Ty, then flipped through the book until something caught her eye. She held it up with the pages spread wide open. Several sheets had been torn out.

The security guard ran out the door. Sophie carried the book out to the desk and Cora followed. Mary stayed with me.

Ty looked at me. "You alright?"

I nodded. "Thank you for stopping him."

A dark expression creased his brow. He took a step closer. "I'm glad you're OK, but this isn't a game. You need to back off before someone gets hurt."

"Watching out for Liv or watching out for yourself?" Sophie asked from the doorway.

He scowled at her.

"Nice try," she said. "You pointed out the wrong row so you'd have a chance to look at the book yourself."

He and Sophie were in a staring battle. He finally blinked and turned his gaze toward me. "Trust me, you are all in way over your heads. Be careful or someone might drown."

I gaped at him as he strode across the room. Sophie stood in his way briefly, then stepped aside and let him pass.

"What the actual fuck? Did he just threaten to kill one of us?" I asked.

Mary dropped into a chair beside me. "It sure sounded like it."

I stood up. "I'll be right back."

Mary started to speak, but Sophie stopped her. "Let her go."

I caught up with Ty in the courtyard in front of the library. "Ty," I yelled at his back. I was furious.

When I reached him, he turned to face me. His expression was stony, though his stance was casual.

"What the hell was that? First you lie about where the book is, then you threaten me and my friends?"

"I didn't threaten anyone."

"Someone might drown? I suppose it was just friendly conversation."

"Let's call it a friendly warning."

"From The Falcon?" I asked.

His expression became stony. He took a step closer, not in my space, but verging on it. His voice was low and serious. "Like I told you at dinner, I would be careful throwing around names and accusations."

My heart was pounding. I tried to keep my voice steady. "Or what?" I held his eyes. "What kind of man are you, Ty? Are you willing to hurt people to get what you want? Is the payoff the only thing that matters?"

He didn't respond.

"I see. The whole kid with a metal detector who loves a sense of discovery was bullshit. You were telling a story you hoped would get you some information from the—"

"From the what?" he asked, an unpleasant grin on his face.

"The woman who doesn't need to be psychic to see right through you."

CHAPTER SEVENTEEN

I stormed back into the basement. "What an ass." My hands were balled into fists.

I told them what had passed between me and Ty.

"Wow, way to go," Mary said. "That was brave."

I'd never thought of myself as brave. I do have a mama bear protective streak when it comes to people I love, though.

"Do you think he's The Falcon?" Mary asked.

"It's something I've considered. I don't know. I hope he isn't and that I didn't have dinner, and ugh, flirt with, a criminal." I suddenly felt exhausted.

"I don't think he's smart enough to be The Falcon," Sophie said. "He's clearly full of himself. Fancies himself Indiana Jones, but he's not so resourceful after all. He didn't get the book, did he?"

I shrugged. "No, but having the book doesn't help us much with the pages missing."

"Ah, that's where you're wrong," Sophie said with a mischievous grin. "I gave the book to Cora, and she's searching UMW's database for the date in question as we speak. The university has all kinds of historic records from the city available online." She paused for dramatic effect. "Including minutes from council meetings."

After getting our hopes up, we were disappointed to find nothing of particular significance in the missing pages of the minutes. They consisted of a discussion of a proposed underground sewer system in Fredericksburg in 1825 to mitigate the flow of sewage into the streets.

"Well, that's disgusting," Mary said, leaning back against the wall behind the desk where we were all gathered. "They were going to build sewers flowing straight into the river."

"Better than into the streets, I guess," said Sophie, who stood beside her.

"Gross either way," Mary said.

"What we need to focus on is why he was so interested in these particular pages," Sophie said.

I was sitting in the chair at the desk scrolling through the document on the computer. Sophie's coworker was in the reading room putting things back in order. I swiveled my chair to face Sophie and Mary.

"If he thinks there were underground sewers, he might think they're still there," I said.

"The tunnels?" Mary asked.

"Exactly," I said. "Maybe he's heard stories of tunnels under Fredericksburg and is searching for them."

"They don't exist," Mary said with exasperation. "They're an urban legend."

"He doesn't know that," I said. "A lot of people still think they're real."

"And as you discovered, someone found one under the warehouse," Sophie said. "Who's to say there aren't more?"

"Science says," Mary protested. "A study was done in twenty-eighteen after the space was discovered beneath the building where Juan More Taco and Fredericksburg Cupcakes are. People were convinced it meant there was a system of tunnels under the city. HFFI even hosted a tour of the space that was discovered. But the results of the study were disappointing. The space was an isolated storage area under the sidewalk, connected to one building, not part of a series of tunnels."

"And still, Liv was in another similar storage area, and it was connected to one across the street." Sophie seemed insistent that the tunnels existed. I wasn't sure why she was so set on it.

"What if there are tunnels? How would they help us find *Tamerlane*?" I asked.

"Don't you remember what I told you about Wallace Jackson?" Sophie asked.

"He was a cobbler and the publisher of *The Lasting Word*," I said, feeling like I was being given a pop quiz.

Sophie glanced around the room to see if anyone was nearby. "And where was his shop?"

I tried to recall our conversation the night Bailey came home. I gasped. "Oh, my gosh. I knew the warehouse had come up recently. I just couldn't remember when."

"Wait, he had a cobbler's shop there? I thought they sold tobacco out of it then," Mary said.

"No, we knew it was near there, but we hadn't figured out where yet," I said.

"If his shop was across the street on the corner of William and Sophia, above where the storage space was, I bet some of the scraps of paper you found in the boxes were from copies of *The Lasting Word*." Sophie was gleeful.

"Do you think the treasure hunters have discovered the journal?" Mary asked.

I leaned back in my chair, taking in all the information and trying to allow my brain to sort through it. "I think they might have. Ty asked Jane about local journals the day I met him at her shop." I spoke my thoughts as they arose. "I was hoping they hadn't. Sophie had hit on such an obscure connection to the process of cobbling and the word "lasting" in the title, I doubted they'd have dug deep enough to find the same connection. Though it's possible they discovered the connection to Wallace another way."

Sophie's brow was creased in a scowl.

"What if it wasn't *The Lasting Word*? What if they found *Tamerlane* in the box? We could be searching for something that's already long gone," Mary said.

"I don't think anyone's found it," I said. "From what Ty told me, the treasure hunting community is fairly small. If someone had discovered it, the others would have heard and left town."

"So where does that leave us?" asked Mary.

"It leaves us at the building across the street from the warehouse," Sophie said. "If Jackson's cobbler shop was there, he may have used the storage area under it or stored personal things in his shop. Cora and I weren't able to find any records associated with the property yet. There's a lot to go through, and there are big gaps in time without records." It was clear she'd been working this angle while we were in the research room.

"It's not surprising. Lots of old records are destroyed in fires or damaged by bugs, or around here, by floods," Mary said.

"So are buildings. Do either of you know the age of the one there now?" I asked.

Sophie shook her head.

Mary pulled her phone from her purse. "I can find out." She selected a number in her contacts and waited for someone to answer. "Regina, hi, it's Mary. I need you to look something up for me real quick. Do you have a second, or are you swamped?" She listened to Regina's response. "Great. Thanks. I'd like information on the property at the corner of Sophia and William across from the Old Stone Warehouse. I think it's a salon. I need to know how old it is." Mary pressed the mute button on her phone. "She's checking. It should be easy to find in the database since it's in the historic district." She unmuted herself and listened. "Oh. Uh-huh." She was silent again and her expression lost its previous hopefulness. "OK, thank you."

"Not good news?" I asked as she disconnected the call.

"I'm afraid not. There were several major fires in the downtown area in the eighteen hundreds, and the previous structure across from the warehouse was destroyed by one in eighteen thirty-six."

"Damn," Sophie said. "Anything left behind by Wallace was either destroyed in the fire or was in those boxes."

I wiped sweat from my forehead, while in my mind I pictured the room with the rafters and hardwood floors. "Not necessarily. The shop was where he worked. It's likely he lived somewhere else."

"That's a good point," said Mary. She looked at me more closely. "Any ideas where we should start looking?"

"We could go back to searching for the room I saw when I was with you, the one with the rafters."

"Yeah, but it wasn't much to go on, and you also said it could've been in France, didn't you? Have you seen any more detail?"

I shook my head.

"How else can we find out where he lived?" Mary asked.

"Tax records?" suggested Sophie.

I did a quick Google search. "Not federal income tax. There wasn't one until 1861."

"Local tax records? He must have paid taxes for his business or had to file some kind of paperwork for it. Did they have business licenses then? He probably had to list his home address on whatever he submitted," Mary said.

Sophie grabbed her phone and called someone she knew while Mary got back on the phone to HFFI. I smiled at their enthusiasm.

⸺⬥⬥⬥⸺

All we discovered in our search was that tax and business records from the 1800s were few and far between by the 21st century. As Mary had warned, many had been lost, burned, or rotted due to flooding or bug infestations. We gave up for the day, promising to keep searching whenever we had time.

The next morning, before I got busy with the next manuscript on my list for work, I was sitting on my stoop drinking a cup of tea when Lucia walked out her front door.

I waved and called, "Good morning. You're out the door early."

She smiled and came to sit beside me. "What are you doing out here in your PJs?"

I nudged her with my shoulder. "It's one of the benefits of working from home. I can work in my PJs."

"Ah, and you do seem to be working pretty hard."

We sat in the sunshine in companionable silence for a few minutes.

"I wish I'd seen your text about going to the warehouse the other night. I would've done something to help."

Lucia had called me as soon as she'd seen my text the next morning. I'd been too tired to fill her in on all the details, and we hadn't had an opportunity to catch up since then.

I leaned against her. "I know you would have."

Lucia took a sip from the travel mug in her hand.

"So, who's this Ty I've been hearing about?" she asked.

Chalk up another point for the grapevine.

I sighed. "He's the dead, not-quite-dead guy from my vision."

"And?"

"And what?"

She turned to look at me. I kept my eyes focused straight ahead.

"What's he like? Was he worth saving? Did he want saving?"

I considered her questions. "Those are very different questions."

"Uh huh," was all she said.

"Yes, I think he was worth saving and no, he may not have wanted to be saved. You were right about that. Not everyone wants to be saved. I think he would have been happier if I hadn't found him and gotten the police involved."

"You did, though."

"I did. He was not thrilled."

"I wonder why not," she said.

"It's not hard to figure out. He didn't want the police to know what he was up to and definitely didn't want to be caught trespassing, while whoever attacked him got away with—"

"Got away with what?"

"There's no way to know for certain. The general consensus is it wasn't *Tamerlane*, or news of its discovery would've leaked by now."

"And my other question?" she asked. "What's he like?"

I stared into the distance, wondering how to answer the question. "He's nice, I suppose. Some of the time."

"Well, thank you for the very detailed description. I feel as if I know him already."

I laughed. "Point taken." I looked down at my hands. "I had dinner with him the night before the incident at the warehouse."

She just nodded. I had a feeling she already knew we'd had dinner together.

"I didn't tell him then."

"About your vision?" she asked.

"Yeah. I felt so guilty afterwards. Do you think I should have?"

"Would he have believed you?"

"I think so. He asked about my visions at dinner."

"Did he? That's curious."

"It wasn't too surprising once I found out why he asked. He wanted me to use them to help him find *Tamerlane*."

"He asked you to help him?"

"Not exactly. He suggested we might be able to help each other."

"Did you like him?"

"Yes and no," I said. "He's infuriating and arrogant."

"That's the no part. What's the yes part?"

She was like Sophie, always paying attention. "He made me laugh. It felt comfortable and a little flirtatious. Until—" I remembered the text he received at the end of dinner.

She waited for me to continue.

"Until he received a text, presumably from his partner, and jumped up to leave like he was the clown in a jack-in-the-box."

"His partner?"

"Yes, a gorgeous redhead, who is not of an age to have to deal with hot flashes."

"You're so ageist. Have you ever stopped to consider hot flashes might be an indicator of a bright internal flame?"

This was the kind of mystical-edged question Lucia often posed.

"Not once," I responded.

"Well, you should. Nothing's sexier—"

"Than a sweaty upper lip?" I interjected.

She laughed. I enjoyed the sound of her laugh, light and melodic.

"That's not quite what I was going to say. Nothing's sexier than confidence. It doesn't matter how old you are or what you look like. Confidence, not arrogance," she clarified, "is definitely sexy."

"You think I lack confidence?" I wasn't sure I wanted her to answer the question honestly.

"I don't think you lack confidence. I think you find reasons not to risk your heart. Hiding behind your age or your menopause symptoms allows you to avoid the idea of connecting with anyone romantically."

We sat in silence for a few moments. With Lucia, silence was always a partner in our conversations.

"It's scary."

She put her hand on mine. "I know."

"Losing Nate was unbearable. When he died, I felt like I lost my compass. It's taken me years to try to find my way again without him. My whole plan for the rest of my life went up in flames in a moment. A single moment. We had plans—" A lump rose in my throat and I had to stop.

Lucia put her arm around my shoulders and pulled me close. "Your compass was always there. It just lost track of its true north. And I don't think Nate was your true north; I think it was, and is, love. The thing you have to remember is love doesn't have to end because you're no longer together. It doesn't even have to end if you offer it to another person."

She spoke over the protest I began to make.

"You love your daughters, right?"

I nodded.

"You love your friends and me and your parents. Does continuing to love them diminish the the feelings you have for Nate?"

"Of course not, but my love for them was different than my love for him."

"I have no doubt it was special and unique."

I rested my head on her shoulder. "I wish you could've met him."

"I do, too," she said. "All I'm trying to say is I think you are capable of more than one special love in your lifetime. And I know you're worthy of it." She kissed my cheek, then rested her head against mine. "You know what's almost as nice as a great love? Great sex. I bet you're capable of that, too."

I sat up, laughing. "I hope I still am."

"They say it's like riding a bicycle, but I've lived a lot of life and I've never seen that kind of bike."

I snorted. "Lucia! Sometimes you astound me."

"Good," she said standing up. "Life should have some astounding moments. They're memorable."

"Well, that image certainly is."

She laughed as she walked down the steps, then turned back to face me with a more serious expression. "I don't know if Ty is someone you want to take a chance on, but sooner or later you'll have to take a chance on someone and make some new plans."

I watched her walk away, knowing she was right. It was time for my compass to point me in a new direction.

CHAPTER EIGHTEEN

After the incident at the library, I didn't hear anything else from Ty, and things settled down around town. No significant Poe-related finds had been announced in the weeks since the news of the letter had broken. Some of the Typoes even packed their black clothes and left. It was nice to have some normalcy, though it didn't last as long as I would've liked.

I had lingering questions about what Ty suspected his rival had found in the box, but since he hadn't been willing to share information, I didn't think pushing would get me anywhere.

I also had to pause and consider why I was searching for *Tamerlane* in the first place. It had nothing to do with me. I wasn't a treasure hunter. Why would I put myself at risk the way I had by going into the warehouse alone? I knew how upset Bailey and Izzy had been last year when I'd nearly lost my life in the search for the Monroe letters. Why would I risk hurting them again?

I walked along the canal path in the evening sun hoping to find some answers yet not feeling particularly hopeful I would.

One of the things no one warns you about in relation to hot flashes is they make exercise infinitely less enjoyable, not that it was overly enjoyable to begin with. I admit a workout that leaves me hot and sweaty can be satisfying. But once I started having multiple hot flashes a day that left me hot and sweaty (and confused by visions), I found it more difficult to get excited for a workout. If you caught me in the middle of an internal temperature fluctuation, I might look like I was working out, when all I was really doing was sweating—and cursing a lot on the inside. Now, if hot flashes burned fat, I would've looked forward to menopause.

"Liv."

I felt a tap on my shoulder and jumped, startled.

"I've been calling your name," Gomez said. "Didn't you hear me?"

"Oh, Detective Gomez. No, I guess I was lost in my thoughts. Sorry."

She fell into step beside me, wearing a simple periwinkle blue T-shirt, tapered black sweatpants, and gray Nike sneakers.

"I've never seen you in anything other than your official detective clothes."

She smiled. "It's my day off."

"I thought you were always on."

"It can feel like I am." There was a heaviness to her tone I hadn't heard before.

"Because of people like me?" I asked.

"While you can occasionally be trying," she said, the lightness returning to her voice, "you are the least of my worries."

"And what are the greatest of them?" I didn't think I'd get an honest answer, but I was curious.

We walked a few more steps in silence. "The greatest of them are not work related," she finally said. "My mom has dementia. Her cognitive abilities are rapidly deteriorating." Her voice sounded weighed down, as I'm sure her heart was.

"I'm sorry, Detec—"

"You're supposed to be calling me Gina, remember. At least when I'm not threatening to arrest you."

I tried not to let my surprise show, both at the intimacy and humor.

"I'm sorry, Gina." It felt strange and also comfortable to use her first name.

I felt heat beginning to radiate from my back, which had nothing to do with the setting sun. I had a sudden flash of her in uniform with her gun raised, breathing hard, an intense expression on her face. Her hands trembled. I shook off the image.

"My dad's mom had dementia. It was an awful thing to witness in someone we loved," I said.

She nodded, no words arising for what she was feeling.

"Does she live in Fredericksburg?" I asked.

"She lived up in northwest DC until last year, then my siblings and I decided it would be better to move her here."

"Do your siblings live nearby?"

We paused where the trail crosses Princess Anne Street to wait for cars to stop for us at the crosswalk. She turned to me and shocked me by saying, "I could use a drink. Do you want to walk down to the meadery?"

"Hell, yeah," I said, surprised by the invitation.

We turned to our right instead of crossing the street. A car had been waiting for us to cross, and the driver honked when we changed direction. I waved an apology as they drove past, wondering if they would behave differently if they knew who they were honking at.

"Ever tempted to arrest people just for being idiots?"

She looked at me with an eyebrow raised, and I laughed.

"I withdraw the question." As we approached the meadery, I asked, "Would you prefer to sit inside or outside?"

"Inside," she said without hesitation, and I wondered why it was such a strong preference. I didn't know anything about the life of a police officer or detective, which is what I said when we found a table in the back corner of the dining area. She sat facing the door.

"It's not like they portray it on TV," she said while glancing at the menu. "It's not all chasing down bad guys. It's a lot of paperwork and meetings." She looked up at me. "And we don't always catch the bad guys."

"I imagine that's incredibly difficult."

"You have no idea," she said, and I knew I didn't.

We perused the menu until the waitress came to take our order.

"The honey nut Brie is delicious," the waitress said.

"It really is," Gina added.

We ordered one to share. Gina ordered a drink called a Gold Hive, with mead, peach, orange, and a honey sugar rim. Since I had never been there, I opted for a flight of meads.

"Thirsty?" Gina asked.

"What? I've never tried mead, I didn't know which I would like."

"You've never had mead before?"

"Nah, I'm more of a whiskey kinda gal," I said.

She made a noncommittal sound. "What people drink can tell you a lot about them."

"It can? What does whiskey tell you about me?"

"Well, it depends on if you like it neat or in a cocktail."

The waitress returned with our drinks and moved on to another table.

"Depends on my mood. If G.G.'s around, I like it neat. If I'm having a lot of hot flashes, I like it with cold lemonade."

"So, it depends on your menopause mood," she said, raising her glass and taking a sip.

I picked up the small glass of blueberry mead and lifted it in return. "And what does drinking mead say about you?"

Putting her glass down, she spun it on the table for a moment. "It means I'm sweet as honey, of course."

"I bet that's what all your detainees say. It's probably scratched into the walls in some holding cell."

I realized I'd never heard her laugh. It was higher pitched than her speaking voice. I liked the sound.

"How old is your mom?" I asked, hoping she didn't mind returning to the subject.

"She's eighty-five. She'd been healthy until she hit eighty, when things started to go downhill. In the past year, the deterioration has increased dramatically. That's why we decided to move her out of the city."

"Where is she living now?"

"With one of my sisters out in Spotsy. I help out as much as I can," she said, with what sounded like a touch of defensiveness in her voice.

We were interrupted for a moment when the waitress brought out the Brie, along with some fruit and slices of baguette. We snacked as we talked.

"I'm sure you do," I said while spreading some cheese on an apple slice. "How many siblings do you have?"

"Six. Three sisters and three brothers."

"Wow. That's a big family."

"Mexicana yyyyy Catolica," she said, switching to Spanish and bringing a little sass.

"Ah, yes, and based on her age, she was having kids when the Pope didn't approve of birth control."

"Go forth and multiply. They took it literalmente." She smiled and took another sip of her drink. "Plus, no había tele," she said with a chuckle.

My Spanish was rudimentary at best. "No television?"

She smiled and explained. "With lots of kids there was too much fighting over what to watch at night. So, no TV before bed, which meant we went to sleep early and our parents had—" she paused, searching for the appropriate words. "Tiempo libre. Free time," she said with a laugh.

I laughed with her. "I would guess free time was a rare commodity with seven children. Good for them."

I was honored she was opening up to me about her personal life. We lapsed into a comfortable, momentary silence.

I tasted the cherry mead next.

"What do you think?" she asked, pointing to the flight of drinks.

"I like the blueberry better. They're both pretty sweet." I paused for another sip. "Where do the rest of your siblings live?"

"Two of my brothers are still in DC and NOVA, and the other is in Raleigh. One of my sisters is in Northern Virginia and the other is nearby in Stafford. My brother Matteo did a lot of the caregiving for mom for a few years, but he was pretty burned out. He's a nurse practitioner, so while he knows how to care for her, his schedule is crazy busy."

"Where do you fall in the birth order?"

"What is this, twenty questions?"

"Are any of them bigger than a bread box?" I asked, laughing.

"How many kids today would get that reference?" she asked.

"Does anyone even play twenty questions anymore?"

"Doubt it. Unless there's an electronic version."

I picked up a napkin to wipe hot flash-generated sweat from my forehead.

"So, these hot flashes," she said. "There are interesting rumors about them."

My face flushed even more at the direction the conversation had taken. The rising heat also brought with it an urge to check my phone. I pulled it out of my pocket and checked it, then set it on the table.

Concern must have showed on my face, because when I looked back at Gina she asked, "Everything OK?"

"Yeah, I just felt—" I stopped because a text from Bailey popped up on my screen. *How's Den doing?* It was a system we'd agreed on long ago. If they needed me to call them ASAP, they would text, "How's Den doing?" and I would drop everything because Den stood for drop everything now. So, I dropped everything, including what was left of the apple slice I'd been eating.

"Excuse me, I have to call Bailey." I stepped outside. She picked up immediately.

"Mom, something's happened to Ronnie." She sounded frantic.

"What do you mean?"

"I was listening to her latest episode after it dropped last night, and she said she would have a special episode live tonight to reveal a big story related to *Tamerlane*." Her breathing was rapid. "I texted her this morning to see if she would give me a hint before the show. I didn't think she would, but I figured she would at least reply with something sarcastic. She never responded. I started to get a bad feeling about it, so I texted a couple friends of hers down there. They hadn't heard from her either. One of them texted asking her to check in because we were worried, and she hasn't replied."

"OK, slow down and take a breath. It's been one day. She could be busy with preparations for tonight's show and is trying to keep a low profile." I doubted this was true, but I was trying to help B stay calm. A part of me was also intrigued by what she described as a bad feeling. As I'd learned last year, psychic abilities do run in the female line of my family.

"I don't think that's all it is. Her friend Carla texted Ronnie's dad, and he wasn't able to get a response from her either. He works in NOVA, so Carla is on her way to Ronnie's place now. She tried tracking her with Find My Friends and Ronnie no longer shows up in her list of friends. I'm really worried."

"Let's not get too worked up yet. Is Carla going there on her own?"

"Yes."

"That's not a good idea. I can meet her there. Send me the address." I turned and looked in the window at Gina. Seeing my expression, she signaled to our waitress for the check.

The text came through from B and I checked the address. "It's not far from here. Let Carla know I'm on my way over. Call or text me if you hear anything before I get there."

"OK. Thanks, Mom." She disconnected, and I turned to find Gina walking out the door.

"What's up? Is Bailey alright?"

"She is, but a friend of hers might not be."

I explained the situation to her.

"Maybe there's something to those hot flashes after all," she said. "Did you know Bailey was going to reach out to you?"

I put her off. "Now's not the time for that discussion. I need to head over to Ronnie's. I don't want Carla there by herself."

"Where does Ronnie live?" She was back to her Detective Gomez tone of voice.

"On the other end of Caroline Street, above one of the shops. My car is near my house. I'll go get it."

"Then you'd have to find parking. You'd be better off on foot." She closed her eyes, silently debating something. "I may regret this, but I'll come with you. How do you feel about jogging?"

"I hate it. But in this case, I'll make an exception. You don't have to come with me. There's a chance nothing's wrong."

"It will save me the bother of having to rescue you later," she said. "Let's go, we're wasting time."

I sighed. I hated running and dreaded how the drinks I'd had were going to slosh around in my belly. "At least we're dressed for it."

It took us ten minutes to get from the meadery to Ronnie's. There were two stops along the way, one for me to catch my breath, which Gomez, being in much better shape, was very impatient with, and one to read a text from B letting me know

Carla was almost to Ronnie's place. I wrote back asking her to have Carla wait for me to get there.

When we arrived at the 600 block of Caroline Street, Carla was pacing the sidewalk in front of the building. She saw me and said, "Are you Bailey's mom?"

"Yes. And this is my friend Gina." When we'd paused for breath on our way, we decided not to introduce her as a detective since she was off duty. "No word from Ronnie?"

"No. I'm so worried."

"I can see that." I put my arm around her shoulders. "We will see what we can find out."

"When did you last see her or have contact with her?" Gina asked.

"We hung out after her show last night. She was so excited by what she'd found out."

"Did she tell you what she discovered?" I asked.

"No. She wouldn't even give me a hint. She said it was going to be a story big enough to guarantee sponsors for a new show she wanted to do." Tears sprang into her eyes. "She was looking forward to starting a show she could put her own name on."

"Let's not get too worried before we know if there's cause for concern," Gina said. "Can you show us where her apartment is?"

She pointed to a door to the left of a window featuring vintage concert T-shirts. "She lives above the shop."

The three of us walked to the door. Carla pulled a key out of her pocket. "Ronnie lets me crash here when I need to get away from my parents for a night or two."

She unlocked the door, but before she walked through, Gina reached out a hand. "You should wait here. We will check to see if anything looks unusual. If it's clear, you can come up."

Carla looked like she was going to disagree with that idea.

"You can wait here at the bottom of the steps so you can hear us," I said. "We just want to keep you safe. We will let you know when it's OK to come up."

Her expression turned fearful at the idea it might not be safe for her to go up. She nodded her consent.

Gina pushed the door all the way open using her elbow and turned back toward Carla. "Don't touch anything else," she said, making the hairs stand up at the back of my neck.

I followed Gina up the steep staircase to the second floor. As soon as we turned the corner, I knew something was wrong.

Gina held up a hand to stop me. With her other hand, she put a finger to her lips.

The apartment door was halfway open. A few pieces of mail lay on the floor just inside, like they'd been knocked off the narrow table that stood inside to the right. Gina stood still, listening. After a few moments, she edged the door open using her elbow. "Ronnie? Are you here?"

A chair was on its side in the room ahead of us. A basket, more mail, and a black beanie lay on the floor beyond the entryway. Gina surveyed the apartment and turned to me.

"This is a crime scene. We need to leave."

Carla's gasp traveled up the stairwell, followed by the sound of her running up the stairs.

Gina reacted immediately, returning to the top of the stairs and holding up a hand, while reaching to her hip for a weapon that wasn't there with the other. "Carla, I'm Detective Gomez with the Fredericksburg Police. I need you to return to the sidewalk without touching anything on your way."

Carla stood frozen on the steps. "You said it's a crime scene. Is she, is she—" the words stuck in her throat.

"I was not able to see Ronnie, but the door was open and there are indications of a struggle. I need you and Ms. Wilde to wait across the street. I need to call for backup prior to sweeping the apartment to verify there's no one inside."

Taking her cue, I walked down the steps with Carla. Gina was already speaking to someone on her phone when we reached the bottom of the steps.

Back on the sidewalk, I put my hands on Carla's shoulders and looked her in the eyes. "Detective Gomez is excellent at her job. She will let us know what she finds. I promise."

Tears filled Carla's eyes. I pulled her toward me for a hug. She clung to me for a moment, then pulled away to check her phone. I sent a quick text to Bailey, letting her know what we'd discovered, telling her I'd keep her posted.

By the time I'd hit send, a police car was turning the corner from Wolfe Street onto Caroline, approaching at speed. The lights were dark, and the siren was silent. Gomez stood just outside the door leading to the steps. Two officers exited the vehicle and went directly to her. She spoke to them, her expression grim. All three went upstairs, pulling on gloves as they climbed.

CHAPTER NINETEEN

I paced the sidewalk waiting for Gina to reemerge. It still felt strange to think of her as Gina.

We'd ignored her directive to wait across the street. Carla sat on the sidewalk with her back against the brick front wall. It was the first instance when I was glad the stores in the downtown shopping district closed at five o'clock. It meant there were fewer people around since the thrift store Ronnie lived above was closed for the day.

Two more police cars had shown up not long after the first, and the officers had carried in a variety of gear. Each time one arrived, Carla looked more anxious.

After the third arrived, I squatted down in front of her. "There's no point in us sitting here, caught up in worst-case-scenarios. Let's move around."

I placed a hand on the brick wall behind Carla, offering thanks for it as I pushed myself back up. Getting up from a squat wasn't as easy as it used to be.

Carla sprang up without any assistance, damn those young legs, and we did laps in front of the building.

Tom Petty was right; the waiting is the hardest part.

When Gina emerged through the front door, it seemed like an hour had passed, though it was closer to twenty minutes. She approached us.

"What did you find?" I asked.

"Is she dead?" Carla asked.

Gina held up her hands. "Ms. Carter is not in the apartment. However, there are signs of a struggle."

"What kind of signs?" Carla asked.

"I can't go into details, but I can tell you we didn't find anything that would indicate grievous physical harm."

It took us each a second to understand that meant she hadn't found a pool of blood, or anything else I didn't even want to think about. I reached out and took Carla's trembling hand.

"That's good news, right?"

Gina nodded. "I have to get back. You should go home. There's nothing either of you can do here."

"Go home? How can I just go home?" Carla asked. "What about Ronnie's dad?"

Gina pulled a notebook out of the pocket of her sweats. "If you'll give me his name and number, I'll contact him."

"You carry a notepad even while you're exercising?" I asked.

She shrugged. "You never know what might come up."

I thought of the notebook I carried in case a flash of insight came up and understood the sentiment.

While Carla pulled up the number for Ronnie's dad, I leaned against the wall, feeling slightly dizzy. I closed my eyes to steady myself. The bricks were warm on my back, releasing the heat of the day as the air temperature cooled with the sun sinking in the sky. The warmth felt soothing at first, until I felt heat begin to radiate from my own body rather than the bricks. Images began to form in my mind. I saw a flashlight raised, ready to strike. At first, it appeared I was seeing the attack on Ty, until I noticed the hand looked different. When I tried to focus on the image, it shifted to Ronnie. She turned around, shock registering on her face, and lifted her hands over her head as if to defend herself. The vision changed to those same arms, crossed at the wrists and bound with zip ties, which were cinched so tightly they were cutting into her skin. Ronnie's eyes were filled with fear. A hand on my shoulder made me jump, flinging my arms up over my head just as Ronnie had.

Gina moved faster than Neo in the Matrix, defensively grabbing my wrists as I lifted my arms. She held my wrists in a grip that wasn't tight but wasn't loose either. I saw a flicker of fear in her eyes, which she quickly contained. She must have seen fear in my eyes, too, because she said, "Liv, are you OK?"

Her steady gaze anchored me back to the present. I nodded, and she released my arms.

"I'm fine. I felt dizzy for a minute. I leaned against the wall for support and I think the heat from the bricks must have gotten to me." I knew she didn't believe me, but I didn't care. My only thoughts were about the fear in Ronnie's eyes.

Gina broke eye contact with me and turned to Carla, who'd been watching us. "Ms.—," she paused waiting for her to fill in the blank with her last name.

It took Carla a second to catch on. Then she said, "Jennings."

"Ms. Jennings, I appreciate your assistance. I'll reach out to Mr. Carter and apprise him of the situation. After I speak with Ms. Wilde, she will see that you get home safe—"

"I can't go home." Carla broke down in sobs. It was a challenge to understand what she said as she cried. "I have to stay here. It's all my fault."

I put my arms around her. She clung to me, sobbing onto my shoulder. I stroked her hair, letting her cry. Gina walked to the nearest cruiser, opened the passenger side door and rummaged around for a moment. She returned with a packet of tissues and waited for an opportunity to hand them to Carla. I mouthed, "Thank you," over the top of Carla's head.

After a few minutes of crying, Carla hiccupped to a pause and pulled back from my embrace. I kept my hands on her shoulders in case she broke down again and so she would know I was still with her. She reached up to wipe her eyes, and Gina extended the packet of tissues. I dropped my arms to allow Carla to take them. She wiped her eyes and blew her nose repeatedly.

"Detective Gomez, I can't go home." She sniffled and took a shaky breath, on the verge of more tears. "I have to help find Ronnie. It's—it's all my fault she's missing." Fresh tears ran down her cheeks.

I put an arm around her. "We'll figure this out, Carla. I'm sure it's not your fault. Just tell us what happened."

"But it *is* my fault." Carla insisted.

"What makes you say that?" Gina asked.

Carla took another shaky breath. "Everything's been crazy since the *Tamerlane* story broke. All these people have been all over town, and Ronnie's been so distracted. She's my best friend." Her tone begged us to understand. "And all the sudden, she didn't have time for me. All she would tell me was she was onto something big. She wouldn't confide in me. Sometimes I'd help her with her podcast, but she didn't want me anywhere near it over the past week or so. She recorded it in her apartment." She glanced up toward the windows above us.

Gina nodded. "We found the room she records it in."

"I was mad that she was shutting me out, so I went out with another friend and was talking about Ronnie and the stupid podcast and how pissed I was." She looked at us fearfully.

I didn't understand what she was driving at. "I doubt that would have led to her disappearance," I said.

She groaned in frustration. "Don't you see? I was talking about her and the podcast, and I used her name. What if someone overheard me? Or my friend could've told someone. I'd sworn to Ronnie I'd never tell anyone she was the one behind *Tea with Jam*. And now, and now—" She broke down before finishing the thought.

Gina spoke gently, but firmly. "Carla, I need you to listen, if anything happened to Ronnie it's the fault of whoever broke into her apartment, not you. And all we know for certain right now is someone broke in. We don't know if any harm has come to Ronnie."

Carla looked up.

"I'm going to need you to tell me everything you can remember from when you went out with your other friend." Gina looked over her shoulder at an officer near the door and waved her over. "Grab a recorder from the vehicle and a notepad."

Carla's eyes widened.

Gina didn't say anything else until the officer returned. "This is Officer Trench. She will take notes, and we will record our conversation so we don't miss anything. Even something that seems unimportant could lead us to Ronnie. Normally I'd have you come to the station to give your statement, but we need to act quickly in a case like this."

I noted she had stopped calling Ronnie Ms. Carter. I guessed she hoped the familiarity would help Carla remain calm.

All the familiarity fell away as soon as Gina pressed record on the handheld device. Trench stood to her right with a pen poised over a spiral bound notepad.

"This is Detective Gomez at 602 Caroline St. on 20 September at," she checked her watch, "nineteen twenty-two with Ms. Carla Jennings and Ms. Olivia Wilde. Officer Trench is also present. There has been a break-in at the residence of Veronica Carter, and Ms. Carter's whereabouts are unknown." She turned to Carla. "Ms. Jennings, please tell us about the conversation you had with a friend."

Carla looked scared, and I was concerned she would freeze up. I squeezed her shoulder.

She began haltingly, but the words began to flow as she told us about having coffee with a friend at Hyperion downtown. Given my own experiences there, I knew it would be easy for someone to have eavesdropped on their conversation.

"Who was with you?" Gina asked.

Carla said the name of her friend, which Officer Trench wrote down.

"We'll follow up with her. Did you notice anyone sitting nearby?" Gina asked.

Carla paused to visualize the scene. "I didn't pay attention to who else was there. I was too upset. Too focused on myself." She trailed off, tears resurfacing.

"It's natural you were upset," I said. "We know you wouldn't intentionally hurt Ronnie."

I looked at Gina, hoping she'd back me up. She didn't say a word. She was in full detective mode now. If Ronnie was in danger, everyone was either a suspect, a potential witness, or both.

It didn't take long for Carla to share all she could think of, including the fact that Ronnie no longer showed up on her Find My Friends app.

"It wouldn't help anyway," Gina said. "We found her phone in the apartment."

Carla shivered. "She would never have left her phone behind."

"Speaking of phones, I need to call Mr. Carter now. You are free to go, Ms. Jennings. I'll be in touch if I have any follow up questions." She pulled her cell and her notebook back out of her pocket.

"Detective," Carla said. "Earlier you said in these kinds of cases. What kind of cases did you mean?"

Gina was slow to respond. "I don't want to draw any conclusions yet. There may still be a simple explanation for why Ms. Carter has been unreachable." Carla looked skeptical, and Gina sighed. "Due to the state of her apartment and since we know there were extenuating circumstances in relation to the big reveal she had planned for her show, we're treating this as a missing person case."

Carla nodded, appearing suddenly much younger than she was.

"We'll do everything we can to find her. If anything else comes up for you, if you remember anything, no matter how inconsequential it seems, please reach out. I don't have my business cards with me, but Ms. Wilde can give you my number. Call me if anything new occurs to you."

She walked away, phone in hand, entering the numbers of Ronnie's dad's cell phone.

I took Carla's hands in mine. They were cold.

"We need to get you home. How did you get here?"

"On my bike." She gestured toward a space between Ronnie's building and the one beside it.

"Where do you live?"

"On Woodford, across route one."

It was getting dark and given the circumstances, I didn't want her to ride home alone, but my car was blocks away at my place.

As if anticipating my concerns, Officer Trench approached. "Detective Gomez asked me to give you a ride home."

"I have my bike."

"That's no problem. All our vehicles have bike racks. We have officers assigned to bike duty, and occasionally they need to transport them by car."

Carla shook her head. "My mom will lose her freaking mind if she sees me getting out of a police car."

"I will be happy to explain the circumstances to her if it will help." Trench smiled. She was gentle and calm, which I knew Carla needed right now. I was grateful to Gina for sending her over. She was very good at her job.

"You'll be OK," I said. "Detective Gomez will let us know when they find Ronnie." I gave her a quick hug, her eyes watery but not leaking, and she walked away with Officer Trench.

I wasn't able to gather my thoughts before my phone rang. I answered on the second ring. "Hey, B."

"You were supposed to call me back," she said, stress obvious in her voice. "Get out of the way you idiot!" A horn blared. "Sorry, I'm on my way home. I had to run a couple errands after work. How is it possible no one in all of Northern Virginia except me knows how to drive?"

I grimaced, hearing my own words reflected back to me. Bailey and Izzy often displayed the driving habits I'd inadvertently taught them. Not my proudest mom moments. Though I admit there are times when it makes me grin rather than cringe.

"What's the news about Ronnie?"

"It might be better if we talked when you're not driving."

"You have to tell me what's going on."

The worry and strain were evident in her voice. At this point in their lives, my youngest daughter Izzy was the more dramatic of the two, channeling her penchant for drama into acting in college theater productions. So, when B was ratcheting up the emotion, I knew there was a good reason for it.

"Calm down. Take a breath. I—"

"I don't want to take a fucking breath!"

I was taken aback by the vehemence of her words and didn't respond.

"I'm sorry. It's just that I've known Ronnie for so long, and you hear all these stories about people going missing on true crime podcasts, but you never think it will be someone you know. I'm so afraid for her." Her voice trembled. I knew she was close to tears. Both my daughters have empathetic hearts. "I keep thinking how scared she must be."

My breath caught in my throat as I recalled the fear in Ronnie's eyes. "Detective Gomez is doing all she can. I was just at Ronnie's place with Carla. It looked like someone had broken in, so they are treating it as a missing person case." Hearing a sharp intake of breath from B, I added, "Gomez found no sign of any serious injury in the apartment, just some furniture turned over and pictures disturbed on the walls."

"If she was home, wouldn't she have called for help?"

"I don't know. There's a chance she did and no one heard her. You know it's not the busiest part of Caroline Street, and we don't know if it was day or night when the break-in occurred. Her neighbors may have been sleeping."

"Mom?" Her voice was hesitant, which wasn't like my normally direct daughter.

"What sweetie?" I asked, preparing for how to respond to a question about what she would do if Ronnie was killed.

"Well...I mean, couldn't you, you know, use your visions to help find Ronnie?"

The last few words were spoken so fast I almost didn't catch them. When they registered with my brain, I was stunned speechless. I didn't know how to respond.

"Mom? Are you still there?"

"Uh, yeah. I'm still here. I'm just, well, you took me by surprise."

"Did you really think we didn't know?" she asked.

"We? Does Izzy know too?"

Her voice exuded impatience again, "Of course she knows. Everyone knows. There were all kinds of rumors after you found the letters."

"Helped find the letters," I interrupted.

"Whatever."

Now she was verging on flippant, which brought me back to my senses.

"What's going on? Are you angry at me?" I asked, wary of the answer.

She was silent for a moment. Then a torrent of words broke over me. "Yes, I'm angry. Why wouldn't I be? You have psychic superpowers and you never bothered to mention it to me or Izzy? We had to hear it from friends and through social media. What the fuck?"

It was killing me to hear the hurt in her voice. "I'm sorry, sweetie. I just didn't know how to bring it up. I tried once or twice, but—"

"But what?"

So much for her empathetic heart. She could also be a real hard-ass when she wanted to be. Though it kind of made me feel good knowing she would stand up for herself.

"I was afraid."

"Afraid?" Her tone softened. "Afraid of what?"

I'd never articulated the fear holding me back from sharing my abilities with them. So, it surprised me when the words came tumbling out. "Afraid of losing you and Izzy. I already lost your father. I couldn't bear losing both of you too."

She sounded incredulous. "Why would you lose us by talking to us about it?"

"I'm not saying it's a rational fear. It was just so new and unexpected. I never had a vision until a couple years ago, and I had no clue what was going on at first. How the hell do you all the sudden in the middle of your adult life start having psychic visions in the midst of hot flashes anyway? I mean, what kind of freakish thing is that? And that's what I was afraid of, you thinking I was some kind of freak. My mom, the would-be psychic. And you being embarrassed in front of your friends. And—" I trailed off. I was rambling.

"Are you done?" she asked.

"Maybe," I said.

She laughed at my petulance.

"You could never, ever lose us, Mom. Not in a million years."

"Only a million?"

"A million squared, times infinity."

Now I knew she was smiling. "Thanks, B. I love you. I'm so sorry I hurt you and Izzy."

"It's OK, but you have to know you can trust us with whatever is going on in your life. Just like we trust you with what's going on in ours."

"A little too much sometimes," I said.

She snorted. "Yeah, well, too bad." She paused before continuing. "So, you have them during hot flashes?"

"Yup. Some people don't know how lucky they are to just get sweaty and red-faced." I sighed. "Lucia is helping me learn to interpret them and, hopefully, make them useful."

"Have you seen anything about Ronnie?" she asked, almost whispering.

I hesitated. Then I heard her saying I needed to trust them echo in my head and heart. "Yes. It wasn't much to go on, and I haven't been able to sit with it since it happened to see if I can glean anything useful from it. All I saw was her sitting in a dark space with her hands bound and her mouth covered with tape." I chose not to share how scared she was. "She was alive and I didn't see any obvious injuries."

We sat in silence until B's voice came shakily through my phone. "Please, Mom. Help her."

CHAPTER TWENTY

I'd promised Bailey I would do all I could for Ronnie, and I intended to keep my word.

I stood on the sidewalk, frustrated by my inability to do anything. The police, including Gina, were still inside Ronnie's apartment. I vacillated between going home, staying, and getting a very large glass of whiskey somewhere. I looked up at the window of the apartment facing the street and paused.

All along the windowsill on the outside of the curtain stood a line of small, colorful figures. I smiled remembering Ronnie and Bailey as five and six-year-olds playing with their Powerpuff Girl dolls and acting out scenes from the show, chasing the evil Mojo Jojo all around our backyard. I wondered if Bailey knew Ronnie had a collection of them. Looking up at the dolls, an idea occurred to me.

I approached the officer standing beside the front door and realized I knew him. "Oh, Officer Clark. I remember you from the break-in at Jane's store. It's good to see you."

"Good to see you too, ma'am," he said without enthusiasm.

"I need to speak to Detective Gomez. May I go up?"

"No, ma'am. It's a crime scene. I can't let you in."

It didn't seem likely he would change his mind. So, I pulled out my phone, which was getting low on battery, and called Gina. I walked away from Clark to stand below the window.

"Yes?" She drew out the word.

"I'm sorry to disturb you. I just need you to do me a quick favor."

"Right now? I'm a bit busy."

"There's no need for sarcasm," I said.

"Isn't there?"

I smiled. "Humor me for a minute. Walk to the window on the left in the room facing the street. Wait, your right, my left."

She sighed and began moving. "OK, I'm standing in front of the window."

"This may sound odd, but can you look behind the curtain and grab one of the dolls there? One of the Powerpuff Girls."

"You're joking."

"I don't joke about the Powerpuff Girls," I said, trying to keep a straight face in case she was looking down at me.

"I don't have time for fooling around." She was getting impatient.

"I'm not kidding. I feel like having an object of Ronnie's might help."

"Help with what?" she asked.

"Let's not go into that now. Please, Gina. She and Bailey used to play with those dolls together when they were little. There's something about them—"

She huffed into the phone. "I'll be right down." I thought she'd hung up, until she quietly asked, "Buttercup, Bubbles, or Blossom?"

I glanced up and saw her looking down at me from the window. "What? I have nieces," she said.

"Buttercup," I said, unable to suppress a small grin. "She was Ronnie's favorite."

"I'll be right down."

❧

I called Lucia on my way home and when I got there, she was waiting for me on the steps outside my door with a book on her lap. She stood and gave me a hug.

"Thanks for coming over," I said.

"Of course."

I unlocked the door, and we headed for the couch. She kicked off her shoes, pulled her legs up, and sat cross-legged. Her mostly gray, wavy, shoulder length hair was swept up in a clip at the back of her head, and she wore loose, green linen pants and an ivory short-sleeve T-shirt. She smelled faintly of cardamom, which tickled a memory buried somewhere in my brain.

"Where is it?" Lucia asked, placing the book on the couch between us. I'd told her about the doll on the phone.

I read the title aloud. "How to Develop and Use Psychometry. So, that's what it's called? When you touch an object and can sense something from it?"

"Yes," was her illuminating response.

I pulled a napkin from my pocket. I'd wiped my face with it at the meadery and put it there to throw away later. I unwrapped the Buttercup doll it now held. She was three inches high and wearing her signature green and black dress and had short, black, plastic hair. "I didn't want to touch it with my skin, so I had Gina put it in the napkin." I looked at it as if hoping it would speak. "What are the chances of someone having more than one type of psychic ability?"

"I don't know. It's not unheard of, but I don't know how common it is either."

"What if I can't get anything from it?" I asked.

She raised her eyes from the doll to my face. "Darling, Liv, you can't put so much pressure on yourself or your abilities. The world does not hang in the balance based on whether or not you can sense something from this tiny doll."

"What if one life does hang in the balance?"

She put a hand to my cheek. "Then we will figure out another way to help her."

I took a deep breath and pulled the doll from the napkin I'd wrapped it in.

Absolutely nothing happened.

"I don't feel a thing."

"Well, at least you gave it some time," she laughed. "Try giving it more than three seconds."

I closed my eyes and touched the doll with both hands, turning it with my fingers, feeling every aspect of it. All I saw in my mind was a memory of Bailey and Ronnie as children playing with the dolls.

I must have been squishing my face in concentration because Lucia said, "Relax. You must learn to trust your gifts and to trust that if there is a message for you in this object, you'll be able to receive it." She placed her hands on top of mine. "You must also accept the possibility this isn't yours to do. That she's not yours to save."

My eyes flew open at her words. "But she's so young, and she's in trouble. It would be such a waste if—" I stopped, not wanting to say it out loud. "And Bailey would be devastated."

"I didn't say she couldn't be saved. I said she might not be *yours* to save."

I let her words sink in.

She continued, "Just because you have a gift, doesn't mean you're meant to use it to help everyone in the world. You will need to be able to discern what is yours to do and what isn't."

"And how the hell do I do that?"

"Well, I fear if I told you to be patient with it, that it will take practice, you would kick me out on my backside."

"You're probably right," I said laughing. "I'm sorry. I'm just so worried about Ronnie."

"And Bailey," she said. "I would guess it would be difficult to see things with clarity when your emotions are so involved." She unfolded her legs and stood up. "My best advice is to take a shower and go to bed."

"A shower? Why?"

"Flowing water is good for removing obstacles. And I always get my best ideas in the shower."

She hugged me and then held me at arm's length. "You have a good heart. Let it guide you." She paused, doing the mysterious listening thing she does. "You know, it would do you some good to remember that while your visions happen in your mind's eye, I think they originate in your heart." She placed her hand over her own heart. "It wouldn't do any harm to sleep with the doll under your pillow either."

"I don't know how I will ever get to sleep tonight," I said as we walked to the door.

"I bet a little whiskey and chamomile will do the trick." Her eyes sparkled.

CHAPTER TWENTY-ONE

I followed Lucia's advice. While my tea was steeping I took a quick shower, pausing to notice the feeling of the water flowing over me. No inspiration came.

After I'd wrapped myself in my robe and wrung out the tea bag, I poured a generous shot of Glenlivet into the tea and placed the cup and saucer on my nightstand. I pulled little Buttercup from the pocket of my robe, stood her beside the teacup, and sat on the edge of my bed.

Before showering, I'd called Bailey and reassured her Detective Gomez was doing everything in her power to find Ronnie. Afterward, I sat thinking of Ronnie and wishing with all my heart I knew how to help. I reached for the doll, holding an image of Ronnie in my mind.

Nothing happened. Again.

Looking at Buttercup's tiny face I said, "I think I'm going crazy. I must be. I'm talking to a doll." I set her back on the nightstand and picked up the teacup. I wrapped my hands around it and let the warmth seep into me before taking a tentative sip. It was warm without being hot, so I took a deeper drink and enjoyed the sensation of the warmth moving through my body. I breathed in the mingled scents of Scotch and tea. Sooner than I'd like to admit, the cup was empty.

I exchanged the cup for the book Lucia had loaned me and propped myself up with my pillows to read. My eyes kept drifting to the doll. I grabbed her and tucked her under my pillow, feeling embarrassed by what others would think even though I was alone.

I didn't get far into the book, which was a bit drier than I would have expected, being about psychic powers and all. After the heat started to rise in my body, prickling on my skin, I wished I could emulate the book in all its dryness.

When a hot flash begins, all I want to do is scream in frustration. Those are some of the Grumpy Gal moments. G.G. also shows up at unexpected moments, dripping with snarkiness in addition to sweat. I try to control her, but every now and then it feels better to just let her loose. Admittedly, it doesn't always feel better to those on the receiving end of the snarky attitude.

I don't blame G.G. though; it's infuriating when my body loses control of its internal thermostat. I break out in sweat and anxiety, the former beading on my upper lip, forehead, and various other locations, and the latter settling in my chest. I don't even like to put moisturizer on my face before going to bed anymore because I know it will just make my sweat feel greasy when the furnace kicks in.

This time, I felt more of the anxiety than the sweat. I closed my eyes to try some of the calming breathing techniques I'd learned in yoga class. I scooted my backside farther up toward the pillows to find a more comfortable position. Instead of comfort, I felt Buttercup's tiny form poking me in the butt. I reached under the pillow, told her I was sorry, and tossed her across the room.

I spent a restless night, filled with dreams involving the Powerpuff Girls. One was particularly disturbing, as it featured me as Blossom having a romantic moment with Mojo Jojo—who is a monkey, by the way. I had no desire to hear what Lucia's interpretation of that would be.

What woke me was a dream featuring Ronnie's frightened eyes. I remembered the vision when I'd first seen those eyes. I sat up and picked up my journal, hoping writing it down would help me stop seeing them.

I did what Lucia had taught me. I took note of everything I'd seen, not just Ronnie. I saw again the zip ties binding her wrists. She was sitting with her legs straight out in front of her, zip ties around her ankles, too. I tried to ignore her face and the bindings and focus on details about her surroundings. I also ignored the heat radiating from my back, raising beads of sweat that dripped down my spine and made me shiver.

What was she sitting on or leaning against? I strained to bring the vision back to mind. It seemed the harder I tried, the less I could see. I was getting nowhere and realized I'd dropped the pen in my lap because my hands were clenched in fists.

I put my notebook and pen aside, pulled my legs up, wrapped my arms around them, and rested my forehead on my knees. I felt tears welling in my eyes. I let them fall, hoping it would help release the tension.

Once the tears abated, I opened my eyes, head still resting on my knees, and saw the rivulets my tears had left on my legs. The image of Ronnie lingered in my mind. There were puddles on the ground beside her legs. The space was dark, but enough light filtered in to glint off the water beside her. Water, that I now realized, was sitting in puddles in dirt, not on a finished floor.

Getting out of bed, I began pacing. I started talking aloud to process the many questions running through my brain. "OK, it's not a brick or cement or wooden floor. Is she in another tunnel? No, I don't think it's likely there are more undiscovered tunnels around town. It could be an old shed or barn or outside somewhere."

As I turned to continue my path back toward my bed, I noticed Buttercup on the floor just under my dresser. I reached for her. "Please. Help me find Ronnie."

I closed my hand around her and a scene flashed across my mind of a carnival of some sort, with music playing in the background, people dancing, dressed like it was early in the 20th century, and an old-fashioned amusement park ride. It didn't resemble the Fredericksburg Fairgrounds. The closest amusement park was Kings Dominion, forty miles away. I threw the doll back across the room, where she bounced off the wall above my bed and landed upright on one of my pillows, as if she didn't have a care in the world.

---◦∞◦---

It was pointless to try to go back to sleep, and I knew I wouldn't get any work done until I felt more alert. Perhaps drinking Scotch and tea late at night was not the best combination for a clear head in the morning. And the idea of sitting down to work and searching for typos after our conversation with Momma M just made me laugh.

I pulled on a pair of jeans and my favorite Carbon Leaf T-shirt and was out the door. Strong, coffee shop coffee was calling my name. The morning was cool. I figured a walk in the crisp air would do me some good, too.

I bypassed Hyperion, which was closer but usually busier early in the morning and headed down Caroline towards Agora. I was going to text Sophie, then decided some quiet time alone with my caffeine would be the wiser choice.

I ordered a cup of light roast and a cinnamon chip scone. I wandered toward the back of the building and out a door into the courtyard. There were a couple of people sitting outside. I stopped to say hello to an adorable chocolate lab sitting on the ground beside a woman I vaguely knew, then made my way to a table in the dappled sunlight under the arbor.

While my coffee cooled, I sent a preemptive text to Bailey, letting her know I'd had no updates from Detective Gomez overnight. Then I texted Gina to see if she had any news about Ronnie. With the check-in texts out of the way, I broke off a piece of the scone and took a moment to enjoy the scent of warm cinnamon before putting it in my mouth. I closed my eyes and let childhood memories of the warm, cinnamon brown sugar Pop-Tarts I had each morning fill my mind.

I must have been making happy noises while I enjoyed my scone, because the next thing I knew I heard, "Must be one hell of a good scone."

Ty stood in front of me, wearing faded jeans, a plain navy-blue, long sleeve T-shirt, and dirty hiking boots. He raised a hand as if signaling a waitress and said, "I'll have what she's having."

I laughed at the unexpected *When Harry Met Sally* reference. "Aren't treasure hunters too cool to watch rom-coms?"

"Well, since I was, what," he thought for a moment as he sat down across from me uninvited, "twenty-two when the movie came out, I wasn't quite a professional yet."

I did some calculations and was pissed though not shocked to find he was a few years younger than me.

"They do make good scones here," he said, reaching across the table to help himself to a piece of mine.

I slapped his hand away. To be honest, it felt more like G.G. had arrived and slapped him, but I couldn't be certain which of us it was without more caffeine. She made more frequent appearances when I was tired.

He raised his eyebrows. "Maybe you should finish your coffee before we continue our conversation."

"Hey, I wasn't inviting a conversation. I was just enjoying my breakfast and the cool air."

He put his hands up in surrender and started to stand up.

Despite still being angry at him for his threatening comment at the library, I felt bad for my sharpness. "I'm sorry. I didn't sleep well and I'm a bit grumpy. I get that way sometimes. It's a hormonal thing." I felt like an idiot. Why was I talking to this handsome, albeit annoying, man about my hormones, for God's sake?

"I hope you were losing sleep for a fun reason," he said with that cocky smile of his.

G.G. reared back up. I opened my mouth to speak, thought better of it, and snapped my mouth shut.

He laughed. "You almost took the bait."

"Bastard," I said and balled up a napkin to toss at him. He batted it away and it fell to the ground beside me.

"So, what's got you out so early?" I asked.

"The early bird gets the worm," he said.

Before I could think better of it, I said, "Or the early worm gets the treasure."

"A worm? I didn't realize you'd developed such a low opinion of me. What've I done to incur your wrath?"

"Hmm, let's see. Do you think it might have something to do with finding you apparently dead in a tunnel, which was terrifying, by the way, and rescuing you with barely a word of thanks?" I knew he didn't truly owe me anything for finding him, other than a little genuine gratitude perhaps. "Then there was your comment at the library." I was aware I was being slightly unreasonable. I held my ground anyway because stubbornness is a family trait. Or he could've been right about me not having conversations prior to finishing my coffee.

He nodded. "I see. I'm sorry for my comment at the library, but I guess our ideas of rescuing are different. I wouldn't say you saved me, considering you threw up on me and got me in trouble with the police. Luckily, I have an excellent lawyer, a necessity in this business, and it looks like I'll just have to pay a fine for trespassing. So, I'll forgive you."

His lips twitched. I knew he was baiting me again, but I rose to it anyway.

"Forgive me?" I said with indignation.

"Hold on before you eviscerate me."

I was having none of it. "I didn't make you trespass, so don't try to blame your trouble with the law on me." I crossed my arms over my chest like a petulant child.

He appeared bemused by my behavior. I forced myself to take a breath, uncrossed my arms, and tried to redirect the conversation. "Did you learn anything new based on what we found in the box under the warehouse?"

"Unfortunately, the scraps left behind by the bastard who knocked me out didn't provide much illumination."

I sensed frustration in his voice and was childishly glad he hadn't made a discovery based on the slips of paper we'd found in the box.

"Good morning," a voice said.

We must have been very focused on each other because neither of us had noticed Sophie approaching.

She looked perplexed. "What brings you two here?"

"We're not here together," I said.

Ty stood and gestured to one of the other chairs at the table.

Sophie extended her hand to him. "I don't know if you remember me. I'm Sophie Grace. We met on the rooftop of Castiglia's and I was with Liv at the library last week." Her tone was chilly. She sat in the chair to my left.

He grinned in recognition. "Oh, I remember you." He put emphasis on the word you. She'd made an impression.

His jeans had barely touched his seat again when someone called his name from across the courtyard. We all turned in the direction of the voice and saw Perry approaching with a to-go cup. A cinnamony scent preceded her. I wasn't sure if it was emanating from her or her drink.

"You ready to go?" she asked him, without acknowledging Sophie or me.

He looked up at her for a moment before standing. "It was great to see you, ladies."

She nodded at us and put her arm through his, leading him out of the courtyard toward the street.

"He may be a jerk, but damn, he looks Kevin Costner fine in a pair of jeans," Sophie said, watching him go.

"You can say that again," a feminine voice said.

We turned to see Claire approaching. She watched Ty go, her blond bob catching the morning sunlight.

I guess Sophie and Claire had wanted to avoid the morning crowd at Hyperion, too. My quiet time alone with my caffeine wasn't working as I'd planned.

Claire sipped from the cup in her hand as she sat in Ty's seat. "Mmmm, the chair's still warm from what's inside those jeans." She wiggled her butt in her chair as if rubbing up against him.

"Claire," I said, astonished.

"What? I can appreciate a fine ass as much as you two."

"Yeah, but you usually don't say it out loud," I said.

"Or do a lap dance on the patio furniture," Sophie said, laughing.

"Who was he?" Claire asked.

"That was Ty," Sophie said.

"Oh. Now I understand why Jane wanted you to have a little fun with him," said Claire.

"Or a lot of fun," added Sophie.

"Mm, hmm," said Claire with a faraway look in her eyes.

"You're starting to sound as bad as Hannah," I said. "You two are terrible. Objectifying the poor man."

"I don't think he's the type who'd be bothered by it," said Sophie, the slight edge back in her voice.

"And nobody's as bad as Hannah," Claire said. She leaned back and sipped her coffee.

"No matter how hot he is, we can't forget what he said to you at the library," Sophie said.

"I haven't forgotten."

"Who was that with him?" Claire asked after a moment of collective silence. "Was she the woman you mentioned seeing him with at Jane's store?"

"Yeah. Her name's Perry," I said.

"He sure jumped at her command," Sophie said. "Is she his boss, or his something else?"

"She's something else alright," I said.

"She could be a descendant of Commodore Perry," Claire said. "He was very commanding."

"I wish she looked like him," I said, grinning.

"Is Perry her first name or last name?" Sophie asked.

"I don't know," I said. "It hadn't occurred to me. I'd just assumed it was her first name."

"Maybe it's short for something," Claire said.

"Persephone," Sophie suggested.

"Hades's Queen?" I asked. "Hmm, sounds pretty accurate. She seems to think she's queen of some kind of kingdom."

"You sound jealous," Sophie said, her tone lighter.

I smacked her arm, but I was the one who felt the sting of the truth of her statement.

"Some people use Perry as a nickname for perimenopause," Claire said.

"Women like her don't get hot flashes," I said, with a trace of bitterness.

"Well, she lit a fire under him," Sophie said.

"Yup. She seems to be able to do that. He told me they're business partners before anything else, but it appears to be a lopsided partnership."

"It looked like it was the only thing that's lopsided about him," Claire said.

While Sophie laughed, I searched for the napkin I'd thrown at Ty to throw at Claire. Glancing under the table for it, I remembered his muddy boots and saw again the muddy puddles I'd seen beside Ronnie.

"Even though I came here for some peace and quiet," I glared at them, "I'm glad you both showed up."

Sophie feigned offense.

"I need to pick your brains. Do either of you know of a fairground around here other than the one they use now? A place with an old-fashioned carnival ride?"

They had similar confused expressions. "Where did that come from?" Sophie asked.

Swearing them to secrecy, I told them what happened the previous day and about my vision of Ronnie.

"How terrible," Claire said. Her hand was over her heart and I knew, just like me, she was trying not to imagine the same thing happening to one of her daughters.

"I'm confused," said Sophie. "If the images you saw were old, how do they relate to where Ronnie is now?"

"I wish I knew."

"Tell us more about what you saw," Sophie said.

I told them everything I could remember.

"It doesn't ring any bells, but I will ask around at the museum," Claire said. She worked part-time as a guide at the James Monroe Museum in town. They'd been getting a lot more visitors since the Monroe letters were discovered last year, much to the delight of the museum's staff.

"I will do some digging at the library," Sophie said, standing up. "Speaking of which, I'd better get going."

"Me, too," said Claire. "I didn't plan to stay until I heard your unmistakable voice when someone opened the side door." She looked pointedly at Sophie. "Once I got outside, well, I felt a sudden need to sit down." She smiled as she took a sip of her coffee.

We gathered our things and walked to the street.

"Thank you, for helping with the research and for—so many things," I said.

"We've always got your back," Sophie said and gave me a side hug.

"Though it's more difficult when you run off on your own in the middle of the night," Claire said, a tone of admonishment in her voice.

"Ah, so next time I should call you first?" I asked, joking.

"Next time?" Claire asked.

"I'm in," Sophie said.

CHAPTER TWENTY-TWO

In spite of the sense of disquiet which had settled in my chest for the day, I was able to work a normal schedule for a change. I even showed up to our Zoom staff meeting at the appointed hour and appropriately dressed. There were good-natured expressions of shock from my coworkers, which, to be fair, I'd earned over the years.

Claire contacted me around midday. None of the museum staff knew of an amusement park near Fredericksburg or knew of a different fairgrounds. It wasn't until evening when Sophie reached out. She sent me a text which read: *Sorry, busy day. Good news. I found this…* The next text included a link to an article in the local paper about Scott's Island.

I texted her back. *Thanks. I'll check it out. I feel like someone mentioned Scott's Island recently.*

Three dots blinked and then she said, *Let me know if it fits with what you saw. I'll be at Kevin's soccer game. Don't do anything stupid.*

Who me?! I responded.

I clicked on the link to the article and read the history of the island. A memory surfaced of Mary and Momma M talking about Scott's Island when I was at HFFI.

The article delved into the island's uses over the years. Since the 1800s, it had been everything from a place to hold dances and celebrations honoring war veterans, to a casino, to a venue for boxing matches. In the early 1900s, a few rides were added. The amenities had been rebuilt many times due to floods which had submerged the island.

Goosebumps rose on my arms. I knew this was it. This was where I'd seen Ronnie. It had to be. It was even located behind the Old Stone Warehouse, so whoever had broken in and attacked Ty might've discovered it.

As far as I knew, there weren't any buildings still standing on the island. I scrolled through the article again, looking at the old photos.

I opened the map app on my phone and zoomed in to see if the satellite imagery picked up any ruins even though it had been a hundred years since the island had been in regular use. Where could the kidnapper be holding Ronnie? Any remaining structures would have been washed away in floods long ago. I recalled the photograph of the river overflowing its banks I'd seen at HFFI and my pulse increased. Late summer had been rainy, but luckily the river wasn't much higher than normal.

I recalled the puddles I'd seen around Ronnie and wondered when high tide would occur.

While we're a hundred miles or so from the Chesapeake Bay, the Rappahannock River is still tidal up to the fall line above the city. The tide can make the river rise and fall up to three feet. I didn't want to consider what that meant if you were underground on an island in the middle of the river. And if it was The Falcon who'd kidnapped Ronnie, would they know about the tides? Knots formed in my stomach.

I pulled up a tide chart, then checked the time. It was almost eight o'clock. The peak of high tide would be just before nine. I had an hour, but I also knew the tide had already been rising for hours. I gasped as I remembered that high tide happens every twelve hours. It had already been high at least twice since Ronnie had gone missing.

My hands trembled as I laced up a pair of old hiking boots and pulled a sweatshirt on over my tee. The nights were getting chilly after the sun went down. As I turned to walk out of my bedroom, I caught a glimpse of Buttercup. On impulse, I picked up the little doll and shoved it in the pocket of my jeans.

In the kitchen, I dug through the junk drawer and found a flashlight small enough to fit in the front pocket of my sweatshirt and still strong enough to provide decent light. My phone's charge was only at thirty percent and I didn't want to drain it by using it as a flashlight.

My family, friends, and Gomez would all give me hell if I went to the island on my own, so I called Gina. It went straight to voicemail. My anxiety increased. I sent her a text filling her in on what I'd learned, where I was going, and why I needed to go now based on high tide.

I didn't have any kind of weapon to bring, and despite the one I'd seen being swung at Ty, I didn't think my flashlight would be of much use in that department. I dug back through the detritus in the drawer and grabbed a pair of scissors to use on the zip ties I'd seen binding Ronnie. I shuddered at the idea of trying to use them as a weapon. I'd have to use them at close range, and I didn't know if I'd be able to do it.

"Here's hoping I don't have to find out," I said as I picked up my phone and keys and headed for the door. "Besides, Gina will meet me there," I reassured myself.

I checked my phone and saw no response from her yet.

She still hadn't replied when I reached the corner of Sophia and William streets, so I sent a quick text to Sophie, too. Not hearing back from Gina left me feeling uneasy. I decided I would just check things out until she arrived.

Finding a way to get down to the riverbank behind the warehouse without being seen this time of night wasn't as hard as I'd imagined. There were several brand-new No Trespassing signs posted on the building and on the wall fencing it in. So, I walked to the parking lot further down the block and waited until no one was around. Once it was clear, I was able to disappear into the trees behind the other buildings on the block.

Safely under the cover of the trees, I let my eyes adjust to the gloomier light. The ambient light from the surrounding properties allowed me to see fairly well. I didn't want to use my flashlight yet, fearing it would draw attention to my presence. I stood still behind a large tree in case anyone happened to look out a back window. They were all businesses which were closed by now, so I wasn't too worried. I was more concerned by the sound of scurrying coming from the brush nearby. I was also not too thrilled by the scents of wet earth and what I was sure was a faint smell of urine. I wondered uneasily if people lived among these trees. I doubted anyone would be living rough on the island given it flooded so often, but I still felt wary of who else might be around. And what if I was wrong and Ronnie wasn't even on the island? I'd be putting myself at risk for nothing.

Shielding its light with my body and hands, I pulled out my phone. It was 8:20 and still no word from Gina or Sophie. My screen saver caught my eye. It was a photo of Bailey, Izzy, and me at the Jersey Shore over the summer. We were standing with our feet in the water and our arms around each other in a group hug. I knew waiting for Gina wasn't an option. I had to at least see if I could find out if Ronnie was on the island, for her sake as well as B's. And if she was, I would find a way to ensure The Falcon was held responsible.

I put my phone on silent and looked around. The undergrowth was thin enough for me to pass between the trees. I walked down the gentle slope to the edge of the river. Ahead of me, a three-foot drop down a steep, muddy slope led to the water, where I'd have to cross a finger of the river about forty feet wide to reach the island. I didn't have any idea how deep it was, but the current didn't appear to be strong.

From the cover of the trees, I peeked up at the bridge fifty feet over my head to the left. The cars traveling across it wouldn't be able to see me over the railing. However, anyone crossing the span on foot who looked over the edge on this side of the bridge could spot me. I was going to have to move across the distance between me and the island quickly so I wouldn't be noticed.

I took the precaution of tucking my phone into my bra. I didn't want it in the pocket of my sweatshirt or jeans in case the water got deep as I crossed.

Wishing there was another way to get to the island, I slid down the short slope and stepped into the water. It was colder than I expected. I ignored the chill and started wading across. Between the mud and submerged branches, the footing was tricky. Halfway across, the water came up to the middle of my thighs and I felt the push of the tide as it flowed upstream. I made it across in a minute or so.

As I reached the shore of the island, I thought I heard someone on the bridge overhead, so I scrambled up the bank and crawled into the undergrowth. I huddled there for a minute, listening and worrying about all the poison ivy I'd probably just crawled through.

I didn't hear any identifiable sounds from the island, but realized it was going to be difficult to navigate by sound with the traffic noise and the way sounds bounced and echoed off the bridge and the water. It might work in my favor, giving me cover and an element of surprise, or it might work against me since I wouldn't hear anyone coming and no one would hear me scream.

From the quick research I'd done on Scott's Island, I knew it was around 200 feet across at its widest and a third of a mile long. It tapered off to an elongated spit at each end, which narrowed my search. I stood and began to make my way through the underbrush toward the center of the island.

The further I went, the thicker the undergrowth got and the less light reached me from the properties on the riverbank. I withdrew my flashlight and began to explore, pausing frequently to listen and to look for the remnants of the fairground..

After five minutes of moving stealthily through the trees, I heard voices not far off and froze. I turned off my flashlight and strained to listen. They spoke too softly for me to be able to identify them, even by gender.

When they began to walk through the trees to my left, I squatted down and held my breath. I hoped they wouldn't turn in my direction and couldn't hear my heart pounding.

Their conversation stopped, and the sounds of movement faded as they moved past me. They appeared to be heading toward the edge of the island, where I'd come from.

I waited until I could no longer hear them before I moved in the direction from which the voices had originally come. Since I had no way of knowing if they'd crossed back to the riverbank, I decided not to turn my flashlight back on.

It was a challenge making my way in the dark. Yet, I also felt safer with the cover of darkness and foliage. I jumped at any sound, fearing the kidnappers were coming back, which meant I jumped frequently given the way the sounds were bouncing around me.

Once my path led me under the bridge, I chanced turning on the flashlight, reasoning it was less likely anyone would spot it there. I didn't see anything resembling a ruined building. My anxiety ramped up as my temperature rose, regardless of the coldness of my damp clothes. I recalled Lucia's advice, and ignoring the urgent voice screaming in my brain, I paused and closed my eyes, allowing the heat to move from my back out into my whole body.

Lucia's gentle voice echoed in my head, "What you resist, persists." I took a couple of deep breaths, trying to calm my rushing heart rate. I let my arms hang at my sides and rest on my thighs. My right hand brushed a lump in my pocket. Touching it, I realized it was the doll. I drew it out, holding it in my palm.

I didn't know if it was the hot flash or the doll, but an image of Ronnie arose. Sounds accompanied the vision - dripping water and echoing traffic. In my mind's eye, Ronnie looked up and cocked her head, like she was listening too. I followed her gaze and noticed a narrow crack in the surface above her where light was able to get in. I saw someone peering down at her through the crack from above. I wasn't able to see who it was before they glanced over their shoulder and disappeared.

The vision vanished as abruptly as the person looking down at Ronnie, leaving me no closer to finding her than I was before.

I listened intently for dripping. The sound of water seemed to be coming from every direction. I heard something else too, someone moving through the brush. It was quieter this time but still audible. I dropped to my knees, switched off the flashlight, and froze.

The person drew closer. I was afraid they would be able to hear me because my trembling made the leaves around me rustle. The footsteps paused a few feet to my right. I knew I couldn't outrun anyone through the dense bushes and briars, so I remained where I was, barely breathing. After a pause which felt like a lifetime, the footsteps moved on straight ahead of me about another fifteen feet. I lifted my head to try to see who it was. All I saw was a form in the darkness with no detail. I watched as the person bent over, intent on something on the ground.

They began to reach toward the ground when a voice yelled, "Liv. Where the hell are you? If I came out here for nothing, I'm going to kill you!"

The other person stood up at the sound. They appeared frozen.

Loud movements through the brush, a lot of swearing, and a dog barking set them in motion again.

They sprinted to the right, crashing through the brush. I stood up and turned on my flashlight, shining it on their retreating back to try to identify them. They never looked back and were soon hidden by the trees.

"Liv?" The voice was more tentative now, but the barking was louder.

Turning in the direction of the voice, I called, "I'm here, Soph."

Then several things happened at once. At the sound of my voice, Sophie must have let the dog loose because he came bounding through the trees in my direction. When he reached me he jumped up with such enthusiasm he knocked me to the ground, making it easier for him to lick my face. While lying on the ground trying to push him off, I heard an outboard motor start downriver. Sophie loomed over me and the dog, scowling at us. Beyond her, a bright spotlight switched on at the edge of the bridge.

"Are you a complete fucking idiot?" Sophie asked, hands planted on her hips. I noticed her pants were wet to the top of her thigh from wading through the water to get here.

It was high tide.

CHAPTER TWENTY-THREE

People yelled from up on the bridge. Spotlights swept the area. Rather than being focused on us, they seemed to be directed downriver, where the sound of the boat's motor moved farther away.

"I knew you'd come out here on your own," Sophie said. "What the hell were you thinking? What a stupid—"

"You can give me shit later. Right now, we need to find Ronnie."

By the light of our flashlights, I saw Sophie's eyes widen. "Whoever that was didn't have her with them?"

"No, and I still don't know where she is."

Sophie's dog Treat whined as he circled around us. She'd chosen the dog's name because she'd had an ongoing crush on Treat Williams ever since she saw him in the movie *Hair* as a teen. It turned out to be a challenging name for a dog because whenever anyone called him by name, he got very excited thinking he would receive a treat. As a consequence, he was what the vet politely called overfed.

"Sit," Sophie said, and Treat obediently sat, though his tail would not remain still.

Looking down at Treat, I had a sudden inspiration. I still had the Buttercup doll in my hand. I held it out to the dog and let him sniff it. "That's a good boy. Now go find her." I gestured ahead of us. "Go on. Go find Ronnie." The dog just looked from my hand to my face and continued to wag his tail.

"That's your whole plan?"

"Well, it was worth a try." I shrugged. "The guy didn't wave his arms and point to where she was being held before he ran off."

"Yeah, but you know Treat. He couldn't find his own ass even if he was licking it at the time."

I groaned in frustration.

"What was he doing before he ran away?" Sophie asked.

I was aware of more yelling from the bridge and also from the direction of the riverbank. My heart was still pounding and my thoughts were jumbled.

"Give me a minute. Let me think." I went back over the person's actions. "He moved past me a few feet away. Then he bent over to look at something." That's when I remembered the vision.

"Wait. He wasn't looking at an object. He was looking through a crack at Ronnie."

I turned in a circle. "Between turning to watch him run away and Treat knocking me down, I've lost track of where he was." I took a few steps, scanning the ground with my flashlight. I glanced up at the lights on the bridge and tried to reorient myself.

"Use your flashlight and move forward slowly. There should be a hard surface with a crack in it. She's underground. We have to hurry."

"How can I move slowly *and* hurry?" Sophie asked.

"Just move cautiously. I don't want either of us falling through whatever she's being held in and landing on top of her. But we have to move fast because it's high tide and she's below ground. I don't know how the rising water affects the space she's in."

Sophie nodded. After reconnecting Treat's leash to his collar, she moved forward, scouring the ground as she went.

"Listen for dripping water too."

Sophie raised her eyebrows in a question then gave me a nod and continued on. Treat was sniffing the ground by her side.

It sounded like people were calling out from the shore of the island. One was definitely Gina's voice, but I was too intent on finding Ronnie to wait for her.

Sophie and I were a few feet apart, sweeping our flashlights across the ground in front of us as we went.

Gina's voice grew louder from behind us now and there were sounds of people moving to our right in the direction the man had run.

Treat strained against his leash, pulling Sophie forward. "Hold on, you crazy dog," Sophie said, stumbling after him. I hurried after them, trusting in whatever was drawing him forward. He stopped and began digging at the ground.

"Oh, my God." Sophie dropped to her knees.

I ran up beside her. She was shining her flashlight through a crack in the ground. I looked over her shoulder, and saw the light reflected back off of frightened eyes.

"Hold it right there. Don't move." Gina's voice was deep and commanding.

I wasn't much for commands. I fell to my knees, putting my mouth near the crack. "Ronnie, it's me Liv, Bailey's mom."

Beside me, Sophie stood up at Gina's command. When I didn't do the same, I felt hands reach under my arms and haul me up.

"Mierda! Are you deaf? I told you not to move. You may be destroying evidence," Gina said.

"Ronnie's down there surrounded by water." I pointed at the ground at our feet. "We have to get her out now. I don't give a damn about evidence."

Gina knelt and peered through the crack. Rising, she pulled us away from the scene and said, "We'll get her out."

She issued orders to the officers who had arrived and I took one step forward. Gina put a firm hand on my shoulder. "Stay," she said.

I felt a new sympathy for Treat.

Officers set up spotlights and shot a video of the area. Then they cleared the ground in a six-foot area around the crack. From where we stood, it appeared they'd uncovered a wooden surface of some sort, which was confirmed when the foot of one of the larger men fell through a rotted board and he sank to his knee below the surface. Gina ordered the other officers to back off while she pulled him out of the hole.

"We can't risk anyone falling through on top of her," Gina said. She paused to consider her options then said, "We'll treat it—"

Treat barked at the sound of his name, earning a glare from Gina. Sophie soothed him into silence.

Gina continued, "—like an ice rescue. We'll need rope. Get a trauma kit and stretcher down here now." An officer relayed the orders on his walkie-talkie.

Gina pulled a flashlight from her pocket, got on her hands and knees, then laid face-down and inched forward on her stomach. She spoke soothingly as she moved. "Ronnie, I'm Detective Gomez with the Fredericksburg Police Department. We will get you out of there." She continued moving forward. "Can you hear me, Ronnie."

"There's tape over her mouth," I called out.

"OK. I'm almost to where you are. Try to stay calm. You're going to be alright."

We watched in silence as Gina made it to the crack in the wood surface. She aimed her flashlight into the crack. With the spotlights trained on her, I saw her body tense. She gave hand signals that caused one of the officers to drop to his stomach and move toward her.

When he reached her, the two of them spoke in low, urgent voices and began looking around. They ran their hands over the surface like they were searching for something. The male officer called out and started brushing dirt away. Gina slid over and lifted a small metal ring from the ground. She gave the officer instructions and he crawled away.

Gina turned back toward the crack, looking down at Ronnie without the flashlight this time. "We're working on getting you out of there, Ronnie. Hang on." She remained where she was, talking to Ronnie as the others carried out her instructions.

An officer tossed a rope with a teardrop-shaped weight at-tached, over a sturdy tree branch overhead. He lowered the weighted end to the ground. The officer who'd found the metal ring held the rope as he crawled back out to Gina. He removed the weight and tied the end of the rope to the ring. Once it was secured, he gave a signal, and his counterpart holding the other end of the rope began to pull it. With a creak, what looked like a trap door was lifted from the dirt. The officer lying beside Gina guided it until it was resting on the ground, revealing a three foot by three foot opening.

A rescue sled arrived. Two EMTs pushed it out to the officer at the trap door, who sat up and swung his legs into the hole. We heard water sloshing after he disappeared below ground.

It was a long ten minutes until they had Ronnie freed from her bindings and secured on the stretcher. Gina continued to talk to her throughout the process, letting her know what they were doing as they worked.

Ronnie's eyes were closed as they pulled the rope attached to the stretcher, guiding it to a sturdier surface. Gina crawled by her side, still talking to her until they could safely pick up the stretcher.

While the EMTs checked out Ronnie's vital signs, Sophie and I went to her side. She didn't appear to be conscious of our presence. I smoothed back her hair and told her she was safe now. Then I reached out and placed the tiny doll in the palm of her hand, closing her fingers over it.

I met Gina's eyes. She nodded, recognizing the doll, and walked beside Ronnie as they carried her away. Looking back over her shoulder at me, she said, "Meet me at the hospital."

It was not a request.

CHAPTER TWENTY-FOUR

Sophie walked me home, each of us clad in wet pants due to our slog back through the water to the riverbank. Treat didn't seem to be bothered by his damp fur. I gave Sophie a towel for her and another for Treat and changed my clothes. We were too tired to discuss the night's events, but Treat was not too tired to give me sloppy goodbye kisses when I dropped them off at home.

"We'll talk tomorrow," Sophie said with a serious expression that said I would not be able to escape the conversation.

"I'll text you from the hospital as soon as I know how Ronnie's doing."

She nodded and followed Treat, who'd run toward the house.

I'd texted Bailey from home and promised to call her on the way to the hospital.

She picked up immediately.

"Have you heard how she's doing yet?"

"No," I said. "I haven't had any updates from Detective Gomez. I'm on my way to the hospital now."

"Tell me everything," Bailey said.

The drive to the hospital was short, so I had to give her an abbreviated version.

"Oh, my God, poor Ronnie. She must have been petrified. How deep was the water?"

"I don't know for certain. As far as I could tell it was up around her waist."

"Holy shit. And they didn't catch the asshole yet?"

"Not as far as I know."

"I hope they do." Her voice was quiet when she spoke again. "You don't think he saw you, do you Mom?"

It hadn't even occurred to me to wonder. "I don't think so. He wouldn't have known I was there until I shined the light on him while he was running away." I thought through the sequence of events and stopped when I remembered Sophie calling out my name. There was no point in mentioning it to B. It's possible he didn't hear it. "I'm pulling into the parking lot at the hospital. I have to go. I love you."

"I love you, too. Thanks for not giving up." Her voice broke. "Thank you for finding her."

I parked and texted Gina to let her know I was there. She was in the lobby waiting for me when I walked in.

Without preamble, she said, "I'm tired of seeing you here." Her voice was sharp, not friendly, like at the meadery.

"I'm not too thrilled about it either."

She gestured to some chairs in an empty corner of the waiting room. One person got up and moved away. Apparently, people in the emergency room weren't all that keen on hanging out with the police.

"How's Ronnie?" I asked.

"She's stable, but unconscious."

"Oh no." I hadn't expected this news.

"The doctor thinks it's traumatic shock. She said the body can go into a kind of hibernation after an experience like this. She doesn't expect it to last long, though obviously she can't predict when Ms. Carter will regain consciousness."

"Were you able to talk with her? Is her father with her?"

"She was unresponsive the whole time. Mr. Carter is sitting with her. He'll be spending the night here. They're in the process of moving her to a regular room, which will be much more comfortable for him."

"How's he doing?" I didn't remember him very well, but I did recall how he looked at his wife's funeral. I was grateful he didn't have to lose another family member. I didn't even want to imagine the grief of losing a child.

"He'd like to see you. He wants to thank you for finding Ronnie." Her expression was dark, but she didn't say anything else.

"Were you able to find the person from the island?"

Gina shook her head. "No. We located the boat they escaped in, though. We're hoping he left behind fingerprints or something else to give us a lead." She held up her hand as I opened my mouth with more questions. "I can't tell you anything else. What I need from you at the moment is any description you can give me of the person you saw."

"I'm afraid I can't help you much. There were two people at one point when I first arrived on the island. I wasn't able to see them from where I was hiding. They walked toward the shore together. I couldn't hear what they were saying or identify their voices as male or female. A little while later, one of them came back alone and knelt down at what I now know must have been the trap door. The sound of Sophie and her dog arriving scared him and he ran off. I'm guessing it was a man based on the broadness of his shoulders. I never got a look at his face. I did shine my flashlight on him as he ran away but only saw his back."

"What was he wearing? Can you guess an approximate height?"

I considered her questions, picturing him as he ran. "He wore a dark colored baseball cap and some kind of jacket with the collar turned up. His footsteps were pretty heavy. Based on the trees he was running past, I would guess he was six feet or more. He did have to duck to avoid branches."

"I assume his pants were dark too?"

I nodded.

"That's a start. Thank you." She stood, her expression serious. "I'll take you to see Mr. Carter, then I'd ask that you go home and not discuss the case with anyone. I will expect to see you at my office at eight-thirty tomorrow morning, where you will make a full statement about your actions on the island. You should write down some notes tonight, while the memories are fresh in your mind."

CHAPTER TWENTY-FIVE

I arrived at the police station at 8:15 the next morning. Sitting on the bench in the waiting area after checking in at the desk, I was acutely aware how much I disliked coming here on my own. It felt much less intimidating last year when I'd been here with Jane by my side, and if I'm being honest, with her being the focus of the detective's questions rather than me.

I didn't have to wait long before Gina appeared at the door leading to the secure part of the building. She waved me back and I followed her down the hallway to the detective's division on the right and through the maze of cubicles to her office. She closed the door behind her as I sat in front of the desk.

Nothing had changed since the last time I'd been there. Her office still had a sterile feeling to it, nothing personal on the walls or on her desk. Now that I knew her a little better, I wondered if she chose not to have photos and personal items around as a safety measure to protect her family. I realized how different her life must be from mine. Every now and then, I chose to put myself in risky situations. She did it as part of her job, a job which might have serious consequences for the ones she loved.

Gina cleared her throat. "Ms. Wilde—"

"Uh oh, we're back to Ms. Wilde."

She was not amused.

"Ms. Wilde," she began anew. "Please take me through what happened last night." Her notebook lay on her desk, and I noticed a recorder similar to the one used to record Carla's statement outside Ronnie's apartment. She followed my gaze and nodded. "Yes, I'll be recording our conversation." She pressed a button on the small device. "Detective Gomez with Ms. Olivia Wilde at 8:34 a.m. on September 24 regarding case number five two zero four five. Ms. Wilde, please describe the events of last night as they happened."

I explained everything, beginning with my text to Gina letting her know where I was going and why and ending with meeting her at the hospital. She asked for a couple of clarifications along the way.

When I stopped, she turned off the recorder.

"Thank you for being so thorough," she said.

"Your advice last night was good. I wrote everything down, before the details faded."

It felt like a wall had risen between us where there had been the beginning of a friendship two evenings ago.

"I will have your statement transcribed and sent to you electronically for your signature. If you remember anything else, any details about the person you saw or the voices you heard, please let me know immediately."

I wasn't ready to be dismissed.

"Gina—"

She gave me a hard look but didn't say anything.

"I know you're upset with me. I did try to reach you before I went to the island and—"

"You sent me one text. One. Then you turned off your phone."

"I silenced it so I wouldn't alert anyone to my presence if I received a message or a call, which seemed wise in the moment."

When I'd returned home, I'd found multiple messages and missed calls from Gina and Sophie.

Exasperation was written all over her face. "If you'd left it on, you wouldn't have been in a situation where you needed to avoid alerting someone to your presence."

"You're right. I'm sorry."

Her expression softened.

"I was just so worried about Ronnie and with the tide rising—" I stopped when I saw the look of exasperation return.

"And if you'd waited for us, we might have been able to apprehend whoever is responsible for kidnapping Ronnie. As it is, we have almost nothing to go on. Nada."

Now I was feeling frustrated. "You act like I went rogue again. I let you know where I was, then did what I thought was best given the circumstances. If you'd gotten back to me sooner, I wouldn't have had to go alone." I was afraid I'd crossed a line, but felt I had to defend myself.

Her hands were tightly clasped on her desk. "Not that I owe you an explanation, but I was with my mom. It's the only time I feel I have a right to silence my phone. Being with her right now takes a lot of focus." She glanced at her hands, and her grip slackened. "When you weren't able to reach me, why didn't you call 911?"

I was torn between sympathy for Gina's situation and anger. "And tell them what? I had a vision of their missing person and knew where to find her? They would have sent someone to find me, not Ronnie."

"Trust me, people at the department know who you are."

I didn't like the idea of them talking about me around the police department, and I didn't like her making light of it.

"You don't understand what it's like." My voice became hoarse with emotion. "I saw her, Gina. I saw the terror in her eyes and the water around her. I couldn't just sit at home and pretend I hadn't seen it. I didn't know if anyone else here would take me seriously." Tears had run down my cheeks. I hoped they masked the fear I felt at having said more than I'd wanted to.

When I dared to meet her eyes, I was surprised to find compassion, not anger or disbelief. She picked up a box of tissues from her desk and leaned across the desk to hand them to me. She opened her mouth to speak, then closed it. As I wiped my eyes, she leaned back in her chair.

After an extended pause, she said, "I've never imagined what it would feel like for you to see something before it happens."

"Mostly it's just disconcerting. Sometimes it's—" I paused, searching for the right word.

"Frightening," she offered.

"A little, though I think the word I'm looking for is heavy." I blew my nose and put the box of tissues back on the desk. "It feels like a big responsibility to see someone else's future. I have to learn to stop and ask if seeing it makes me responsible for changing their future or if, as my friend Lucia says, not everyone wants to be saved from what I see."

"I wouldn't have thought of it that way. I think my instinct would always be to save them from it."

I offered a half smile. "It's mine too, as you may have noticed. But I'm starting to think Lucia has a point. While Ronnie did need help, Ty wasn't too thrilled with what he saw as interference. There seems to be a line between help and interference I need to figure out."

Her expression was serious. "It doesn't sound easy."

I shook my head signaling my agreement and remained silent.

"Despite your unsanctioned actions, you did help save Ronnie, which we are grateful for." It sounded like she had to force the words out. "Once the doctor thinks it's alright to question her, I hope we'll be able to get a description of who abducted her."

"And find out who she thinks The Falcon is," I added, immediately regretting it based on the frown it provoked.

I tried to divert Gina's attention. "Has she regained consciousness yet?"

"She hasn't. The doctor I spoke with this morning said the signs are good. He thinks she may have lapsed into a deep sleep at this point due to exhaustion. I'm going to the hospital after this."

"Would it be OK for me to visit her this afternoon if she's awake and feeling up to it?"

"Why?" she asked, suspicion in her voice.

"To check on her and pass along Bailey's messages," I said. "What nefarious reason do you think I'd have for wanting to see her?"

"Oh, it wouldn't be so you can ask her about The Falcon yourself, would it?"

I crossed my arms.

She appeared to weigh her words before she spoke. "I think we both need to remember we're on the same team. We have the same goals - to keep Ronnie safe and make sure no one else gets hurt. It makes it much harder for me to keep *you* safe if you're investigating on your own. I can't impress upon you strongly enough how dangerous this Falcon can be. Law enforcement officials have been injured working on cases involving The Falcon. You are not trained to deal with a person like this. I need you to stay out of it for your own safety."

I uncrossed my arms and rested my hands in my lap. "I appreciate your concern. And believe it or not, I don't set out to make your job harder."

"It just comes naturally?" she asked, a smile tugging at the corners of her mouth and eyes.

"What can I say? I'm gifted." I let my smile have free rein.

She shook her head in mock resignation.

I was hoping to ask her something else but wondered if now was the time. She must have seen the internal debate on my face.

"Come on. Out with it."

I felt like a child trying to figure out how to get an extra cookie.

"I wondered what you've been able to learn about some of the treasure hunters. Not The Falcon," I said quickly. "Some of the others who are in town."

"Why?" She stretched out the word, somehow filling it with accusation.

"Curiosity," I said.

"Uh-huh." She rolled her eyes. "There's not much I can tell you. Believe it or not I can't use police resources to dig up information on law-abiding citizens just because I'm curious."

"What if they aren't law-abiding?"

"Is there anything you'd like to report, Ms. Wilde?" Her voice was tense once more.

"I had a little run-in with one of them at the library."

"Define a little run-in?"

I described being trapped between the library shelves by the long-haired man and how Ty stopped him, then tried to hide a book from us.

She threw her hands up in frustration. "You have a hell of a knack for getting yourself into trouble. Now you've started dragging your friends into it too. Caray! Someone's going to get hurt."

"Why are you blaming me for what he did? I was the victim, not the cause of the problem."

This prevented whatever tirade had been coming next.

"You're right. What he chose to do was not your fault."

She raised a hand to silence me, when I opened my mouth to speak.

"However, you must admit you have a way of putting yourself in the midst of dangerous situations without much thought for the consequences."

She stopped, waiting for my response, but I had no rebuttal.

She sighed. "If this pattern continues, you or someone you love may get hurt. I'm worried you won't be able to live with yourself if that happens."

I was finding it hard to swallow due to another lump forming in my throat.

"What happened to Ronnie was not your doing; however, your friend Ms. Grace could have been harmed following you to the island." I was starting to tear up again. She pushed on anyway. "I'm asking you to take into consideration that what you see in your visions is not the whole picture. Piensa. Think."

Her frustration had bubbled up again. She paused and took a breath before continuing. "How you respond to them involves others in ways you might not be able to foresee."

I didn't know what to say. I reached for another tissue and blew my nose. Loudly.

"I hear you, detective. Honestly, I do, and I appreciate you sharing your perspective. I hadn't thought about it that way." I met her eyes and did my best to hold her gaze. "Thank you. For everything."

"You're welcome. And it's Gina, remember?"

After a more comfortable silence, I said, "I would like to see Ronnie, if it's OK with you."

"There will be an officer outside her room twenty-four seven." She paused. "I will put you on the list of authorized visitors. We'll need to talk to her first once she is conscious. Even then, I'm not sure how cognizant she'll be. She'll also be low on energy. We don't want to wear her out."

"Of course not. Thank you."

I stood to leave, and she rose with me.

"Don't ask her anything about The Falcon," she said.

I nodded.

When I reached the office door she said, "I hope you'll take my warning seriously. I don't want to have to search for you next."

CHAPTER TWENTY-SIX

Gina might not be able to investigate law-abiding citizens, but I could, and digging for a little information wouldn't put anyone in danger. So, I did some research on The Falcon. However, without access to the dark web I didn't have much luck.

I found two newspaper articles on a series of art thefts in New York City between 2010 and 2014. At each crime scene a single falcon feather was found. After 2014 the mysterious thief dropped off the radar. Then in 2020, *The Boston Globe* ran a story on a break-in at a house museum in the area. Thanks to a quick-thinking security guard, the FBI was able to give chase. An agent was critically injured when the suspect fired on one of the two pursuit vehicles, causing a crash that ended the pursuit. A source who spoke on condition of anonymity within the Bureau said the suspect, who was known as The Falcon, escaped with a small sculpture.

I found no other references to the mysterious thief.

With almost nothing to go on, my thoughts turned to Ty and the Boston theft. Could he be The Falcon? I hadn't seriously considered him until now. I'd been thinking whoever it was would want to stay in the background pulling the strings, not be out searching for *Tamerlane* with everyone else. Now I wondered if it was Ty I saw on the island. I would have recognized something about him, wouldn't I? Surely I would've sensed it at dinner if he was dangerous. Maybe my psychic abilities were clouded by emotions or by attraction. Logic could be obscured by emotions, why not psychic capabilities?

Out of frustration and a need for distraction, I also did some general research on falcons. The most interesting fact I discovered was they mate for life, which wasn't particularly helpful, though it made me think of Ty again, and by association, Perry.

When I dug a bit deeper for information on Ty, I found a short Wikipedia page listing his biggest independent find as a cache of first century Roman coins he discovered in Wales. I smiled; happy little Ty had finally found his Roman coins. I shook off my foolish grin, reminding myself there was a chance he was a dangerous criminal.

I found the website for Ty's business, F & P Recovery Services. Under the company logo it read, "To Find and Protect." I scoffed at the lame attempt to make them sound like the good guys. "F and P? Foley and Perry?"

I clicked on the About Us link. Up popped a description of the work F & P did. As I scrolled down, photos of Ty and Perry appeared side by side with their names below them, Tynan Foley and Perry R. Cooper.

Under each photo was a short bio. Ty's included much of what I already knew. Perry's said she'd been in the recovery business for decades, starting out as a teen working in her father's recovery business, Cooper & Sons.

It didn't take me long to find Cooper & Sons had been a thriving business in Boston in the 1980s and 90s, until Perry's father was killed on a recovery dive off the coast of Jamaica in 2001. The family business dissolved after his death, but no reason was specified. I discovered an interesting tidbit in the father's obituary. Cooper & Sons was a misnomer. He had only one son and one daughter.

The alarm I'd set on my phone put a stop to my search, as I'd intended it to do. I'd lost hours going down the rabbit hole of Internet research many times, and I had work to finish if I wanted to visit Ronnie in the afternoon.

I arrived at the front entrance to the hospital, a nice change from the emergency room entrance, which I seemed to be frequenting. Despite what Gina might think, I didn't want to make a habit of hospital visits.

Gina had sent me Ronnie's room number, so I went straight to the third floor.

As I approached the officer outside Ronnie's door, I recognized her as the one who had taken Carla home the evening we'd discovered Ronnie was missing. "Hello, Officer Trench," I said.

"Ms. Wilde." She nodded in greeting.

"How's Ronnie doing?"

"She was awake a couple hours ago when Detective Gomez was here, but from what the nurses have said, she's been sleeping soundly all day."

"Can I go in?"

"Yes. Detective Gomez said you need to keep your visit short. No longer than fifteen minutes."

"OK. Thank you."

Hospital rooms are the same wherever you go. Sterile, of course. They all had similar vinyl, uncomfortable easy chairs (oh, the irony). The walls were invariably painted in bland blues or grays and other neutral colors. There was the endless hum of machines and fluorescent lights. None of it was restful or healing from my perspective.

Ronnie was lying on her back, the bed raised slightly, with a blanket pulled up over her chest and tucked under her arms. Her eyes were closed. I took a moment to study her even though I knew I had limited time for my visit. She seemed younger than when we'd seen her on the street. In my mind I pictured her with pigtails, playing with Bailey in our backyard. I smiled and offered silent gratitude to Gina when I noticed little Buttercup on the tray beside her bed.

I pulled a chair up next to her. The vinyl fabric squeaked as I sat down. Ronnie stirred at the sound but didn't open her eyes.

In a motherly instinct, I reached out and brushed the hair from her forehead.

Her eyes fluttered open. She looked at me hopefully at first, then appeared confused.

"Mom?"

A tiny crack appeared on my heart. I reached for Ronnie's hand and rested mine on top of it. "Hi, Ronnie. It's Liv Wilde, Bailey's mom."

I waited to see if who I was would register with her. I wondered if any of the medication she was being given was affecting her cognitive abilities, especially since she thought her mom was in the room.

Her eyes closed. I thought she'd gone back to sleep, but after a moment she opened them. "Ms. Wilde," she said, a rasp in her voice.

I squeezed her hand. "Please, call me Liv."

She smiled and cleared her throat. Her voice was stronger when she spoke again. "Liv, I don't know how to thank you."

"I'm just glad you're OK. Don't waste your energy on thanks. Focus it on healing and recovery instead. That's what's important right now." I squeezed her hand.

Her eyes drooped. It seemed to take some effort for her to keep them open. It wasn't hard to imagine the toll the trauma of being kidnapped and held captive with cold water rising around her twice a day had taken on her body and mind.

As much as I wanted to ask her about what happened, I knew now was not the right moment. I simply sat with her, holding her hand. If the love of a mom was what she needed, I would be happy to be the surrogate.

Ten minutes later, with Ronnie still sleeping, I kissed her forehead and left.

I closed the door behind me and thanked Officer Trench.

I was nearing the elevator when someone called my name.

I turned to find Ronnie's dad, Shane Carter, walking toward me.

"I'm so glad I caught you," he said. "The officer told me you were here. I didn't want to barge in on your visit with Ronnie, so I went outside for some air."

"How kind. Thank you."

When I'd seen him at the hospital the previous night, he'd been disheveled and distraught. This afternoon, he was much calmer. His short, dark hair was spiked in the front and combed down on the sides. He was dressed in faded jeans, a bright red, V-neck T-shirt, and black Chuck Taylors. I'd failed to notice the night before how handsome he was. I tried to ignore it now.

"How are you holding up?" I asked.

He gestured to an alcove with two chairs with a low, round table between them. We walked over and sat facing each other.

"I'm doing better since getting to talk with Ronnie this morning. She was groggy, but just hearing her voice was such a relief."

My heart went out to him for the fear he must have felt at the news of Ronnie's disappearance.

"I can only imagine," I said. "I was able to talk with her for a couple minutes, and she seemed to be doing OK. It will take time for her to recover from the shock and trauma."

"Yes, the doctor said it's likely her body shut down in self-defense so she wouldn't have to experience the trauma so directly. She said some people's bodies become hyper-aware if there's a chance or at least a perceived chance of escape. In Ronnie's case, since there didn't seem to be anything she could do to save herself, her mind and body distanced themselves from the situation the only way they could."

"She's lucky she'll have your love and support to help her heal."

"Thank you. I've already reached out to the therapist she saw after Erica passed. She's coming by to check on her tomorrow, if Ronnie's up for it."

"I'm glad to hear she's willing to visit her here. Do you have any idea when Ronnie will be able to go home? I know Bailey would love to come down to see her once she's settled."

He leaned back in his chair. "They won't say yet. I think the doctor expected her to be a bit more alert by now."

The all-too-familiar fire began to kick in at the center of my back. I closed my eyes and drew in a slow breath to calm the unsettled feeling accompanying the heat. When I did, I saw a glimpse of a hand pulling the tape off Ronnie's face and giving her a drink from a plastic water bottle.

When I opened my eyes, Shane was staring at me.

"Are you OK?" he asked.

I wiped my brow with the back of my hand and tried to brush off his concern, "I'm fine. Just a hot flash." I hesitated. Not sure how to bring up the question the hot flash brought with it. "Have you or the doctors—" I paused, uncertain if I should go on. I didn't want to cause him more worry.

"Go on," he encouraged.

"Well, I wondered if her captors drugged her to keep her quiet, to sedate her."

His eyes grew wide.

"I'm no expert, but it might explain why she's still experiencing some grogginess." Now that I reflected on her mistaking me for her mother and her general confusion it made perfect sense.

Shane was on his feet. "I'll be right back. Please, wait if you can." He disappeared through the door to the wing where Ronnie's room was.

I didn't get very far into the day's *New York Times* crossword puzzle on my phone before I heard his quick steps returning.

"The doctor said she was starting to suspect the same thing. She drew some blood and is having labs run. It won't take long to run a basic toxicology screening. Plus they will prioritize it because of the police investigation."

"I hope it provides some answers."

His eyes were intent on me. I stood. It was time for me to go.

"Please let me know if there's anything I can do. I'd be happy to bring you some food if you're spending the day here."

He rose and put his hand on my arm. "I don't know how you found her or how you knew to ask about the drugs, and I don't care. I'm just so grateful to you for saving my girl." His voice was husky. "I couldn't have—" His words came to an abrupt stop as he suppressed the sob in his throat.

I stepped closer and hugged him. It felt as if there were a lot of unspoken words in his embrace when he hugged me back. We stayed there until his breathing became steadier. When we stepped back, he kept his left hand on my shoulder, looking me in the eye.

"I don't know how to repay you."

"You don't owe me anything. The only thing that matters is she's going to be alright."

He nodded and dropped his hand.

In the back of my mind, I knew there were other things that mattered. I needed to know what Ronnie remembered about who had done this to her. My intuition told me the information she found on The Falcon was what got her into trouble and if she hadn't been on the right track, none of this would have happened.

A question occurred to me. "Do you have Ronnie's phone?"

"The police still have it, as well as her computer," he said.

"Good. I hope they can find something on them to help catch the bastards who did this to her."

"Thanks," he said with a grim smile. "I do too."

I pulled a pen and scrap of paper from my purse and wrote down my phone number. "Call me if you need anything, OK?"

He said he would and I walked away. I needed to talk to Gina.

CHAPTER TWENTY-SEVEN

I called Gina as I walked to my car. She picked up after three rings.

"Yes, Ms. Wilde?" She sounded harried.

"I thought we'd gotten past the Ms. thing."

She spoke to someone other than me, her voice muffled.

Returning to me, she said, "I'm in my office."

"Ah, understood."

"What can I do for you? Have you seen Ronnie?"

"I just left her room." I filled her in on the toxicology screening the doctor ordered.

While she was silent for a couple of breaths, I heard the scratching of a pen on paper.

"It would explain some things. I'll reach out to the doctor for the results. Thank you for letting me know."

"Of course. We're on the same team, right?"

She chuckled. "Throwing my words back at me, huh?"

"Well, they were wise words." I wondered if she could tell I was buttering her up.

"I assume this isn't simply a social call. What can I do for you?"

I guess she could tell.

No point in beating around the bush. "I wondered if you've been able to get into Ronnie's phone or laptop yet."

"Why?" Her voice was guarded.

"I think we can agree she wouldn't have been abducted if she hadn't been onto something in relation to The Falcon."

"And you think there's evidence of what she found on her phone or computer." It was a statement not a question.

"It's a logical assumption," I said.

"Not a feeling?"

"No. I do use logic as well, you know."

"I meant no offense. Just trying to figure out if you already know something I don't."

"I wish I did."

"I'm afraid I can't tell you much in relation to what we've found so far. But before you start to give me grief about being on the same team, I can disclose that we haven't found anything to lead us to make an arrest."

I was frustrated at the lack of news and amused she was getting to know me well enough to predict my reactions.

Before I could respond, my phone vibrated with a call from Mary. I decided to let it go to voicemail. If it was important, she'd leave a message.

"With Ronnie's impending announcement, I was convinced there'd be useful information on one of her devices to indicate who she thought The Falcon was," I said.

"We're still searching, but my guess would be if she didn't want anyone else to know, she would have deleted any references to it, including her search history."

"Would she have been that worried about hackers?"

"Maybe not hackers as much as thieves. You'd be surprised how easy it is to steal someone's phone. And it would be a big story to break if it was an exclusive, so it would make sense to be cautious."

"Especially after teasing her discovery on her podcast."

"Yes, I'm now going on the assumption that's what led to her disappearance."

"Now?" I asked, confused. "What else did you think might have led to it?"

She sighed and I knew she hadn't meant to bring this up. "We have to consider all possibilities in cases like these."

"What other possibilities are there?"

"She could have staged her disappearance to heighten interest in her announcement."

I bristled. "What the hell? You think she—"

"Hold on. Don't say something we'll both regret. I said I had to consider it when we first discovered she was missing, not that I believed it. It's part of my job to look at cases from every angle."

"I guess so," I said. Once more, I was struck by the difficulty of her job. "It must suck to have to be suspicious of people all the time."

"You have no idea," she said.

My phone vibrated again. It was a text from Mary: *Call me!*

"You won't be able to tell me if you find anything on her devices, will you?" I asked, knowing her answer.

"No." At least she sounded conflicted. "Will you tell me if you discover anything using your...internal devices?"

I swear I heard a smile in her voice.

I didn't respond right away. I wanted to encourage our friendship and partnership, but I also wanted it to be a two-way street. "If I think it will help you catch The Falcon, you can count on it."

"I'm glad to hear it."

We said our goodbyes, and I called Mary.

"What's up?" I asked when she picked up.

"The Richard Johnston Inn," she said without preamble.

"What about it?"

"It has a room called the Fréjus, named after our sister city in France. It even has a mural on the wall of a French château." There were some muffled sounds. "I just sent you the link to the page for the room on their site. It has pictures."

I put her on speaker and waited for the text to arrive. When it did, I pressed the link and found a photo of the room I'd seen in my vision. "That's it," I whispered. I still wasn't used to seeing things in reality I'd seen previously in visions. "What could that room have to do with Wallace Jackson? What's the history of the house? Was it a boarding house in the eighteen hundreds?" I asked.

"I know Richard Johnston was a mayor of Fredericksburg, but I don't remember when." I heard the clicking of a mouse. "It says the house was built in seventeen seventy." The volume of her words dropped as she continued reading. "Richard Johnston owned it in the eighteen hundreds. So, he would have been living in it when Jackson was alive."

I felt disappointed. "Does it say he rented out rooms?"

"I doubt as mayor he'd have needed to. It says it was his home, so I don't think he was taking in boarders."

"Now what?"

"Are you sure it's the same room you saw?"

I took another look at the picture on my phone. "Yes, definitely."

"Then, I guess we need to see if we can find a link between Richard Johnston and Wallace Jackson."

"I'll call Sophie and see if she can help," I said.

"I'll call the ladies at HFFI and see if they can come up with a connection. I'll let you know the minute I hear anything."

She hung up without saying goodbye.

CHAPTER TWENTY-EIGHT

I called Sophie and filled her in. I'd bet money she was on her way to the Virginiana Collection in the basement to check with her friend Cora before I'd even hung up.

It was better to let the experts do the searching for a connection between Jackson and Johnston. I would have to just trust they'd discover it. Otherwise, we would be no closer to finding *Tamerlane*.

In the meantime, I had some research of my own to do.

I drove home and settled on the couch with a notepad, my phone, and my laptop. I pulled up the Apple podcast app and found Ronnie's podcast, *Tea with Jam*. The latest episode was at the top of the list.

It started off with a teaser for a big announcement she'd be making during the next episode. "I'll have a little more to say about it at the end of today's show, so, stay tuned."

If I didn't already know it was Ronnie, I never would've recognized her voice. There was some electronic distortion that gave it a deeper pitch, with a more nasal quality, and her words flowed faster than her normal speech pattern.

I listened to the half-hour show, which was quite entertaining, even if it was short on the information I was hoping to hear. At the end, she made good on her promise.

It sounded like she was signing off with what I assumed was her standard closing line. "Remember, there's no point in crying over spilled tea..." Then after an extended pause she went on. "Come on, you didn't think I forgot did you?" She chuckled. "Join me tomorrow night at eight p.m. eastern for a special live episode of *Tea with Jam*." I got goosebumps realizing the episode would have aired the night she went missing.

"I'll be sharing the clues I've uncovered that led me to the identity of an infamous thief known as The Falcon. It took some digging, but I found this person has a list of high-profile thefts to their credit in the U.S. and Europe, and now they're here in the small city of Fredericksburg. Why? You'll have to tune in to find out what I've discovered, but I'll leave you with one hint. The words of Poe himself gave away the notorious thief."

After this cryptic pronouncement, the recording cut to descriptions of the show's sponsors.

"The words of Poe himself," I mumbled.

I grabbed my laptop and began searching for famous quotes from Poe. I read through the whole of *The Raven* and skimmed a couple stories. I even found a site with poems from *Tamerlane*, but there were no references to a falcon.

After a half-hour of fruitless searches, I pushed my computer aside and flopped back on the couch. "How could something Poe wrote in the eighteen-hundreds identify a thief today?"

I replayed the end of the podcast. "The words of Poe himself gave away the notorious thief."

I closed my eyes and let Ronnie's words repeat on a loop in my mind. I felt beads of sweat begin to form on my arms, forehead, back, and other places I won't mention. I groaned in frustration. *If I have to get all sweaty, the least you can do is show me what I'm missing.*

An image arose before my eyes of a website Bailey showed me when she was visiting. I sat back up and did a search based on what I remembered about it. It took two tries to find the right combination of search words. I scanned down the page and drew in a sharp breath when I found what I was looking for.

"The words of Poe himself," I said, smiling at Ronnie's cleverness.

I had some more research to do. Luckily, I'd followed up with Sophie about her knowledge of the dark web. I downloaded and installed the secure Tor web browser.

⸺•◦∞◦•⸺

My research was interrupted by the sound of Sophie calling from the front door.

"I found it!"

She arrived in the living room breathless with excitement. "I found the connection," she said with triumph. "Mary's on her way over." She wore her Contrarian Librarian T-shirt we'd had made for her, along with jeans, and navy-blue Chucks, which brought Shane momentarily to mind. She sat in the chair facing me, her knees bouncing with excitement.

"You're going to make me wait?" I asked.

She grinned. "Yup."

I threw a pillow at her. As the minutes ticked by, I longed to throw something heavier. Luckily, Mary's arrival stayed my hand.

She walked in, not in her customary casually elegant clothing, but in yoga pants, a baggy T-shirt, and sneakers, all clear signs she had rushed over from her tai chi class, which she said she needed more than ever to maintain her calm with all the Typoes in town. She sat next to me on the couch. "What's the big news?"

"I found the connection between Richard Johnston and Wallace Jackson. Well, if I'm being honest, Cora found it—"

"Who cares who found it?" I interrupted. "Tell us."

"Patience is a virtue," she chided. "Wallace Jackson was Johnston's nephew."

Mary and I looked at each other and back at Sophie.

"So, they didn't just know each other. They were related," Sophie said.

"His nephew. How fascinating," Mary said.

"How does it help us?" I asked. "Did you find any indication Jackson lived with him?"

"No, but it has to be important. You saw a room in the house Johnston owned, and he was related to Jackson. There must be a connection," Sophie said.

"Now we just have to figure out what it is," Mary said.

I leaned back into the cushions. "Even if they are related, how does it lead us to *Tamerlane*?"

"If he lived with his uncle, there's a chance it's still there." Sophie said.

"Yes, but how do I know if it was related to *Tamerlane* or just some random premonition having nothing to do with this?" I was feeling frustrated by my own lack of clarity.

"Come on. The owner of the house you saw was related to Wallace Jackson. It can't be a coincidence." Sophie was insistent.

"Let's go on the assumption we're on the right track," Mary said. "If Jackson lived there, could he have hidden *Tamerlane* in the house? In the room you saw?"

"What do we know about the room?" Sophie asked as she picked up her phone.

"We know it has exposed beams, a painting of a French château on the wall, and hardwood floors," Mary said.

"I feel like there's something I'm missing," I said.

"From your vision?" Mary asked.

Sophie preempted my response by jumping up and sitting between us on the couch.

"I found a video of the room," she said, holding her phone in front of her.

She pressed play on a video of the Fréjus room a visitor to the inn had shared. I had a moment of not being sure if I was watching it on the screen or in my mind. After a couple minutes, I closed my eyes, trying to focus on what I'd seen in my vision as I half listened to the traveler's description of the room.

"The room is at the top of the building, probably a former attic. The ceiling has exposed beams, and there are beautiful hardwood floors. An antique armoire has plenty of space for clothes storage. There's a cozy seating area for reading or watching TV. Two dormer windows let in lots of..."

I tuned out the sound when I felt a fluttering in my back. In my thoughts, I replayed the words she'd spoken, trying to understand the message my body was sending me.

"Liv?" Mary spoke my name quietly.

I held up my hand to silence her and kept my eyes closed. I was almost there, I knew it. The montage from my vision flew past my mind's eye. The parade of images paused at what I had thought was a brown leather pouch, but which I now saw was a pocket on a leather apron, the kind a tradesman might have worn. It was hanging on a hook in the room with the rafters. It felt like it belonged there. The room looked quite different from the one in the video. The floors and ceiling beams were the only things similar. A single bed with a simple wooden bed frame stood against one wall, opposite a dresser with a basin and pitcher on top. A round wooden table with a candle in the center, papers scattered across it, had a chair pulled up to it.

I opened my eyes. "I think Wallace lived in the Fréjus room."

"What did you see?" Sophie asked.

I told them how the room looked in Wallace's time and what I'd seen in it, including the leather apron. "It had to be him," I said.

"Do you think he was working on *The Lasting Word* there?" Sophie asked.

"It's possible," I said.

Sophie was up and walking around the room now, working off the nervous excitement. Mary was calmer.

"Say he did work on it there," Mary said. "The house has been owned by many people since then. Don't you think they would have found something when they did renovations to convert it to an inn?"

Sophie stopped pacing. "You're right. Now what do we do?"

"Do you know who owns the inn?" I asked Mary, but it was Sophie who reached for the phone she'd put down on the coffee table. She pressed on the screen a couple of times and handed it to me with the About Us page pulled up. It wasn't a name I recognized.

Mary read it and said, "Let me call Momma."

CHAPTER TWENTY-NINE

I needed to make a phone call too. The phone rang three times before it was answered.

"Hello. Who is this?" said a sharp, male voice.

"Hi. I'm trying to reach Ronnie. This is Liv Wilde."

"Oh, Liv. Hi. It's Shane."

"Is it a bad time?"

"It's no problem. I'm sorry if I sounded rude. I'm feeling overly protective of Ronnie and wasn't expecting any calls." He paused. "Can I call you back from my cell phone?"

It seemed like an odd request, but I said, "Of course."

The background sounds were different when I answered his call.

"Sorry. I wanted to be able to leave the room to talk to you."

"Is everything OK? Is Ronnie alright?"

"She's fine. As soon as they figured out what she'd been given, they were able to counteract it, and she's been much more alert. She's even complaining about the food, so that's a good sign."

"It sure is. I'm glad to hear it."

"The police still have an officer outside her room, and they've said to be wary of phone calls in case whoever did this to her tries to threaten her."

"They think she's in danger?" I asked.

"Possibly. The kidnappers could try to get to her before she can reveal their identity to the police or anyone else."

"Has she been able to tell the police who did this to her?"

"She had another visit from Detective Gomez an hour ago. Ronnie didn't want me in the room, so, I don't know what she shared. I don't think she wanted me to hear the details of what happened to her."

As a parent, I silently thanked Ronnie for sparing her father that pain. "If she was able to speak with Gomez, maybe they'll arrest whoever did this soon and she'll be safe."

"Better they find them than I do," he said. "I suspect that's another reason Ronnie didn't want me in the room. So, I wouldn't be able to find the bastards myself."

I didn't like the suppressed rage in his voice, though I understood where it came from. I'd feel the same way if it was one of my daughters.

"You're all she's got," I said. "She wouldn't want you to do anything that would keep you apart or get you hurt."

"It's taking all my willpower not to insist she tell me." His voice cracked with the depth of his emotion.

"I understand your desire to see the people who did this punished. I would feel the same way in your shoes. Hell, I'm not in your shoes, and I already feel the same way. But Detective Gomez is very good at her job, and she's a good person. She'll find the people who did this."

"I hope it's soon," he said.

"You sound tired. Have you had any sleep?"

"Not much, but I'm fine. There's no way I'm leaving her alone right now."

And I knew he wouldn't.

"Can I bring you anything? Food? A pillow? One of those weird Snuggie blankets?"

He laughed in a tired way. "I'm fine for now, thank you. I brought some things from home. The doctor thinks she'll be able to discharge Ronnie tomorrow or the following day."

"Feel free to call me if there's anything I can do."

"Thank you. I'm so grateful to you." His voice broke again. He cleared his throat before continuing. "You called to talk to Ronnie, right?"

"Yes, if she's up to it. I'd love to say hello." I didn't want to cross a line, yet I needed to ask her a question. "I won't keep her long."

"It should be fine. Let me see if she's awake."

I heard footsteps as he moved into the room. He had a muffled conversation with Ronnie.

"I'll let you two have a moment," he said.

"Thanks, Dad," Ronnie said away from the phone. Then she spoke to me. "Hi, Ms. Wilde."

"It's OK for you to call me Liv," I reminded her. "How are you feeling?"

"I'm ready to get out of here," she said, taking a deep, shaky breath.

"That's not surprising," I said. I paused before asking, "How are you really?"

"I'm alright. A little anxious. I can't sleep much without nightmares."

"I'm so sorry. I can't even imagine how difficult your experience was. Your Dad will be there for you every step of the way, whatever you need."

"I know. He's barely left the room. I can't get him to go anywhere for more than ten minutes."

"He was so afraid he'd lost you."

She sniffled, and her voice softened. "I was, too."

"You're safe now. He's watching out for you. There's an officer outside your door around the clock, and Detective Gomez is going to catch whoever did this."

"I hope so. I want to go home and not have to worry about—" She didn't finish. "Liv." Her voice was so quiet I almost didn't hear her.

I smiled to hear her use my first name.

"Yes?"

"Thank you for finding me." She sounded just like the little girl I used to know.

My eyes filled with tears, and a lump formed in my throat. "You're welcome. I just wish I'd found you sooner. I'm so sorry you were put through this ordeal."

We were both sniffling now. I wiped the tears from my eyes.

"You're going to be OK. It may take a while, but you will be able to feel safe again."

She took a deep breath. "I hope so."

While I didn't want to pressure her with questions, I knew I was running out of time. Not knowing what to do, the silence stretched on.

Finally, Ronnie said, "I told Detective Gomez who I think The Falcon is."

I was so relieved. "I'm glad to hear you told her." I rushed on. "I won't ask you to tell me, but I think I can help her with the case against The Falcon if you can answer one question for me."

"Will it help put them in prison?"

"I think so."

"Go ahead," Ronnie said.

I had mixed emotions after we said goodbye. I felt elated that I'd figured out her clue, certain I could help Gomez with the case, worried about Ronnie's wellbeing, and scared knowing what I needed to do. More than anything, I was angry, knowing who had done this to her.

CHAPTER THIRTY

Two days later, early in the morning before the streets were too busy, I sat beside Gina in her unmarked police car in the alley behind the Juvenile and Domestic Court on Princess Anne Street. We were beside the one hotel on Caroline Street downtown, though we were purposefully out of sight from any of the hotel room windows on this side of the building. Other officers were positioned out of sight in a variety of places along Princess Anne Street. They were in place in case everything went according to plan. I tried not to imagine what would happen if things didn't go according to plan. Gina had assured me she had different probabilities covered, and I trusted her.

"Are you certain you can do this? Segura?" Gina asked me for the hundredth time.

"I wish you'd stop asking me the same question. It makes me more nervous."

"Sorry."

I took a deep breath. "We've got everything covered, right? There's nothing to worry about. The first arrest has been made already, right?"

"I wish you'd stop asking me the same question," she said with a half-smile.

I smiled too. It helped me feel a little calmer.

"Yes, I've had confirmation," she told me again.

"But we don't know if they were able to communicate about it?"

"We're relatively confident they didn't. However, they may have alternate means of communicating other than by phone or watch."

I didn't like the phrase "relatively confident," but it would have to do. Gina raised her hand for silence, listening to someone through an earpiece.

"Confirmed. Suspect is on the move. Turning left out of the hotel and walking toward Princess Anne Street. Check in." She listened. Then to me she said, "We were right, they're heading out early. Everyone is in place. It's time." To her team she said, "Hold your positions until you hear from me or see my signal. Notify the team of any changes in the suspect's course."

We got out of the car. Gina was wearing a bulletproof vest. We'd considered having me wear one but thought it would be too obvious. I didn't think it would come down to a shoot-out anyway. This wasn't the Wild West.

Prior to parting, Gina gave me one last look. I gave her a nervous thumbs up and walked down the alley and onto Charlotte Street. I knew she and her team would be watching over me, but I still felt strange and very alone.

I caught up to them just after they rounded the corner onto Princess Anne Street. I was glad the court wasn't open yet. We had the street to ourselves.

"Ty," I called.

He paused before turning toward me. Perry faced me too. Uncertainty altered her features momentarily.

Ty put a hand in his pocket and waited for me to approach.

"I think we've said all we need to already," he said.

I stopped a few feet from them. "Have we?"

He shifted on his feet. "Maybe more than we needed to once or twice."

Perry slipped her right hand into his left, leaning closer to him as she did so and whispering into his ear, just as I'd seen it happen in a vision.

Ty nodded at her, and they turned to walk away.

This was the moment. I could let them walk away or stand up and no longer let The Falcon prey on our town.

"It would be a shame to leave without *Tamerlane*, wouldn't it?"

They paused, their backs still to me. Perry tugged his hand to pull him onwards, but he turned back toward me.

I turned my focus to Ty. "It doesn't strike you as a bit strange that The Falcon has been one step ahead of you, getting to the next clue right before you did? Seems too coincidental to me. Almost as if the information you found was being passed on to someone else before you could act on it."

"You're saying The Falcon has been spying on us?" Ty said.

"Not exactly."

Perry said, "She's playing some kind of game, and we don't have time for games. She doesn't know where it is any more than we do." She slipped her hand back into his, and I stole a glance at her arm for confirmation of the tattoo through the fabric of her sleeve.

"You're close, Perry." I pronounced her name deliberately. "Though it's more truthful to say I think I know where it is. The same as you think you do."

She threw her free hand up in the air. "Word games. All it means is that none of us know for certain where it is."

"It's interesting you bring up word games."

Her left hand became still at her side, while the other still held Ty's.

"Has she ever told you Perry is a nickname, Ty?"

It appeared this was news to him because he took a moment to glance sideways at her. "What the hell does that have to do with anything?"

"It's the most important thing. The one thing you should've asked."

I didn't know how much I could say before Perry reacted, or how she would react if I pushed her too far. It was another of those moments when I wished I had the ability to choose what or who to have visions about. I took a breath and hoped they didn't hear how shaky it was. "It's short for Peregrine." I let it sink in for a beat. "Like the falcon."

Perry's laugh was derisive. "So what if it is?" she asked. "What does that prove?"

They were still holding hands, but each of their bodies had tensed.

"I trust Perry with my life." He didn't look at her, though, continuing to hold my gaze.

"That's all you've got?" she asked. "That my name is Peregrine? Let's get out of this Podunk town." She pulled Ty's hand as she started to turn. Ty didn't budge.

"It's not all I have," I said.

I tried to feel my feet on the earth, to feel the energy flowing up through my feet like water through roots, just as Lucia had taught me to do when I was anxious.

"She's trying to get you to leave town so Caleb can recover *Tamerlane* while you're gone. They've been working against you all along. Probably on other recoveries, too. They've been partners for years."

Ty's expression shifted, and I knew I had to play the last card.

"Have you ever noticed the tattoo on Caleb's neck? Those paw prints disappearing under his collar? I learned some things about the paw prints of canines recently. The ones on Caleb's neck had slender toes. It stood out to me." I took a breath. "It turns out foxes have slender toes. It's one way to differentiate their tracks from other canines. You have a fox tattoo, don't you, Perry?"

The color drained from Ty's face.

"You know the female fox is called a vixen, right?" I continued.

Perry said, "Yeah, and you know a female dog is called a bitch, right?"

The anger behind her words hit me like a gust of wind. I kept going anyway. "An interesting fact about foxes is they mate for life. In this case, it's not mate for life, as I first suspected. It's more accurate to say bond for life. From birth, in fact."

Ty turned toward Perry, who continued to stare at me, no longer trying to disguise her emotions. Her loathing for me was palpable.

I pushed on, in spite of the warning I felt rising. "They're brother and sister, Ty. They've been working together since they were teens, first with their father and then on their own." I was wandering into guesswork at this point, but I knew I was on the right track. "Their father died when they were in their twenties, and from what I found out, he left his family with enough debt that they had to find creative ways to raise money. So, they took the business underground and found it was a lot more lucrative to steal treasure than to find it through legitimate channels. And I would guess Perry here had a knack for working with the less scrupulous clients. It would've appealed to her sense of self-importance and drama to give herself a persona. So, Peregrine became The Falcon."

"Bullshit," Ty said. He looked at Perry. "Tell her it's bullshit."

Her free hand moved at her side ever so slightly, but she didn't act on the motion.

"But the rest of your name is what gave you away to Ronnie, isn't it? It's where the foxes come in, too."

"I don't know what you're talking about," she said. "You're right, Ty. This is absolute bullshit. C'mon." She pulled his hand and started to turn.

"You can find an awful lot of information on the dark web," I continued.

Seemingly against her will, she turned back toward me.

"Yet, it was what I didn't find, that struck me as odd. It seemed strange there were no hints from The Falcon about being on the trail of the manuscript. Nothing designed to drum up interest for a copy of *Tamerlane* to help raise the selling price. I didn't understand why at first. Then I remembered something Detective Gomez said. She mentioned the target was fairly inconsequential, except perhaps in the eyes of the Poe fanatics. That made me wonder if you and your brother had a more personal interest in finding the document. I asked myself what reason you might have for recovering it and not selling it. So, I dug deeper and discovered a connection between your middle name and Edgar Allan Poe."

Ty glanced between us. Perry and I kept our eyes fixed on each other.

"Perry R. Cooper," I said. "It was the R that gave you away in the end."

Loathing emanated from her. I'd never been so scared of another person in my life. I sensed we were near a precipice. One of us was going to have to fall, and I hoped it wasn't going to be me.

"Was it a family obsession? To find out what Poe meant?"

"I have no idea what you're driving at," she said.

"The wording of Ronnie's hint led me to the last element I needed to put the pieces together. She said the words of Poe himself. Not Poe's words, but the words of Poe. Something he spoke, not something he wrote. One word in fact. One of the last things Poe ever said was the name Reynolds. Did you know that, Ty?" I sensed his focus shift to me, but I only had eyes for Perry. Her glare could've melted steel. My heart pounded. I hoped I'd have the courage to say the rest of what I needed to.

"And did you know Perry's full name is Peregrine Reynolds Cooper? Reynolds was her mother's maiden name. It wasn't easy to find, but birth records and obituaries are difficult to eliminate. Even for clever criminals," I said to Perry. "By all accounts, the Reynolds were an old Boston family going back to the mid-seventeen hundreds. They go even further back in England, where there's a fox on their coat of arms." I let the words hang in the air for a moment. "There were Reynolds living in Boston when Poe was born there in eighteen-o-nine. Maybe the family knew Poe's mother, who was a well-known actress. There's a chance they even met the young Poe. Or perhaps his last words were driven by delirium, and he spoke a random name."

Part of me relished the idea she was chasing a non-existent connection.

"But if there's even a possibility he meant one of your ancestors, what a lure it would be for treasure hunters like you. An ancestral connection to the mysterious death of one of the most well-known writers ever? The allure must have been irresistible. I bet you even have a private collection of Poe artifacts." Her brows furrowed and I knew I was right.

"I think you had no intention of selling it. Another piece for your personal archive. His first poetry collection, and it was published in Boston. It would take an item that personal to draw you out in the open to our little *Podunk* town."

Her mask dropped and her face transformed into a sneer. "As clever as you think you are, you're too late. Caleb will have found *Tamerlane* and be long gone by now."

Ty dropped her hand. "You bitch. All this time—"

"Sorry, Ty. It's been fun. Truly it has, but you know the most basic rule of treasure hunting: There are no rules," she said with a frighteningly mirthless smile.

"So, it was you who attacked me in the tunnel?" he asked.

I chimed in. "I wasn't sure if it was Perry or Caleb who attacked you," I said. "Until I realized you were hit on the left side of the back of your head. So, if someone came up behind you and hit you there, they would've been left-handed."

They each refocused on me, which wasn't necessarily such a great plan, based on the expressions of fury on their faces.

"Which of course you are, right Perry?" I didn't wait for an answer. "I also noticed a scent in the tunnel that made me think of Christmas. When I remembered seeing you at Agora,

I finally made the connection. You wear a scent with a touch of cardamom in it."

She turned toward Ty. "Sorry, Ty. I wouldn't have had to take such drastic action if it hadn't been for—"

"Wait, let me guess. If it hadn't been for those meddling kids?" I asked.

Her focus returned to me. "Close." There was venom in her tone. "I was thinking more along the lines of the ridiculous podcaster with her lucky guess. I'd heard about her show around town. I figured I'd get some local tidbits to help us in our search. I got more than I bargained for. Lucky for me she's no poker player. She showed her hand too soon."

The tiniest of smirks widened the sour expression on her lips as she turned and started to walk away. Ty just stared at her back.

"Now so have you," I said.

She stopped walking but didn't turn around.

"You and Caleb won't get to add *Tamerlane* to your collection. He's already been arrested."

In one smooth motion, Perry spun around, reached under the back of her jacket with her left hand, and pulled out a handgun. Before Ty or I had time to react, Detective Gomez emerged from an alleyway to our right and armed officers appeared from three different directions. All plainly visible to Perry.

"I'd think twice about that if I were you," Gomez said with quiet intensity

"Trust me, I've already thought about it more than twice," Perry hissed, with the gun still pointed at my chest. Without breaking eye contact with me, she lowered the weapon.

Gomez reached her in a few swift steps and removed the gun from her hand, gesturing for the closest officer to handcuff her, which he did with efficiency.

"What are you arresting me for? You've got nothing on me," Perry said to Gomez.

"Last I checked, brandishing a weapon is a crime, not to mention kidnapping and attempted murder, both of which you just confessed to in front of witnesses, including several police officers with body cams." Gomez held up Perry's gun. "Plus, I'm wondering if you have your concealed carry permit with you. Or did you leave it in your other purse?" Gomez looked at the officer holding Perry's arm and jerked her chin to the right.

He led her to a police car parked out of sight in an alley.

Ty, who had been uncharacteristically silent, came back to life.

"Wait." He walked to Perry and faced her. His expression vacillated between rage and what appeared to be genuine pain. In the end, he just shook his head and stepped out of the way.

After verifying I was OK, Gina turned to Ty. "I'll need you to come down to the station, Mr. Foley."

He looked in my direction.

Gina said, "I'll give you a ride to the station, but you can have a minute before we leave." Then she followed the officers towards the entrance to the alley, pausing where she could keep us in sight.

Ty and I stood on the sidewalk in awkward silence. When he spoke, his voice was filled with anger.

"You couldn't just leave it alone."

I was shocked. "Leave it alone? She knocked you out and has been betraying you for years."

"What if she was? It was none of your damn business."

"Seriously? That's the thanks I get? None of my damn business?"

"You think I owe you thanks?" he asked.

G.G. took the reins. My hands went to my hips. "I saved your ass from continued betrayal and financial losses, possibly even saved your life, and the best you can do is tell me it was none of my damn business? She lied to you, nearly killed you, and was working with her brother to beat you to treasures for years. They were stealing from you." I realized I was yelling and brought my voice down a couple notches. "Tell me, did she let you take the lead on projects, let you be the public face while she worked behind the scenes? I'm sure it sucks to find out, but she played you."

He leaned close to me, and I knew I seen this moment previously. "Maybe she did and maybe she didn't. And maybe I'm not as dumb as you think I am."

He turned and stalked away.

CHAPTER THIRTY-ONE

"What the hell did he mean by that?" Sophie asked.

She, Mary, and Bailey were sitting on the couch. Bailey had left for Fredericksburg as soon as she'd heard the news and had made me swear I wouldn't tell Sophie anything before she arrived.

I was facing them from the armchair after filling them in on the confrontation with Ty and Perry.

"I have no idea."

"You don't think he knew she was The Falcon, do you?" Bailey asked.

I threw my hands up. "I find it hard to believe he was pretending to be angry at her. But on the other hand, I can't believe he never suspected anything." I went back over what he'd said and how he'd reacted. "He did seem genuinely surprised by Perry being The Falcon. He might've suspected Caleb was the mastermind and Perry was spying for him. After all, he was arguing with Caleb the first night we saw him. He may have

known something was going on behind his back, just not what."
I felt uneasy when Lucia's face sprang to my mind. "Maybe he
didn't need saving after all."

"You thought he was in danger and did your best to help,"
Sophie said. "And it doesn't sound like the bastard, hot or not,
was appropriately grateful for your help."

It was good to know my friends always had my back. However briefly.

"Though you did throw up on him. Not what I'd call kind
solace in a dying hour," Sophie added.

"Kind solace in a—What are you talking about?" I asked.

"It's from *Tamerlane*, right?" B asked.

"Yup. It's the first line from the title poem. Geez, didn't you
even read any of it during all this?" Sophie asked.

"I skimmed some of it."

Sophie rolled her eyes, and we were all quiet for a moment,
lost in our thoughts.

"It could've been his bruised ego talking," Mary said. "I
mean, if he hadn't known, he would've felt pretty embarrassed
finding out like that."

"Could be," Sophie said. "Or maybe he has a very small penis."

"Sophie!" I said.

Mary laughed, and Bailey snickered.

"I'm just saying, sometimes guys with oversized egos have
undersized other stuff." She turned to me.

"Don't look at me. I have no idea what size his stuff is."

"OK, if we can stop discussing penises now, that would be great," Bailey said.

"Sorry, B," Sophie said, but the grin on her face told me she wasn't.

"I always suspected this was the kind of stuff you guys talk about at your Monthlies," Bailey said.

We looked at each other sheepishly.

"I knew it," Bailey said, shaking her head.

Mary went for a change of subject. "Do you think you'll ever hear from him again?"

My smile faded. "I doubt it. His last words to me were slightly menacing, and I don't think he's my biggest fan at this point."

Mary said, "It's kind of a shame."

"A shame she won't be hearing from a man who knowingly associates with criminals?" Sophie asked.

"Well, you have to admit his accent is hot. I'd love to find out—"

Bailey stood up. "I don't want to hear the end of that sentence."

Mary shrugged and laughed.

"I'm going to visit Ronnie at her Dad's place for a while. She asked me to stop by her apartment and pick up some stuff on her front windowsill, but she wouldn't tell me what it was. I need to get going."

I smiled, thinking of her surprise when she found the dolls. I stood and hugged her. "Give my love to Ronnie."

"To her dad too?" Bailey asked.

"What?" I asked.

"Ronnie said he's asked about you a couple times."

"Oooo, I wonder what size—" Sophie said.

Bailey covered her ears. "La la la, I can't hear you."

After Bailey left, Sophie turned serious.

"Do you think *Tamerlane* will ever be found?"

"I don't know," I said.

"Well, there might be a little hope," Mary said with a smile. "After we made the connection to the Richard Johnston Inn the other day, I reached out to the owner and to a professor at UMW, who put me in touch with a couple archaeologists. They were intrigued by the idea of helping with the search. So, I connected them with the owner of the inn. They're working on a plan to use infrared devices to examine the walls and floors in the Fréjus room."

"That's wonderful. You're a miracle worker." I said, feeling equally excited and apprehensive.

I didn't want Mary to coordinate a search only to find I'd sent them on a wild goose chase. It would make me look so foolish. Who would take my visions seriously if they didn't find anything?

CHAPTER THIRTY-TWO

It had taken some wrangling, but within a month, Mary had been able to coordinate a search of the Fréjus room with funding through HFFI. After two full days, the archaeologists had given up on discovering *Tamerlane* there. They'd found nothing in the walls, ceiling, or under the floors.

We were back to square one.

We met at the library again to pore over old records, diaries, newspaper stories—anything we could find referencing Richard Johnston.

"I'm still grateful there wasn't anything under the floorboards," Mary said, shuddering at the Poe nightmares playing in her head.

"I'm not," I said for the millionth time.

Lucia had accompanied me on this visit. Her calm, steady influence was what I needed.

"It doesn't mean what you saw was not related," Lucia said. "It may simply mean we've misinterpreted what you saw. It's not an exact science, you know."

"It's not a science at all," I retorted, and regretted my words as soon as I'd spoken them. "I'm sorry. I shouldn't take my frustration out on you."

She put her arm around me. "It's OK, G.G."

I rested my head on her shoulder. "I wish I understood it. If they didn't find anything in the room, what does it mean? Why did I see it so specifically?"

Sophie was searching on the computer at the desk, but we had the door open between the spaces so we could talk to each other. "Guys. Come here. I think I found something." Her voice rang with urgency.

I jerked my head off Lucia's shoulder, and we hurried to the desk. We gathered around the monitor, leaning in to see the tiny font filling the screen.

Sophie laughed. "I will need to be able to breathe."

Mary, Lucia, and I stood a little straighter to give her more room.

"What did you find?" I asked.

"I decided to search through government records related to Robert Johnston and came across this page on Revolutionary War pensions. It documents letters written by Johnston's son and the deliberations over whether his father qualified for a pension as a Revolutionary War soldier."

"How is it related?" Mary asked.

"It's not directly related, but in one of his letters his son says, 'He placed his papers in an old paper case not much used in a part of the house remote which case together with everything in that part of the house was destroyed by fire in eighteen twenty-three.'"

"The archaeologist said some of the rafters still showed signs of charring from a previous fire," I said.

"If it was destroyed in a fire, it still doesn't help us, does it?" Mary asked.

"And now that I think about it, eighteen twenty-three was before *Tamerlane* was published. So, it couldn't have been stored in the same case," Sophie said.

I'd stopped listening to what they were saying. Something was nagging at me. Something I'd seen. It wasn't in the room with the rafters. What was it?

I felt a hand on my back, where heat was rising, and knew it was Lucia's gentle touch. I closed my eyes, trying to resist the urge to force the memory to arise. I tried to recall the other images I'd seen the day I'd had the vision of the room. So many of them had been accurate—the tunnel, the flashlight, the person leaning so close to me. Why was this one not accurate? What had I missed? I went over and over them in my head: the tunnel, the room, the door, the raven, the tunnel, the—I inhaled sharply. The tunnel. It was different. I tried to hold the picture in my mind for as long as possible.

"It's different," I said.

"What's different," Lucia whispered, not wanting to disrupt my process.

"The tunnel. I saw the one with Ty on the ground, and so when I saw a tunnel again, I assumed it was the same one, but it's different. And it's not the one where the boxes were either. How did I miss it before?"

I opened my eyes to find Sophie turned in her chair and Mary staring at me.

"Miss what?" Sophie asked.

"I saw two different tunnels, not the same one twice. And the raven," I said with excitement, pieces falling into place.

Mary and Sophie looked confused. Lucia stood behind me, her hand still on my back, somehow keeping me tethered to earth.

I took a calming breath. "We know the room I saw was in the inn, right?"

Sophie and Mary nodded.

"So, what if the other tunnel I saw was at the inn too? What if the raven pecking at the ground was telling me to search underground?"

Their eyes grew wide.

"The house was built around the same time as the tunnels. Then it burned down and was rebuilt by Johnston. Now we know it burned a second time, and that he lost important records in the fire. What if afterwards he took precautions with his important documents and kept them in a place that wouldn't burn in case of another fire?"

"Like an underground storage area," Mary said with awe.

"What if he let his nephew store his important documents there, too?" I asked.

"Wouldn't it have been found by now?" Sophie asked.

"Not necessarily," Mary said. "The warehouse was used for a variety of purposes over the years and no one knew the storage space was there. We've been doing some research since the night Liv was there, and our best guess is it was closed up because it was deemed unsafe. Eventually, people probably forgot it was there. The same thing could have happened with Johnston's descendants. They might have closed it off without knowing it held anything important and forgot it was there. Or new owners bought it and were never told the space existed."

We all stared at each other, wondering if it was possible. Was a copy of *Tamerlane* in a storage space under the inn?

Mary had to pull some strings, and Momma M had to use her persuasive southern charm to convince Dr. Dennis, an archae-ologist, and Dr. Benson, a professor in the Historic Preservation department at the University of Mary Washington, to come back to the inn once more.

Jack, the proprietor of the inn, had been happy to be part of the search for *Tamerlane*, mostly due to the spotlight it brought to the property. The idea of anyone digging around in the basement didn't make him happy, but he'd been assured the experts would be using thermography equipment to begin with. If they found anything, his permission would be necessary before any digging commenced.

Mary was there to help document the process for HFFI, and by means I'm unaware of, was able to persuade them to allow me to accompany her. As one of the people involved was a friend of hers since elementary school, I suspect their longtime friendship had won the day. Or she had some dirt on him from their youth. No matter the reason, I was happy to stand in the background and observe as they worked. Part of me watched with a sense of unease knowing my fledgling reputation as a finder of lost things was being tested.

Before they began, the experts went over the process with the inn's proprietor as we listened in. Dr. Benson, whom I estimated to be in her forties, was casually yet professionally dressed. Dr. Dennis was a rumpled man in his fifties with a receding hairline. He was what you would imagine the stereotype of an archaeologist would look like. So, the idea that Mary had some dirt on him only intrigued me more.

"We will begin with a basic thermography technique using infrared technology," Dr. Benson said. "It's what we call a non-destructive testing method. It will do no damage to the walls. In the simplest terms, it reads the heat levels of objects. Above absolute zero, all objects emit radiation. Warmer objects emit more radiation than cold objects. In this case, different building materials and different things in the walls like pipes, wires, or insulation will have different heat signatures."

Dr. Dennis took over. "What we will be able to determine will depend in part on the depth of the concrete walls. For instance, if the walls are two feet thick, we will be able to read very little and nothing beyond that depth."

Dr. Benson added, "If there are spaces in the walls or differences in construction materials—for instance, if cement was put up over brick, we would be able to identify the differences in radiation levels."

"Like if a body had been bricked in behind a wall," Mary whispered in my ear. I stifled a laugh.

With a glance at us, Dr. Dennis said, "I wouldn't get your hopes up. It's likely the walls are typical foundation walls with no secrets to reveal."

They set to work while Mary, Jack and I watched with anticipation. Two tedious hours later, Jack was called away to deal with an issue upstairs in the inn, and nothing unexpected had been found within the basement walls.

As a hot flash kicked in, I wondered if the heat I was radiating would impact the readings on their instruments. I giggled, provoking raised eyebrows from Mary. I used my hand to fan my face, both for relief and to let her know what I was experiencing.

The flapping of my hand brought up the memory of the raven's wings flapping as it came to land on the sidewalk in front of the house. Dr. Benson and Dr. Dennis had begun their search at the back of the house, guessing a storage space or tunnel wouldn't have been built under the street.

I summoned my courage. "Excuse me." They paused, appearing annoyed at the interruption. "I have a thought, or maybe a question." I knew I needed to sound confident and also knew I was failing. I needed them to take me seriously. "I know you're the experts, but when the space was found under the Old Stone Warehouse, it ran under the street, connecting with another building. And the space found on George Street was also under the sidewalk. So, there's a chance we're searching in the wrong part of the basement." I hurried on. "I know you need to be systematic, but you've reached the end of the rear wall. Could we try the front wall next, instead of the one on the side?"

Dr. Dennis's eyebrows rose. It was Dr. Benson who was operating the infrared camera, though. She shrugged. "We can work from the opposite corner along the front wall and work our way back over here just as easily, I suppose."

Somewhat reluctantly, Dr. Dennis followed her across the room. They began working their way along the front wall, which ran along the edge of the sidewalk above.

They were three-quarters of the way along the front wall. Mary was on her phone, and my eyes were getting droopy.

"Hmm," Dr. Benson said.

Dr. Dennis stepped closer to her.

She pointed at the screen. They looked from the screen to the wall and back again.

My eyes were wide open now. Mary and I took a step closer to where they worked.

Dr. Benson worked with slow, deliberate movements, staring intently at the screen as she guided the thermal imaging camera over a space three feet wide. As she reached the top of the wall, her hand moved to the left in an arc rather than a straight line, as if there was an archway.

Dr. Dennis said, "Would one of you please ask Jack to join us?"

Mary and I looked at each other with excitement.

"I'll go," she said and ran up the stairs.

She was back a few minutes later with Jack trailing behind her.

"Did you find something?" he asked.

The doctors turned to face us. Dr. Benson spoke first. "It appears there is an anomaly." She gestured to a space they had now marked with chalk. She held up her hand as we all tried to speak at once. "We are registering different construction materials in this section. We can't tell for certain if there is an open space beyond it."

The more skeptical Dr. Dennis chimed in, "It may be a part of the wall caved in or needed to be repaired, which would explain the difference in material signatures."

"What we'd like to do, with your permission of course," Dr. Benson said, looking at Jack, "is drill a small hole so we can use a borescope to look into the wall and see if there is a space beyond it. If there is no open space, we will drill into only earth beyond it, which has the potential to expose your walls to moisture. If that's the case, it would require some mitigation afterwards to avoid any damage moisture might cause."

Jack's excitement visibly ebbed. "Is there anything you've found to give you an indication of whether it was a repair or an existing opening that was covered?"

After a pause, Dr. Benson spoke. "I don't want to give false hope. It's common when doing a repair to remove some of the existing materials to make the shape of the collapsed or damaged portion more regular, as long as removing them won't cause further damage." She turned toward the wall and raised her hand, tracing the chalk outline. "However, in this case, it appears the top of the opening is arched, which could indicate an intentional opening rather than a repair. But I can't make any promises."

Mary and I waited while Jack debated his options. My hot flash had ended, but the excitement of the moment had my heart beating fast.

"It would be a small hole?" he asked.

Dr. Dennis walked to the cases of tools they'd brought with them and pulled out a battery-operated drill and a long drill bit. He returned and showed the drill to Jack. "This is the bit we would use to make the hole." It was the width of a pencil and about a foot and a half long.

Jack's eyes traveled from the drill to the wall to us and back to Dr. Dennis. "Go for it," he said.

It wasn't quite as simple as saying yes. First, he had to sign a liability waiver absolving the researchers of any blame if the work they did caused any unforeseen damage.

Paperwork completed, they approached the wall. In the center of the space marked with chalk, Dr. Benson drilled a hole. When she removed the drill, they examined the end of the bit and smiled.

Dr. Benson turned toward us, holding it up. "It doesn't appear we have encountered any dirt."

While Dr. Benson showed us the drill, Dr. Dennis walked to the case and came back with a hard plastic box, which he set on the floor in front of the wall. He snapped open the latches holding it closed and extracted a handheld device with a monitor built into it. A long cord extended out of the top of the device with a tiny lens at its tip. They had already run extension cords from an outlet upstairs for the lights they'd brought to illuminate the space. They plugged the device into one of the extension cords, and the small screen lit up with a black and white picture of the wall.

Mary, Jack, and I took a couple steps closer to get a better view of the screen.

With great care, Dr. Dennis fed the thin cord with the built-in camera through the hole while Dr. Benson held the device where he'd be able to see the screen while he worked.

We watched as he pushed the camera through the hole painstakingly slowly.

Dr. Benson provided information as her colleague worked. "While the cord is wrapped in a corrugated casing, the camera is more delicate, so it has to be moved carefully to avoid damaging or dislodging the lens."

The only thing visible on screen was a long circular opening illuminated by a minuscule light built into the camera.

Finally, the image began to look different. The long, narrow tunnel they had drilled now had an opening the lens was approaching, which appeared to get wider the farther the camera progressed.

"I don't see any obstacles," Dr. Benson said.

Dr. Dennis nodded and continued to move the camera toward the end of the passage. He paused just before the end to see how much more cord he had. I guessed another six or eight inches remained.

He pushed the camera through the opening of the hole, but not so far that the camera would tip downward if it moved out into an open space.

There was a collective gasp. The image on the screen, as small as it was, showed an open area beyond the hole they'd drilled. While the view was limited to the left and right, the space straight ahead appeared to be at least several feet across.

CHAPTER THIRTY-THREE

Once the space was discovered, it took months before they began the excavation. There were permits to obtain, engineering and architectural questions to be considered, and ground penetrating radar was used to get a better idea of the size of the space. After all the hoops had been jumped through and plans made, the work commenced.

Doctors Benson and Dennis discovered a storage space, and inside it, among other things, were what they called two paper cases from the 1800s. They were wooden boxes two feet long by one foot wide and one foot deep, with hinged lids.

Jack and Mary had become fast friends, so he texted her as soon as the boxes were discovered and invited us over to watch the opening. He didn't allow reporters in case the boxes held nothing of significance, but a technician was tasked with recording the proceedings.

A portion of the basement had been walled off with heavy plastic and specialized equipment controlled the humidity within the space. The makeshift room held a table, also covered in plastic, and some lights. It was designed as a place to examine artifacts brought out of the storage area.

The boxes sat on the table. One had a delicate inlay design of a peacock on the top of the lid. The other was less elaborate, covered in rich, deep red leather.

Six of us stood squeezed into the space. The doctors both wore cloth gloves.

We faced the doctors across the table. The technician with the camera positioned himself at the short end of the table to have a better angle for recording everything. Dr. Dennis lifted a small metal latch on the box with the inlay on top. He lifted the lid and laid it back until it was held open by the hinges. We all tried to peer inside. He looked up at us and smiled.

One by one, he removed papers from the box. Some were related to Richard Johnston's business dealings, some were personal, and some related to the house. He also extracted a family Bible, which Dr. Dennis carefully opened to reveal a list of family births, deaths, and marriages.

Once everything had been removed from the first box without any sign of *Tamerlane*, all our hopes rested on the second.

Dr. Benson approached the leather box. She turned the simple latch holding it closed and lifted the lid.

Throughout the proceedings so far, a musty smell filled the air, but when Dr. Benson opened the box, the scent of leather reached us as the old covering was reawakened.

The first document Dr. Benson pulled out of the box was an issue of *The Lasting Word*.

I gasped when I saw the title. Everyone but Mary looked at me. Her hand covered her mouth in wonder.

"*The Lasting Word* was a literary journal Richard Johnston's nephew Wallace Jackson published," I explained.

"And Jackson was the person Poe's brother wrote to about *Tamerlane*, wasn't he?" Jack asked.

I nodded, now at a loss for words.

We turned our attention back to the box. Dr. Benson removed two more issues of *The Lasting Word*. The final one was dated August 1828 at the top, the same as the scrap I'd found in the crate at the Old Stone Warehouse.

Dr. Benson held it up as the technician leaned closer to record it. From the cover page she read, "Visit of the Dead, by Edgar Allan Poe."

"That's one of the poems from *Tamerlane*!" I'd taken Sophie's advice and read all the poems from the collection.

Dr. Benson looked up and met my eyes with awe in her expression. She set the document aside and pulled out a long envelope. It seemed like an eternity before she had lifted the flap and with glacial slowness, pulled a document from it.

She held a timeworn pamphlet six inches wide by ten inches tall. Other than a slight browning at the edges, the paper appeared to be in good condition. Dr. Benson's eyes were wide when she turned the cover toward us so we'd be able to read the title, "*Tamerlane and Other Poems by a Bostonian.*" Beneath the title was a quote attributed to Cowper, "Young heads are giddy and young hearts are warm, And make mistakes for manhood to reform." At the bottom it read, "Boston: Calvin F.S. Thomas...Printer...1827"

"*Tamerlane*," I whispered.

CHAPTER THIRTY-FOUR

Our glasses met with a satisfying clink.

"Cheers," I said.

"Salud," Gina said. After a sip, she asked, "Where are they with the process of ownership?"

I sighed. "From what Jack's told us; it's been a legal mess. He owns the inn, but there are still living descendants of Johnston's and Jackson's. They're all trying to claim it. It may be tied up in the courts for a while. Jack's willing to donate it to UVA to replace the one stolen from their library, but I suppose it should go to Jackson's descendants, since it belonged to him."

"If only they'd ask you," she said with a grin.

"Exactly. The world would be so much nicer if people would just let me run it."

Gina almost choked on a sip of her standard Gold Hive drink. "I don't dare imagine it."

"What? I'd be a great benevolent ruler of the universe."

"Uh-huh." Her eye roll expressed her true feelings.

I took a sip of my blueberry mead, my mood becoming more serious. "How soon do you think the trial will happen?"

"Not for a while yet. No matter when it happens, I doubt there's a way for you to avoid testifying."

"Even with Perry's confession on the body cams?"

"Yes. Her lawyers will try to persuade the jury to believe it was entrapment." She held up her hand to forestall the protest I'd made in all our conversations concerning the trial. "While the judge denied their request to throw out some of the charges based on a claim of entrapment, that doesn't mean they can't let the idea slip during the trial to create doubt in the jury. Doubt's all they need. Though I don't think they'll have any trouble showing predisposition, which should help counter any doubts the jury might have."

"So, they need to know how I discovered she was The Falcon apart from her confession in case the defense raises issues with the validity of the confession?"

"Yes," she said and took another sip.

"What if—"

She leaned across the table, keeping her voice low. "Liv, there's no way around it."

I'd tried every argument, every loophole I could think of to get out of testifying. While facing Perry in court would be intimidating, it was the idea of my visions being discussed that scared me the most.

"I know you're worried they'll try to discredit you based on rumors of your psychic abilities. You'll have to trust the prosecutor to object to anything derogatory or based on hearsay. However, if they ask you directly, you'll have to answer honestly."

"Or I could lie," I said, taking a longer drink of my mead.

"I wouldn't recommend it. Perjury will get you a fine and possibly jail time."

"Is it perjury if no one can prove I lied? I mean, no one can know if I actually had a vision or not. So, there would be no way to prove it." I hated the idea of going on the record about my psychic abilities and being ridiculed by Perry's lawyers and the press.

"If you perjure yourself, they may try calling your friends as witnesses to the visions. Then they'd have to contradict you or commit perjury too."

I sighed and stared at my glass. She hadn't used this argument previously. I hated the idea of my friends or family having to testify.

"It's probably best for you to get some independent legal advice," Gina said.

My brows rose in surprise.

"Isn't Ronnie's father a lawyer? You should call him." A smile tugged at her lips.

I ignored the suggestion and her smile. "You think I need legal representation?"

"Hey, I'm not a lawyer, bu—"

"But you play one on TV?" Sophie's voice took us by surprise, quoting an old commercial.

I turned around and saw all the Monthly ladies there with her.

"What the heck?" I sputtered.

"We figured since you and Detective Gomez seem to make such a good team, we ought to get to know her better," Sophie said.

They dragged chairs over to our table for two. I turned to Gina, who appeared to be stunned as well as amused.

"A good team?" Gina asked.

They sat down. "Well, yeah," said Claire. "You've solved two cases together already."

"People are referring to you as the dynamic duo," Mary said.

"Wait, what?" asked Gina. I couldn't tell if she was more shocked or horrified.

"So, we thought you'd need some advice on keeping Liv in line," added Jane.

"That's possible?" asked Gina.

"Not remotely," said Hannah.

"Especially if G.G.'s around," said Mary.

"Aren't your initials G.G. too?" Sophie asked, while raising a hand to call the waitress over.

"Screw G.G.," Hannah said. "No offense, Liv."

I laughed. "None taken."

Hannah continued, "I wanna hear what you were sayin' about Ronnie's dad. He's smokin'."

I shrugged my shoulders when Gina glanced at me for help.

She looked like a deer wanting to bolt yet paralyzed by the terror of knowing she was going to be run down. Awakening from her momentary paralysis, she raised her glass and smiled, surrendering to the unavoidable power of the Monthly.

AUTHOR'S NOTE

While I used the idea of tunnels under downtown Fredericksburg, Virginia in this story, Mary's information about them was correct. One underground storage space was found in 2017. It sparked a lot of interest and tours were briefly offered. A study was then commissioned and no evidence was found of a series of tunnels or additional underground storage spaces. While you may still find websites that suggest the tunnels exist, to the best of my knowledge the idea has been disproven. It was fun imagining discovering hidden spaces, though!

Acknowledgements

There are many people who contribute to the writing and birth of a book.

There are those who help inspire the stories. Thank you to my female friends whose insights and laughter continue to inspire Liv's circle of friends. Special thanks to the dear friends who gather at our home each month for dinner and community. The safe, joyful space we share inspired the "Monthly" gatherings in the stories. Our own shared meals are a treasured time for me. The incredible people in my life are why friendship is a central theme in Liv's stories. You make writing about friendship easy and such fun!

There are those who help guide the words with their feedback. Several people served as beta readers for book two, offering their thoughts to help make the story better. Thank you Kathy Ryback, Jessica Utz, Bill Brooks, Jean Martell, Laura Schmidt, and Lori Roberts Herbst. Lori, thank you not only for your feedback on the story, but for your amazing editing skills as well. Thanks to early reader Brenda Yost for posting the first review of the book! Members of the Royal Writers also provided valuable feedback and invaluable moral support.

There are professionals whose skills help make the story better. My thanks to Barbara Grassey for her insights on the flow of the story and the structure. Tom Allen provided a keen eye as proofreader extraordinaire. The gorgeous cover was created by Abigail Simmons who saved the day with her vision and talent. Dear friend Xochitl Skora served as my sensitivity reader, for which I'm deeply grateful.

There are people in the local community who support authors in so many ways. My thanks to the staff and volunteers at the downtown branch of the Central Rappahannock Regional Library, specifically Nancy Moore and Rose Fanara, for sharing their knowledge of the Virginiana Collection. I'm also grateful for the way Joy O'Toole consistently supports local authors through library events and the annual Rappahannock Writers Conference. My thanks to Scott Walker at the Historic Fredericksburg Foundation, Inc. for his willingness to allow HFFI to be featured in the book. I'm also grateful to Jane Keller at the Barnes & Noble in Fredericksburg for her ongoing support of my work and for being a champion of local authors. Thanks to Fredericksburg legend, Ted Schubel, for providing the opportunity to connect with local readers through his radio show Town Talk. I'm grateful to Cheryl Bosch at Frame Designs for providing a home for my books in her shop! I've lived in Fredericksburg for 28 years. I've stayed so long because the people are some of the most kind-hearted and supportive I've ever met. I also love learning new things about our town as I work on each book.

There are the readers, who make sharing Liv's stories such a joy. Thank you to the book clubs who have chosen to read the books, who've invited me into their circle, and who've had humorous and serious conversations sparked by the stories. And to you, kind reader, thank you for accompanying Liv on her adventures.

There is one person who helps make all this possible. Thank you to my kind, supportive, and beloved husband Bill. My gratitude for your belief in me is beyond words.

About the Author

Lynda Allen is the author of the Liv Wilde Mysteries in which menopause is a superpower! Since she had to put up with hot flashes everyday, she figured she might as well make them useful.

Lynda proudly infuses her writing with her Jersey Girl sensibilities and aims to create stories imbued with heart and humor. She lives in Fredericksburg, VA, where her mysteries are set, with her husband, their cat, and the many incredible eagle friends who pay them frequent visits.

When she's not writing about hot flash-induced psychic visions, she also writes poetry and is an artist.

STAY IN TOUCH

Sign up for Lynda's newsletter at
www.lyndaallenwrites.com
or use the QR code below.